PRESENTS

MISSING PIECES
Untold tales from your favorite Bards in GenCon 2010 Author's Avenue

Volume 1

This is a work of fiction. All the characters and events portrayed in this novel are either fictitious or are used fictitiously.

THIS BOOK IS PUBLISHED BY
Old School Publishing

Missing Pieces © 2010 C.E. Rocco, C.S. Marks, V.J. Waks, Maxwell Alexander Drake, Matthew and Stefanie Verish, Todd Austin Hunt, Tracy R. Chowdhury, Dylan Birtolo.

All rights reserved under International and Pan-American Copyright Conventions. This includes the right to reproduce this book, or portions thereof, in any form.

Edited by Bil White, Jeffrey Schneider, Sandy Garfield, C.S. Marks, C.E. Rocco
Layout and Design by C.E. Rocco and Amber L. Campbell
Cover Art by Larry Elmore with C.E. Rocco
Interior Art by C.S. Marks, Stefanie Verish, Celia Yost
Art Direction by C.E. Rocco

Published in the United States by Old School Publishing,
Old School Publishing
c/o C.E.Rocco
305 Winifred Street East
St. Paul, MN 55107

www.dragonroots.net

ISBN: 978-1-4536878-6-4 (Trade Paperback)
First Printing: August 2010

Foreword

Behold, brave reader: you are on the event horizon of adventure and intrigue, lust and passion, life and death. Before you lies the combined works of GenCon's favorite bards--tales of such secrecy that the knowledge had been buried deep within the confines of their minds, locked away for all time, until one versifier gently lured these long-forgotten tales into the light of day for all to marvel at.

Missing Pieces is a collective of short stories detailing the questions that all readers have regarding their favorite authors' work. Ever wonder about a character's background that wasn't fully detailed in the novel you just read? What happened between the first and the second novels that wasn't fully explained? How did the hero and his sidekick first meet? Why did the protagonist have a change of heart and a soft spot for children? In this anthology some missing pieces of the puzzle are brought to light.

Fans fell in love with one of the main characters, Clytus Rillion, in Maxwell Alexander Drake's first book of the *Genesis of Oblivion* saga, *Farmers and Mercenaries*. Step back in time twenty years and see how he started his career and met his right-hand man, Ragnor De'haln, in "*The Way of the Lion*".

In the aftermath of "Raven's Heart", the tracker named Hawkwing and the former bandit known as the White Demon try to evade a clandestine organization known as the Seroko. "The Hawk's Shadow" tells their tale and bridges "Raven's Heart" with the upcoming Black Earth Trilogy.

"At the Expense of Kings" opens up the possibility of a new world.

"Decisions" explores the beginning of the unusual relationship between two of the fans' favorite characters from Dylan Birtolo's novels. This a world of shifters, people who have the ability to change from human to animal form.

"A Simple Twist of Fate" reveals an altered reality after Adrianna's journey through time. Come see a new destiny unfold while experiencing the fascinating world of Shandahar.

"HUNGER", the tale of a research expedition that finds more than it bargained for, actually had its origins in the author's dreadful nightmares; writing helped make it easier to get to sleep and recover from that sense of dread when you finally turn out the bedroom lights.

"Bringer of Bedlam" details a realm bathed in constant shadow. The world is tidally locked, so the sun always faces one side of the planet and the other is constantly shrouded in darkness. The most hospitable section is where the light and dark meet--in the shadows. "Bringer of Bedlam" offers a look into the past and a glimpse into some of the characters in the future Wizards at War series.

Finally, "The Unbroken Mirror" deals with a pivotal moment in the history of Alterra, the World that Is, providing a glimpse into the foundation of C.S. Marks' "Elfhunter" trilogy. Those who seek understanding of the true nature of Evil risk being ensnared by it.

But wait, there's more. Hemingway was once challenged to craft a six word short story. His story, "For sale: baby shoes, never worn," is now famous. As an added bonus to these wonderful tales contained within, each author has plucked from the fountain of their own mirth a tale so expertly crafted that they too only required six words to tell it. Look for their second work under, "Hemingway's Challenge," before each story.

C.E. Rocco

Acknowledgments

"Missing Pieces" isn't just an anthology; it's the first to feature a piece of my own work. Therefore, please allow me to bask in the limelight for a moment and thank a few people.

First, there are two particular individuals who drove me to my current path of literary genius. Okay, it might be premature to say literary genius, but you know what I mean. I am not sure if they are sirens or muses, harpies or angels, imps or smurfs (er, smurfettes), but one thing is for sure--without these two dynamic young ladies in my life you would not be reading these stories, and I would not have my own story in this anthology with the prospect of my own novel hopefully soon to follow. I won't say which lured me in with song and which inspired me to actually finish, which tried to eat my liver and which graced me with heavenly words of encouragement, which was diabolically evil by example and which was, well, er, blue. Anyway you look at it, V. J. Waks, C. S. Marks, thanks for your constant meddling and devious trappings. Take that as you will.

I would like to thank my children; even though they are too young to appreciate it, they are a great inspiration and everything I do in my life is for them. Ames Augustus Rocco and Joss'Lynn Epic Rocco, this book, as everything, is for you.

I would like to thank Mr. Ames, who taught me the meaning of being proactive. He inspired me so much in my life that I named my son after him. I hope you are doing well in heaven.

Of course I would like to thank the other authors for their own contributions.

There is one individual who really means more to me than words. One person who, months ago, would without question have been first and foremost in these acknowledgments. For reasons I don't wish to share, that person shall not be named, but will understand what it means when I thank Marilyn Monroe in that person's stead.

My brother, Steven, who supported me silently all these years, and Jeffrey, who was at times like a co-author, deserve special mention.

Last, but certainly not least, I would like to thank my mother. Does one ever really need to elaborate about one's mother?

C. E. Rocco

Table of Contents

The Way of the Lion
        by Maxwell Alexander Drake   2

The Hawk's Shadow
        by Matthew & Stefanie Verish   24

At the Expense of Kings
        by Todd Austin Hunt   48

Decisions
        by Dylan Birtolo   58

A Simple Twist of Fate
        by Tracy R. Chowdhury   70

Hunger
        by V.J. Waks   96

Bringer of Bedlam
        by C. E. Rocco   108

The Unbroken Mirror
        by C. S. Marks   130

PRESENTS

MISSING PIECES
Untold tales from your favorite Bards in GenCon 2010 Author's Avenue

Volume 1

Hemingway's Challenge

Devouring power, I starved on loneliness.
                                        -Maxwell Alexander Drake

About the Story

This short story takes place some twenty years prior to the first book of the Genesis of Oblivion Saga, Farmers and Mercenaries. It introduces Clytus Rillion and Ragnor as well as giving the readers hints to some relationships that exist between other characters in the series.

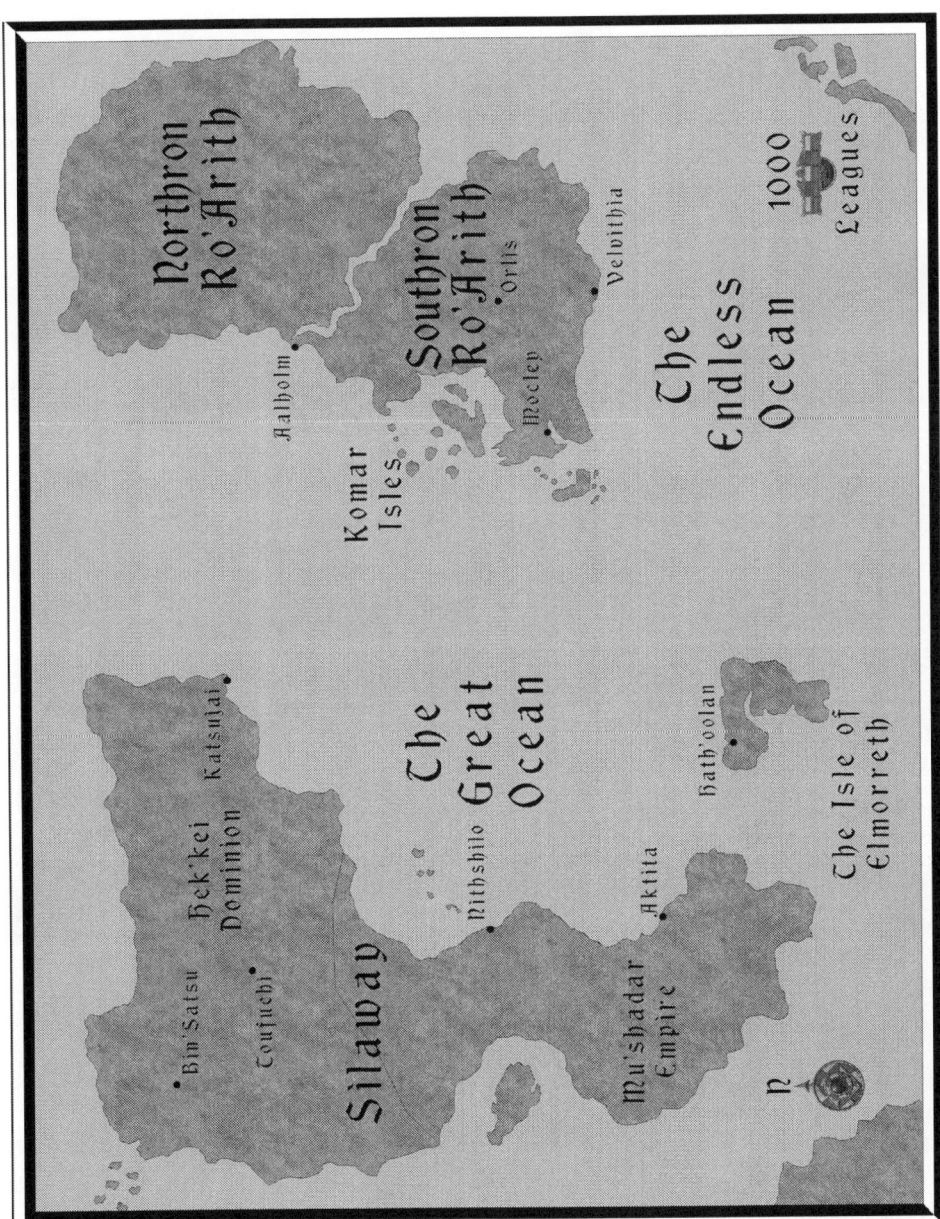

The Way of the Lion
By
Maxwell Alexander Drake

Some people say that blood is thicker than water. Others that honor is the foundation of a man. I say family and honor are funny bedfellows, and if a man is forced to choose between them, he may find that he has no loyalty to either.

MAD

Chapter One

"I still say we have no need of some pale-skinned outlander!" Ragnor De'haln shot a glare at the tall, fair-haired man leaning at his ease against the wall of the royal audience chamber before turning back to his father, the Crown Prince of Mu'shadar.

His father, Bathlin De'haln, was large for a Silawaian. Standing well over two paces in height, Bathlin towered over Ragnor by half a hand. The dark, black skin of his well muscled arms bulged from his sleeveless yellow silk shirt. The long, ornately decorated scimitar resting on the man's left hip was more than ceremonial—the inch-long scars layered below his right eye, seven in total, were testament to that. Each scar had been carved into Bathlin's cheek after he led his people to victory in a major battle of the ongoing war with the Hek'kie. "Be at your ease, son. Your uncle do request that this man help. And what the Oash'ado requests should be heard as law." As he often did when he spoke of his half-brother, Bathlin reached up and fondled the laurel leaf necklace that encircled his throat—a gift from their mother, and one he was rarely without.

"King, my uncle may be, yet you be Yosh'ado, and I, the Hand of the King's Justice. Surely we can no stand by under this insult!" Ragnor no longer tried to keep his voice down. He wanted the outlander to hear, though he did not look back at the man. "This be a matter for the *Royal* family. For the Blood only! How can you let a mere commoner—a foreigner no less!—assist in this matter? It be a slap to the face. A slap to Honor!"

His father's smile simply added to Ragnor's anger. "The King be in great turmoil over this. Turmoil enough to allow even an outlander to assist. Your cousin, Shaith Ku'rin, the High Princess of Mu'shadar, is missing, Ragnor. You can no understand the pain that brings to a father. If your uncle thinks this man can help, what be the harm?"

Ragnor could not believe his ears! His own father, instead of being offended by the insult from his half-brother, was defending the man whose only reason for being here was to shout to everyone that Bathlin De'haln, Crown Prince of Mu'shadar and half-brother to the King, was incompetent! Not to mention Ragnor himself! As the Hand of the King's Justice, it was his *duty* to see that law was served. Aye, Ragnor was in turmoil over the disappearance of his cousin, Shaith. He loved the little girl as if she were his own. The thought of a child who was barely old enough to walk being kidnapped—possibly murdered already—just to further the war... The Hek'kie would stoop to any deed!

His mind raced, anger boiling in him to overflowing.

Anger clouds your mind, you fool!

Bringing his rage down to a manageable boil, Ragnor continued to glare at his father. Yet, even with his temper under some semblance of control, he could not see why his father would allow this, much less approve! If the outlander were to succeed, the insult to his father would be—

Mayhaps this be why my father wants me with him. To insure no dishonor befalls us should this outsider get lucky.

The thought calmed Ragnor somewhat. Somewhat. Turning, he regarded the pale-skinned man while trying to keep the disdain from his face. "Very well. I will do as the Oash'ado... requests." The pause was minimal.

Ragnor did not wish to insult his King. He loved the Oash'ado with all his heart. He would love the man even if he were not his uncle. Vandin Ku'rin was a good man and fair ruler, despite the rift between him and Ragnor's father. Both men shared the same mother, yet, Ragnor's father had been born out of wedlock. And to a common man, no less! The fact that Ragnor's grandfather, Patell De'haln, was one of the greatest generals in the history of Mu'shadar did not save him from the class of a commoner. Only marriage into the Royal Family could raise someone from that class. Yet, after Patell's death, only a year after Bathlin was born, his mother married the then Crown Prince Laydrin Ku'rin, and immediately produced him an heir, Vandin Ku'rin, the present King of Mu'shadar.

Ragnor did not fully understand the relationship his father had with Vandin. He never heard his father say a derogatory word about the King. Yet, Ragnor always felt his father was restrained whenever in the Oash'ado's presence, like a spring wound too tight. Ragnor had heard the rumors, of course. That his uncle's father had had a hand in his grandfather's death. That Ry'ielle, Ragnor's grandmother and mother to both Bathlin and Vandin, had always favored Bathlin over his Royal Blooded half-brother. Even the laurel leaf necklace Bathlin wore, a gift from their mother, was said to be a thorn in Vandin's side. Yet, whatever rift was between the two men, both did their jobs well.

None of that lent itself to the reason behind the outlander now standing before him that Ragnor could see. Still, if his father wanted Ragnor close to the man, that was reason enough.

Crossing the chamber, his hard-soled boots echoing on the tiled floor, Ragnor did not stop until his nose was less than an inch from the outlander's. He had meant the aggressive approach to unnerve the man, yet the outlander stood his ground. The smile that crossed his white face made Ragnor want to growl. He almost grabbed for the man's throat, despite the fact that the outlander wore both sword and dagger and Ragnor was unarmed. "It seems you were correct when you came to me. I shall be accompanying you after all, *Master* Rillion." The fact that Clytus Rillion was a bit taller than Ragnor did not help his mood. He glared into the man's eyes, daring him to call him down.

After a moment, when it became apparent that the outlander was not going to speak, Ragnor turned and glanced back to his father. "With the Yosh'ado's permission, I will attend to the task he did put to me." With the nod of his father's head, Ragnor spun on his heels and strode out of the audience chamber. He did not look back to see if the outlander followed.

Chapter Two

Clytus Rillion had not known what to expect when he crossed Nithshilo, the capital city of the Mu'shadar Empire on the continent of Silaway. He knew he could not sit by and let someone die—the Princess no less—through his inaction. The information he had been given was at best something he should be careful with, at worst it could get his head separated from his shoulders. He did not dare glance at the large black man in the sleeveless yellow silk shirt during the conversation with the Hand of the King's Justice.

When people as important as the Crown Prince, or Yosh'ado as local custom called him, and the Hand spoke, a common man should remain silent unless spoken to.

If the information that had brought him to the Royal Palace turned out to be true, he did not want to give any man an inch of a hint until he knew whom he could trust.

You have been in this country for less than a moon and you are already mired in the affairs of the Blood! Well done, Clytus.

Pushing himself from the wall, Clytus made a formal bow to the Yosh'ado and followed after the hot-headed black man that was the key to his success.

If anyone could succeed at this endeavor.

Clytus had never liked politics. He always tried to stay clear of nobility even in his home town of Mocley on the continent of Ro'Arith. To be mired down with the King himself—the Oash'ado, as *he* was formally called—was not something Clytus appreciated. Still, he could not stand idly by with the information he held.

Hurrying down the wide hallway, he caught up to the dark skinned man just as he rounded a corner that would lead deeper into the palace. The building was massive, and Clytus did not want to risk becoming lost. Falling in a step behind Ragnor—Clytus knew enough of Silawaian nobility to know not to walk next to the man—he did not even bother trying to strike up conversation.

All pomp and ceremony. Likely, this one has slaves to wait on him hand and foot.

The thought of a man owning another disgusted Clytus. Yet, he was in a strange land to learn about strange ways. He had to remember that.

Thinking back to late last eve, Clytus ran over the news he had received. Why they had come to him was simple. He was an outsider and thus expendable, although he did not see himself so. He hoped to live long enough to see the coast of Silaway over the stern of a ship on its way back to Ro'Arith. Yet, for now at least, his apprenticeship lay here.

And apprentice I am.

Newly raised to a Brother of the Tat'Sujen Order, he had no business walking these halls. Yet, his Master was north on what he called 'pressing matters', leaving Clytus to look after his villa here in Nithshilo. From the moment the bedraggled, smelly old man refused to leave the back door until he spoke to the master of the house, Clytus had been trapped. The news was too important to wait. Still, how to use the information was the issue. Use it he must! There was no doubt the old man knew of the Order. What else could his final words have meant?

"The child will never be found!" The old man, frail as he looked, grabbed Clytus' arm with a vice-like grip as he turned to enter his Master's villa. "The Kashi look to the Hek'kie being the Princess' abductors, as do the Blood. And well they should—all evidence points to a Hek'kie plot."

Clytus tried to pry the man's gnarled fingers from his arm without success. "I am sure you are correct, sir. Yet, Master Yoanin is not here. He is north on personal business."

The old dark-skinned man finally released him. "Yet, you be his apprentice. You must be...one of his...type?" The question floored Clytus. No one outside of the Order was supposed to know the Tat'Sujen even existed. Well, no more than rumors and folklore told by old wives to frighten children. How could this man even hint at implying that he knew Master Yoanin was Tat'Sujen? Killing the man quickly and disposing of the body flickered through Clytus' mind, yet the man's final words before he turned and disappeared into the night stayed his hand. "And apprentice or no, you be the one here. This matter can no wait. Any time spent dawdling, and the child grows closer to death. It may already be too late. And that little girl's blood will stain your hands for the rest of your life."

Chapter Three

Without breaking stride, Ragnor De'haln headed for the closed doors of his apartments within the Royal Palace without so much as a glance at the two Kashi guarding the door. The armed men in their blue lacquered armor were charged with protecting all of the Royal Family. They had been on high alert since the young Princess was discovered missing two days past. Several had taken their own lives;

the rest had painted their breastplates blood red to publicize their shame. They were always hard-eyed men. Now their gaze held death.

The guards opened the doors as they made their slight bows at his approach, never taking their eyes from the hall or the yellow haired man following Ragnor. He wished the two Kashi would stop the outlander dogging his heels—or better yet, kill him as a trespasser and cure all the ills the man brought—yet, he knew they would not.

Upon entering the sitting room, Sart, his servant, rushed in from his small quarters just off the sitting room. "Master De'haln." The man had been his manservant since Ragnor was a boy, a gift from his father. Though Sart was property, the man held few formalities with Ragnor when they were alone. However, seeing another person enter in Ragnor's wake, Sart bowed low at the waist, as was appropriate of a servant of the Blood. The formality was almost ruined by the questioning look plastered upon the manservant's face when he rose. Casting one quick glance to Clytus, he turned back to Ragnor. "Is there any news?" There was no doubt as to what news the man was inquiring about.

"Nix. At least—" Ragnor spun to face Clytus. "At least none worthy of hearing." Without taking his attention from the outlander, Ragnor waved to Sart. "Bring us wine." Taking a cushioned chair next to the warm hearth, he indicated to Clytus to join him. "Now, *Master* Rillion, what be this news you say you carry?"

The outlander shot a look to the back of Sart as the man poured two goblets of what Ragnor hoped was warm spiced wine. "You may speak freely, man."

The man had the audacity to hesitate a moment longer before he spoke. "Be that as it may, I would prefer to discuss this in private, Hand."

Clytus' slow drawl irritated Ragnor even more than the notion that the man did not trust his manservant, yet he nodded and remained silent as Sart turned to offer them their drinks. The use of his honorific, the Hand of the King's Justice, said that at the least the outlander was not a complete fool. Ragnor took this silent moment to fully take in this outlander who had intruded on his day.

Clytus Rillion was young, a winter or two younger than Ragnor himself at twenty. More a boy than a man, really. Had he not come with the seal of Master Yoanin, a much honored house of the Mu'shadar Empire, the boy would have been thrown out on his ear before he ever reached Ragnor, much less been able to speak to the Oash'ado himself! Another thing to hold against the outlander—the man should have been brought to the Hand of the King's Justice first, not force the Hand to find out that some outlander with news of the missing Princess was in audience with the Oash'ado! Yet, he wore the sword at his hip with a confidence that either spoke of skill or stupid bravado. Few men, even one as young as Clytus, lived on stupid bravado alone. The man's clothes were plain, if well cut, in the style of the local merchants. Not surprising, since that is where the Yoanin Family drew their power. Other than the fact that he was an outlander—his pale white skin and light brown hair would stand out like a beacon amongst the darker skinned locals—he could have fit in in any district of Nithshilo. And in his plain clothes, wearing no visible jewelry, even the city's lifters would take little notice of him.

Without being told, Sart left the room as soon as both men were settled with drinks in hand. As the door closed, Ragnor raised an eyebrow to indicate his impatience.

The outlander held the cup on his knee and looked at Ragnor for a few moments before he spoke. It was obvious the man did not trust the drink, as if he had no understanding of honor. Then again, few outlanders did. "I know where the High Princess is being kept."

Ragnor scoffed. "Aye, I was in attendance when you did convince the Oash'ado that you had information that may help in our search. However, with the way you rambled about possibilities without actually saying anything did no convince me. I think my uncle did agree for me to help you just to be rid of you. And a broken-hearted father may grasp at straws when all else be gone." He took a drink of his wine, letting the warm liquid sooth his insides.

Setting his cup upon the side table, Clytus leaned forward and rested his elbows on his knees and peered deeply into Ragnor's eyes. "You misunderstand, Hand. I know the exact building where the High Princess is being held."

Just that. No pretext. A simple statement of fact said without a trace of the evasion he had given to the King. Ragnor was on his feet before he knew he had left the chair. "Why did you no say this when you arrived? Why did you elude that you had some information that might be helpful in the search?" The questions flew from his lips before he could stop them, and it was all he could do to clamp his tongue to the roof of his mouth to keep more from spilling out. Surely this man was goading him. Had he had this information, he would have told it when he spoke to the Oash'ado. The wealth that would be lavished upon the man who helped return the Princess unharmed could set him up for life.

He would no have held his tongue!

Anger replaced the shock that gripped him a moment before. "Do you think to coerce me? Or trick me into some scheme? Young I may be, though I think I be a few winters older than you, yet no man lives who plays with the Hand of the King's Justice! No man! Especially an outlander!"

The man just sat there, gazing up at Ragnor. Finally, after Ragnor realized the man was giving him time to cool his rage—giving *him* time!—the outlander slowly rose to meet the Hand eye for eye. "I *believe* my being an outlander is the *reason* I was chosen to bring this news." The man kept his voice low and even, yet there was a layer of anger threaded through it. "Whoever discovered this must have known my Master was away. Must have!" Abruptly, Clytus turned and started to pace. "They would not have put one of their own in this position, and my Master is most certainly one of their own—an old smelly beggar could not know what he spoke of. Yet, why? That is the rabbit I cannot catch." The man spun and pointed at Ragnor. "What damage is done to the Oash'ado over the loss of his daughter?"

"Mad, you truly be." Ragnor could do no more than shake his head. He knew his mouth hung open, yet he could not bring himself to shut it. This man knew nothing. He was rambling. Whatever brought him here, it was not the rescue of the Princess. "What harm do come to any man who loses a child!"

Missing Pieces: The Way of the Lion

The crazy outlander waved a hand as if to dismiss a servant and started to pace once more. "Nix, I can imagine the grief of a father. I mean to the Oash'ado—the King. I understand that your customs forbid a woman from ruling, so how does losing the Princess endanger the Throne? I just don't see it."

The thought sent a cold shiver cascading down Ragnor's spine, and he was glad the outlander was not paying him any mind. He did not want the man to see any weakness, for the man must be insane, yet...

Yet, he be true. The Hek'kie would gain nothing of political value from this abduction.

Had it been a male heir that was taken... Yet, his uncle's only child was Shaith—though his Queen Aunt was with child once more and all hoped for a boy. The only damage would be to the man himself—something that would make any Hek'kie glad to be sure, yet not worth the risk of abducting her.

Still, madman or no, the man's train of thought be headed in a direction I doubt any of the Blood have considered. I never would have thought of it!

If the Oash'ado showed weakness—or worse, fell into a depression and could no longer do his duty—there was a war to maintain! The Oash'ado must be strong at all times to repel the Hek'kie advance. He was the heart and core of the army. Any weakness and the rest of the Blood would begin to grumble, mayhaps even go so far as speak of a succession. It would not lead to in-fighting—over two-thousand winters had seen no infighting amongst the Blood of Mu'shadar—yet it could still lead to—

Nix! I will no go down that path of thought!

Ragnor gave a start. He had no memory of sitting, yet he sat in the plush chair he had vacated in his rage. Glancing up, he flinched again with the realization that the outlander had stopped pacing and was now studying him. Ragnor opened his mouth, though he could find no words to speak.

Crossing back to the sitting area, Clytus sat opposite Ragnor, concern filling his face. "Hand, I do not claim to know the inner workings of the Blood here in Silaway. I have been in your land less than a moon. If I did, I might be able to unravel this puzzle-box I find myself in." Clytus raised a hand to forestall Ragnor from speaking. It was a testament to the level of shock the conversation had put Ragnor in when he realized he was not angered by the outlander's audacity at cutting him off. The outlander continued as if he did not notice the slight. "It is information I do not need. I know in my heart that the man who came to me last eve spoke true. Whoever he was or whomever he represented, I believe he wishes no harm to fall upon the young Princess, nor to House Ku'rin."

Ragnor took a drink to give himself another moment to insure his voice would be under control. "Though we have never met, you told the Oash'ado you needed my help to ferret out the truth. How can this be?"

Leaning back in his chair, Clytus picked up his cup of wine sitting on the side table and took a long drink before continuing. "I was told to speak to you alone. '*The Hand of the King's Justice be the only man to be trusted with this information*' was the exact quote. I now believe they spoke true on this as well."

A spark of anger tried to well up inside Ragnor once more. By force of will he kept it in check. "Any of the Blood would ride into the very heart of the Hek'kie army—all the way to King Thaloman's throne room in the center of Toufuchi itself—if it meant the safe return of my cousin!" By the end of his speech, he was yelling.

Outlanders have no sense of honor!

Clytus gave a shallow laugh. "We have no need to travel far on this quest. The Princess is being held right here in the palace. In something the old man referred to as the old east-wing dungeons."

"Impossible." Ragnor did not believe the man could shock him more. Yet, he was wrong, and the thinness of his voice proved it. "If my cousin be held here, it would mean the abductors were…"

Clytus nodded. "Aye. This is a plot from within Mu'shadar Blood itself."

Ragnor could only stare at the man. It offended him that the outlander would give voice to such an accusation—upset him that he could not give voice to such himself. His blood boiled with the realization that he believed the man spoke true. At least in part. "The east-wing dungeons have no been used in centuries. I used to play there as a child and I doubt any have been down there since. If anyone be using them for any reason, the evidence should be easy to find."

Rising on unsteady legs, he called for Sart even as he crossed the room toward his private chambers.

Chapter Four

Little time passed before Ragnor De'haln, Hand of the King's Justice, strode out of his private quarters to rejoin Clytus Rillion in the sitting room. A long, curved blade hung from his left hip and a thick dagger set with a heavy contre-garde—a mass of thick swooping metal that not only protected the wielder' hand, it would also enable the smaller blade to be used as an effective defense against any sword of a length less than a longsword—on his right. "Shall we go see if your information be correct? Either we shake the very foundations of the Mu'shadar Empire, or you have wasted my time on this fool will-the-wisp chase."

Tilting his head in acquiescence, Clytus motioned for the Hand to lead the way. As they stepped out into the main halls, the two Kashi who stood guard outside the doors eyed the weapons that now adorned the Hand's waist before turning their death gaze toward Clytus.

"Be at ease, men. All be well." The Hand never paused in his stride, speaking instead over his shoulder. "Stay at your post until relieved." How the man had known that the two Kashi guards had started to follow, Clytus did not know. Yet, he was glad when only their hateful stares pursued him as he trailed in the wake of their Hand.

It was a long stroll through the massive palace. Master Yoanin taught Clytus during his lessons of the region that the Royal Palace had stood at the heart of Nithshilo for some three thousand turns of the seasons—older even than his home city of Mocley in Ro'Arith, if one could believe that. Time for a building to grow as new needs arose.

Insuring the Hand maintained a one step lead was easy—the black man strode through the halls like a bear looking for something to kill. Liveried servants, the hand and scale of House Ku'rin embroidered on the left breasts of their pale blue shirts, stopped to gape at the sight of two armed men all but running through the halls. Clytus had to remind himself that the servants he saw were not servants as he knew. Slavery was not illegal in his homeland, yet he knew of none who owned any. This was not the case here. Most of the *servants,* however, had the sense to continue on with whatever they were doing before the two disappeared. Still, Clytus saw a few dart off in a new direction as soon as they thought no one was watching.

So much for stealth.

News that the Hand wore a sword, stalking the halls with a murderous scowl that should have burned any servant who glanced his way, would spread like wildfire. The fact that he was accompanied by an outlander who wore weapons as well would make the tale fly as if carried on wings.

Time was the biggest enemy the little girl had. Too much time had been spent with the Oash'ado convincing the man to allow Clytus to speak to the Hand. Too much time spent in the Hand's private quarters. Enough time to allow the guilty to know there was an outlander with news of the abduction within the palace. Hopefully, not enough time to allow them to do anything about it.

Lost in thought, it took several turns and a few long hallways before Clytus noticed that the two now traveled corridors empty, save themselves. A palace of this size required an army of servants to keep it running, and it amazed him how many were always about. Mirrored stand-lamps still blazed away, casting the same level of light that lit the rest of the palace, and no dust could be seen in evidence on the tapestries that hung in evenly spaced alcoves, nor upon the vases or small bust statues that filled cubbies that lay between them, yet the hallway echoed in its loneliness.

As if reading his thoughts, Ragnor stopped. "This be the main hall to the east wing. The servants do no keep any hall in this building tidy and lit, except this one. As I did say, the east wing gets little use—mostly it be a place to store furniture and such." Continuing forward, the Hand struck up a quick pace once more. "Come. The main doors to the dungeon be at the east courtyard entrance."

Just on the edge of the light cast by the stand-lamps stood a large rough table that seemed out of place in the lavish hall, like might be found in a commoner's workshop. Several lanterns and flasks of oil littered the tabletop and the Hand busied himself with topping off one of the lanterns and lighting it. Enough daylight filtered in through the windows of rooms that lined the hallway, even without the addition of stand-lamps. Yet, Clytus knew their final destination would be sparse of windows—if it had any at all—and the lantern's light would be needed. Handing the lantern to Clytus, he motioned toward a small side hallway. "We can take the servant's passages to the back kitchens. From there we can go through the stables and across to the courtyard entrance."

As the Hand started to go, Clytus reached out and caught his arm. "Do not take this lightly. If my information is correct, whoever is responsible for this already knows I am here."

Ragnor shrugged the hand from his arm. "I take no thing lightly. I want to be done with this business and with you. If your tale proves true, my day will only get worse."

Clytus understood. Traitors, no matter where they are found, were a hard brew to swallow. He did not fully understand all that went on within the political structure of this land. Yet, what he did know was that almost every aspect of life was tied to the war. The Unending War, as it was known by some. An entire House could be brought to trial at the mere suggestion that it may have been involved in such a traitorous act.

And an outlander could quickly find his own fat in a frying pan for no other reason than being in the wrong place.

The servant's passageways were narrower than the hallways they had been traversing. Meant to keep the servants out of sight while they did their duties, a network of them snaked throughout every large palace Clytus had ever been in, not that he had been in many during his life. As they seemed the quickest way to get where one needed to go, he had never understood why so many nobles refused to use them. Casting a glare at the back of the dark-skinned man he followed, he did not think he would ever understand nobility.

The kitchens sat cold. Even though the wood racks were full of split wood, dust covered much of the flat surfaces of the place. The windows that looked out to the stables were in bad need of a cleaning as well. The Hand did not seem to notice as he kept his brisk pace. Reaching the far door, he fished out a set of keys from a pouch hanging on his hip and fumbled with them until he found the correct one. The latch creaked, and as the door swung outward, its hinges complained with a loud squeak that proclaimed they had not seen use for a very long time.

A small alleyway separated the main building from the stables, and even here dust and dirt sat heavy. A few weeds had found root between the paverstones, yet, all in all, the area seemed in good repair, just unused. It had been a little past noon when Clytus arrived at the palace. Now the sun sat barely its own height above the distant mountains, and the early autumn air was crisp and cool. The two men's boots echoed in the open courtyard as they rounded the stable wall. The courtyard itself was surrounded by the lofty four-story building of the east wing. A large portcullis covered a tunnel that was wide enough to admit four horsemen abreast and tall enough for them to have lances or banners held high without hitting the roof of the arched tunnel that led out onto the grounds of the palace proper. Large chains with padlocks wrapped the portcullis in three separate spots—at the ground, in the center and one almost to the peaked top. It was obvious the yard had not seen any recent activity.

Again, as if the Hand were able to read Clytus' mind, he stopped and motioned slowly around the area, pausing to indicate things that spoke of a lack of use, before resting a stern look back on Clytus. "It seems that your credibility be fading with the sun, *Master* Rillion." With a harrumph, the Hand reached out and took the lantern from Clytus, then headed across the open courtyard.

On the north side of the east-wing entrance to the courtyard, a set of large iron-banded doors sat into the stone wall of the building. Each looked as if someone was battling to keep the rust from the bands, though both showed wear from neglect. Setting the lantern on the ground, Ragnor fumbled with his keys for a moment. Suddenly, the Hand froze, staring at the doors. For long moments the man stood there, and an uneasiness settled on Clytus.

The man cannot balk now. I care not what lays down there, we must go on!

Raising a fist, Clytus coughed to break the silence. "It may be as you say. This whole affair may be a will-the-wisp chase. Yet, for what other purpose I do not—"

"Nix!" Ragnor's hiss cut Clytus off and lifted the hairs on the back of his neck at the same time. Fear gripped the word like a vice. "It be gone!" Turning, the black man motioned to the door. "As I said, I played here as a boy. When my father found out, he was furious. He had an extra hasp and lock added to these doors and only he and a few choice people have keys." He indicated to four large holes drilled through the door and a faint rusted square where something had once been attached. "As the Hand, I carry all keys of the palace, including the one that kept me out as a child. Yet this was recently removed." Taking a deep breath, he reached out and grasped the latch without using his keys on the door lock. It lifted without a sound and the door swung out silently, fresh oil glinting from the hinges in the lamplight.

The Hand bent to retrieve the lantern and Clytus was too slow to call warning, as a brass-bound cudgel whipped from the darkness to slam the man in the back of the head, crumpling him like a sack of grain upon the paverstones at Clytus' feet.

"No harm was to befall the Hand!"

A dark skinned face materialized from the blackness of the doorway, the cudgel in his hand lightly smeared with Ragnor's blood. "The Hand no be dead. I do no envy him the headache he will have on the morrow, though." Two other black men followed in the first's wake, one with an axe big enough to fell a tree in one blow—and a massive muscular body that could easily supply the force to insure one blow was all that was needed—the second, a rapier-thin stick of a man. As the three advanced, Clytus backed into the courtyard, sword already in hand. "At least our orders do include killing the outlander." With a gap-toothed grin, the man let the cudgel fall to the ground and slowly drew the thick scimitar from his side as his two companions split left and right.

Not wanting to be surrounded, Clytus lunged at the Thin Man who had gone left. The man brought his sword up to block the thrust with a quickness Clytus would have to attend to when it was time. Now, however, was not the time. Redirecting his lunge into a spin before the two swords ever touched, he slashed his blade in an arc parallel to the ground. Gap-tooth was just as quick as Thin Man, lunging back as Clytus' blade whisked through the air where the man's throat had been.

The big axe wielder was not so lucky, though his massive height saved him a lethal cut. Instead of his neck, Clytus' blade cut through the thin brown cloth of the man's shirt and bit deep across his chest. Blood flowed freely from the wound, yet the man flinched only once before letting out a bellow and charging with his axe swinging in a wide arc. Shifting to the right to position the big man between himself and the other two, Clytus tucked and rolled. The wind sang in his ears as the enormous axe whistled over him. Had he been a bit slower...

Regaining his feet smoothly, he was immediately pressed to the defensive as Thin Man came at him with snake-like speed, thrusting and slashing with his blade. Clytus parried as fast as he ever had. Still, blood soon flowed from several small nicks and cuts on his arms, legs and sides, and Clytus knew he was no match for the man he faced. It would not be long before Thin Man struck with a fatal blow.

Reaching for the inner calm that Master Yoanin had been trying to teach him, he attempted to embrace Sujen. When he was in lessons, with none in attendance except he and his Master, he could only embrace Sujen one out of every three tries. The fear that he would fail now almost prevented him from even trying. Yet, the Sight of Sujen fell on him like water flowing down a plane of glass. Swirling Strands of the Essence danced around him, the three men, everywhere. Everything at once became sharper, clearer. The tiny beads of sweat running down the black man's face as he concentrated on his attacks. The stench of his breath. The slight tilt of a paverstone beneath Clytus' left foot. Even the courtyard seemed brighter with the Sight upon him. Thin Man still pressed his attack, yet as always while Clytus held Sujen, the world seemed to have slowed. Time stretched and he could see each individual attack. He was able to adjust his stance to parry precisely and insure that the other man's blade failed to find its mark.

Though his lessons had just begun, Clytus could do so much more with Sujen since coming to study under Master Yoanin. Wrapping a Strand around Thin Man's blade, Clytus willed the Strand to pull the weapon to the side. Thin Man's eyes widened as his sword failed to obey his body and he lost his balance. His eyes widened more as the tip of Clytus' sword slipped into his throat. Blood sprayed into the air following the sword as it sliced out the side of Thin Man's neck. Clytus did not bother to watch the man fall. His attention was already on the axe wielder.

Lacing one Strand along the blade of his sword, Clytus stretched the Strand so thin, he was not sure it was still resting on the edge of the blade. Leaping into the air, he brought the sword down with all the force he could put behind it. The axe man already had his axe held high with a hand at either end, ready to block the telegraphed attack. The ting of metal on metal rang loud as Clytus' blade, enhanced with the Strand of the Essence, sheared through the metal haft of the axe and buried itself into the large man's skull.

Kicking the man's body away as he wrenched the blade free, he turned to the last. Gap-tooth stared from one of his companions to the other with a look of both disbelief and horror. When he finally rested his eyes back on Clytus, fear dominated them. Licking his lips, Gap-tooth took up an aggressive stance and seemed to be waiting on Clytus' next move.

The strain of holding the Sight of Sujen—or perhaps the adrenaline of nearly being killed or even the loss of blood from the myriad of small cuts that littered his body—began to take their toll on Clytus, and he felt the Sight slipping from him like sand through his hand. Darkness crashed down upon the courtyard as the added luminosity from the Sight of Sujen fled. A momentary dizziness swept him up, and he lost sight of Gap-tooth for a moment. Panic gripped him to the core, yet he stood motionless, still staring at the spot he thought the other man stood.

As quickly as it started, the dizziness vanished and his vision cleared. A fresh moment of panic struck him with the realization that Gap-tooth no longer stood in front of him. His nerves settled once he caught sight of the man running away, disappearing into the stables at the far side of the courtyard.

Letting out a shuddered breath, Clytus walked over to the still form of the Hand.

Chapter Five

Pain.

That was the first thing Ragnor thought of as consciousness crept upon him. That he lay face down upon cold paverstones was the second. Groaning, he put a hand to the back of his head and felt a wet stickiness he knew would be blood. A hand rested upon his shoulder and he tried to flinch.

"Easy, man. It is me, Clytus Rillion."

He thought he recognized the name—the voice. Forcing his eyes to open, he turned his head so he could peer into the face that spoke. It was a pale skinned face, almost white compared to his countrymen. Piercing blue-gray eyes stared back from under rumpled sandy-brown hair. A worried expression filled him and several times the man glanced around as if looking for something.

"What happened?" Ragnor's throat was dry and the words came out in a croak.

"We are still in the east-wing courtyard. You were clubbed over the head."

Memory came flooding back. "Shaith!" Forcing himself to roll over, he grabbed Clytus' arm. "Help me up."

"Are you sure you can stand? That was quite the blow you took."

Even as the outlander complained, he helped Ragnor to his feet. However, it took a few moments before he could release the man's arm. "At least you killed the man who did this to me." He indicated the two bodies lying not far away. Both were big men, and Ragnor knew the sword that was still in the outlander's grip was more than just show.

"Nix, Hand. I am afraid the one who hit you ran off that way." Using his sword, Clytus pointed off toward the stables.

Three! He fought three men and lived! The man be more than he appears.

"He will be dealt with. Come. Let us see what they were protecting." Ragnor leaned over to retrieve the lantern and immediately regretted it. The throbbing in his head intensified and he wanted to sit down, yet he forced himself to continue. The outlander reached for the lantern and Ragnor pushed his arm away. "Nix. I do no think I can use my sword to any good just yet. If there be more down there, you will no need be burdened with holding the lamp."

Clytus nodded. "Stay close to me, then. I do not wish to fight in the dark either."

Both men stepped through the iron-bound door into a large room void of any furnishings. Opposite the doors sat a stairwell that descended into darkness. The outlander made to continue to the stairs and Ragnor reached out a hand to stop him. "Down there be a warren of corridors and rooms. I be no sure how we shall find anything." Just then a high-pitched cry of a child cut through the musty air. Both men reached the stairs at the same time and plunged down. The outlander, however, took them two at a time and was soon well ahead of Ragnor. At the bottom of the stairs, the corridor branched off three ways and it took a moment to realize that Clytus was running down the one to the right. The child was no longer crying, and after only a moment's pause to look down each of the other dark corridors—there was nothing to indicate that the outlander had chosen the correct corridor that Ragnor could see—he ran after his companion.

Reaching a T in the corridor, Ragnor noticed light spilling into the hallway from an open doorway further down. Without pause this time, he ran for the door, fumbling to draw his thick dagger from its sheath.

Before he reached the door, a voice echoed from the chamber beyond, stopping Ragnor in his tracks and freezing him where he stood.

"Get back, outlander, or she dies!"

The voice caused Ragnor's very blood to turn to ice and he almost dropped the lantern.

This can no be!

Clytus Rillion's voice was calm and steady, as if the man had not just been running through a dark dungeon. "I am not sure this is what you wish to do. Let me have the girl and I will say I found her elsewhere. No one need know any of this."

Clytus' words snapped Ragnor from his frozen state. "Nix!" The steadiness of Ragnor's voice surprised him. Steeling himself, he strode into the room and took in the scene.

Clytus stood only a few steps into the large room. A small cot rested against one wall and a washstand with pitcher and bowl rested next to that. A large table and four chairs rounded out the furniture. None of this, however, held any interest for Ragnor. The man standing on the other side of the table some ten paces away held his complete attention. A thin knife was pressed to the throat of his cousin, Shaith Ku'rin, Princess of Mu'shadar, who dangled from the man's grip. The girl looked terrified. Her eyes were wide as they darted around the room looking for some release. Even at just over two winters, the girl knew what was happening—knew that the cold steel at her throat could end her tiny life.

Ragnor thought he had steeled himself for what he knew he would see when he entered the room. Yet, now that it was full in front of him, he felt his heart break. "Why?" It was all he could ask as he stared into the eyes of the man holding his cousin. Setting down the lantern, his bottom lip shook as he spoke. "Why have you done this, Father?"

Tears spilled freely down Bathlin De'haln's cheek before Ragnor had finished the question. "It was no supposed to be this way. I be the eldest, not him! Do you no see, Son?" The hand with the knife came away from Shaith's neck and dropped to his side.

Missing Pieces: The Way of the Lion

"And now his wife be pregnant once more. This time it will be a son for sure!" Bathlin's face twisted into anger, then softened as he looked at his son. "I did this for you, Ragnor. It be your right to rule. You should be King of Mu'shadar." Turning his face to the ceiling, the man let out a guttural yell. "Mother! You said I would be king! That my son would rule after! Why did you no kill Vandin when he was in your womb!"

His father had always been aloof, stood apart from even his son. Ragnor understood, though. He knew the pressure that came with the responsibilities of being one of the Blood. Still, looking back, he now saw the patterns—remembered the times when his father had done things Ragnor had not understood. Those actions did make sense if looked at from another perspective.

Yet, my father be ranting to a woman dead near ten turns of the seasons! He be mad. More than mad for doing this to Shaith.

"Father!" Ragnor pulled every reserve of confidence he held and forced it into his words. "This be done. Release the Princess! Now!" Without waiting on an answer, he started to cross the room.

His father flinched as if he was surprised to find he was not alone. His face contorted into a snarl. "Nix!" The girl's body slammed onto the tabletop and she immediately began to wail. "This will no be over until my son sits the throne!" His father's arm whipped into the air, the knife he held pointing down. "He deserves this! He deserves more than I have given him!"

Stopping just past Clytus, still many paces from his father, Ragnor held up both of his hands. "Father, I be your son. I be here. Do no do this. It be madness."

The anger drained from his father's face and tears began to flow once more as he looked at Ragnor. "Forgive me, son. Oh, Gods! Please forgive me!" With this last yell, Bathlin slammed his knife down. Ragnor's heart leapt into his throat even as he tried to leap the impossible distance between himself and his father. A wordless scream erupted from his throat as he watched the blade streak toward the back of Shaith's small head. Knowing he would never reach his father before the knife struck home, he lunged forward anyway. Letting his momentum carry him on, and not wanting to look at the little girl on the table who had suddenly stopped crying, Ragnor slammed into his father, sending him sprawling to the floor. Whipping about, he gaped at the tabletop—his father's knife stood quivering in the wood. The fact that the outlander stood on the other side of the table holding Shaith protectively in his arms some ten paces away hit him like a blacksmith's hammer. "Yet...How...?"

"How?" Clytus looked puzzled. "How am I supposed to know how your father planned for this to work? I told you, I am not versed in the affairs of the Blood." Rounding the table, he handed the little girl to Ragnor. Tears still streaming down her plump cheeks, she flung her arms around his neck. "However, I think the little Princess would appreciate the company of her parents." Placing his hand upon Ragnor's shoulder, the outlander all but pushed him out the door. "I will bring...the other up." The pause was slight.

Desire as he did, Ragnor could not turn his head back to look at his father. He could hear the man sobbing where he lay upon the floor. Rubbing the girl's back and making shushing sounds, Ragnor headed out of the east wing dungeons.

Chapter Six

Clytus Rillion pulled the last leather strap tight on his saddlepack. The chestnut mare was a gift from his Master and would serve him well back home. The morn was bright, though still a bit chilly for late autumn. The sky shone a bright blue and the courtyard of Master Yoanin's villa was deserted, save for him.

A good omen to start a journey on a clear day!

All was in readiness. The ship that would take him back to Ro'Arith would be leaving with the afternoon tide—plenty of time yet for him to reach the docks and get loaded. The sounds of boots entering the villa courtyard from the street gave him pause and he looked over the rump of his mare. Dressed in plain brown leather with a cloth knapsack thrown over one shoulder, very few would glance at the common man walking toward Clytus, much less recognize him as the Hand of the King's Justice. With a last pat to the horse's neck, Clytus strode out to meet Ragnor De'haln. "Hail, Hand, and well met. I almost did not recognize you without your colorful silks."

"Aye. I did no feel like wearing silks this day." The black man took Clytus' offered hand and shook it. "I heard you were leaving Silaway. Be your apprenticeship at an end so soon?"

"Nix. Master Yoanin felt it was best that I seek a new Master. He feels there may be some who do not fully understand the events that happened at the palace. That someone might take it against me for one reason or another."

The Hand snorted. "Aye. They might at that."

The man looked tired. More so than a lump on the head two days gone would account for. Clytus reached out and touched his arm. "Are you feeling all right?"

Bowing his head, Ragnor's shoulders drooped. He looked like a man who was lost. "Nix. It may be a while before I feel right again." Taking a deep breath, the man looked up at Clytus. "I never got the chance to thank you for what you did." He raised a hand to forestall Clytus. "You left the palace as soon as you turned my father over to the Kashi. I heard you even refused a reward. I have always thought outlanders knew nothing of honor. Yet, it be you who has given me a lesson about honor."

"I was just a man who was in the right place to stop a terrible thing. That is all."

Ragnor did not answer. Instead, he stood eyeing Clytus like a man with a bone to pick. It was a fine time for Clytus to realize the man wore his sword and thick dagger. As the silence stretched, Clytus shifted his feet, feeling a desire to have his chestnut mare between them once more.

Finally, with a snort and shake of the head, the Hand smiled. A smile that never touched his sad eyes. "I was hoping that you would allow me to accompany you. I have never been across the Great Ocean."

Clytus thought the man drawing a weapon on him would have shocked him less! "You are the Hand of the King's Justice. You have duties here. Especially now with your... the trial. Your people need you now more than ever."

Missing Pieces: The Way of the Lion

"Be that as it may, I can no sit in judgment of my own father." Scrubbing the back of his head, Ragnor turned and started to pace. "His guilt be indisputable, of that there be no doubt. He will no survive the trial. Yet, I could no sooner send my father to the headsman than I could my own cousin." Walking back to Clytus, he pulled his knapsack from his shoulder and held it out. "Besides, I be packed already."

This made Clytus laugh in spite of himself. "Very well then, Hand—" Ragnor shook his head and Clytus nodded. "Very well then, *Ragnor*. Let me say my farewells inside and we shall be off." Turning, Clytus headed toward the main doors of the villa. Stopping at the top of the stairs, he called back over his shoulder. "Who knows, perhaps someday we shall even become friends."

Pronunciation Guide
Names in () were never mentioned in the story.
They are added here for completeness

Characters - Silawaians

Bathlin De'haln - [BATH-lin dee-HAL-n] - Crown Prince of Mu'shadar, half-brother to the Oash'ado and father of Ragnor De'ahln

Master (Fylain) Yoanin - [Fie-LAIN yo-ANN-in] - Wealthy merchant in Silaway, Clytus Rillion's Master and a Brother of the Tat'Sujen Order

Laydrin Ku'rin - [LAY-drin COO-rin] - (Deceased) Former Oash'ado of Mu'shadar, husband to Ry'ielle Ku'rin and father to Vandin Ku'rin

Patell De'haln - [PA-tell dee-HAL-n] - (Deceased) General in the Mu'shadar army, first love of Ry'ielle Ku'rin and father to Bathlin De'haln

Ragnor De'haln - [RAG-nore dee-HAL-n] - Hand of the King's Justice and Nephew to the Oash'ado of Mu'shadar

King (Rahn) Thaloman - [RAWN THAL-o-man] - King of the Hek'kie Dominion

Ry'ielle Ku'rin - [rye-EYE-elle COO-rin] - (Deceased) Former Queen of Mu'shadar, wife of Laydrin Ku'rin, mother of Bathlin De'haln (by Patell De'haln) and Vandin Ku'rin (by Laydrin Ku'rin)

Shaith Ku'rin - [SHAITH COO-rin] - Princess of Mu'shadar and daughter to Vandin Ku'rin

Vandin Ku'rin - [Van-din COO-rin] - Oash'ado of the Mu'shadar Empire, father to Shaith Ku'rin, uncle to Ragnor De'haln, half-brother of Bathlin De'haln and son of Laydrin and Ry'ielle Ku'rin

Characters - Ro'Arithians

Clytus Rillion - [CLY-tuss RILL-ee-un] – Apprentice Tat'Sujen under Master Yoanin and originally from the city of Mocley in Ro'Arith

Societies - Titles-Classes - Governments - Nationalities

The Blood - People who can trace their lineage back to the founder of the Mu'shadar Empire, Brun E'angle

Hek'kie - [HECK-kie] - Meaning 'Of the People' Warrior class in Silaway

Missing Pieces: The Way of the Lion

Kashi - [KAH-she] - Men assigned to guard the royal family and any nobles known as the Blood
Mu'shadar - [MOO-sha-dar] - Meaning 'Shelterers of Life' Ruling class in Silaway
Oash'ado – [oh-AHSH-ah-doe] - Meaning 'Father' or 'Giver' it is the official title of the King of Mu'shadar
Ro'Arithian - [row-ARE-ith-ee-an] - A person from Ro'Arith
Silawaian - [SILL-a-way-ee-in] - A person from Silaway
Tat'Sujen Order - [tat-SUE-jen] - A secret organization whose members have a power over Sujen
Yosh'ado – [YOsh-ah-doe] - Meaning 'First Son' it is the official title of the Crown Prince of Mu'shadar

Countries - Towns - Geography

Mocley - [MOCK-lee] - A large port city in south-west Ro'Arith
Nithshilo - [nith-SHY-low] - A port city in east Silaway and capitol of the Mu'shadar Empire
Ro'Arith - [row-ARE-ith] - A large continent on the Plane of Talic'Nauth
Silaway - [SILL-a-way] - A large continent on the Plane of Talic'Nauth
Talic'Nauth - [TALL-ick nawth] - The Plane of existence on which all things reside
Toufuchi – [Tow-fu-she] – Capitol city of the Hek'kie Dominion

The Essence

Strands - What a Tat'Sujen sees while holding the Sight of Sujen. They can use Strands to manipulate the surrounding environment
Sujen - [SUE-jen] - A form of the Essence that surrounds all things

Maxwell Alexander Drake

About the Author

Maxwell Alexander Drake—or Drake as he is known to friends and fans alike—has been writing fantasy for over 28 years.

Currently, he lives in Las Vegas with his wife and two sons.

Find out more about him on his official website, www.maxwellalexanderdrake.com.

Farmers and Mercenaries was Drake's first major novel and has won a 2009 Moonbeam Young Adult Fantasy Award for excellence in literature.

You can read the first four chapters of both Farmers and Mercenaries, and the second book of the series, Mortals and Deities, as well as keep up to date on the Genesis of Oblivion Saga at its official website, www.genesisofoblivion.com.

Each of the six novels of the Genesis of Oblivion Saga are scheduled for release each Summer. You can pre-order your copy at our website, www.imaginedinterprises.com.

Hemingway's Challenge

Co-authors tempt fate, get married, survive.
                              -Matthew and Stefanie Verish

About the Story

In the aftermath of *Raven's Heart*, the tracker named Hawkwing and the former bandit known as the White Demon try to evade a clandestine organization known as the Seroko. "The Hawk's Shadow" tells their tale and bridges *Raven's Heart* with the upcoming *Black Earth Trilogy*.

The Hawk's Shadow
By
Matthew and Stefanie Verish

The flames in the hearth flared, a peculiar violet light staining the amber tongues but for a moment. The surge of heat enticed skinny white fingers from beneath the heavy black cloak to reach for the flames as if to stroke them. The rest of the huddled form remained concealed, though no one else was as near the hearth to pry at the face beneath the hood.

"You're in Braidell," the barkeeper addressed the tall, gaunt man before him. "It's another ten miles before you reach Rasdin, if you head north."

Hawkwing took off his hat and shook his head. "What about south?"

"The Kingdoms?"

"Belorn."

"That's a bit more of a trek."

"I would be willing to pay for victuals, if you can supply them." The tracker set a purse upon the counter, and the barkeeper stared.

"How soon are you leaving?"

Hawkwing met the man's gaze. "How soon can you assist me?" He pushed the purse across the counter and allowed the man to inspect its contents.

The barkeeper looked up and studied him, then gave a whistle to a young man who had been gathering empty tankards from the tables. "I'd like you to tend to this gentleman's needs. Mister...."

"Hawkwing," the tracker supplied, rubbing his thick beard.

"Help Mr. Hawkwing gather what he wants for his journey south."

"A horse?" the tracker asked.

The barkeeper nodded. He turned to the young man. "Start him at the stables."

Hawkwing tipped his hat and followed the youth out of the tavern.

The shrouded figure near the hearth turned its head and reluctantly withdrew from the flames. It slung a pair of boots over a narrow shoulder and left the room without anyone's notice.

Missing Pieces: The Hawk's Shadow

~*~

"Where are we going?"

Hawkwing patted the mare's neck with a shaky hand. "Eventually we'll head north into the mountains." He paused to check the supplies that had been fitted to the animal's back. "Do you remember the old mill we saw before this town?"

The hooded figure nodded.

"Head there, and wait for me. I'll need a few hours." Hawkwing mounted and caught the shadowed frown from his companion. "Trust me, Collin. I'll be back for you." He gave his brother a reassuring smile. "I'll explain everything. Mind you wear your boots."

The Demon said nothing but stepped aside as Hawkwing urged the horse onward and down the road. Slowly he walked the same stretch, watching the snow clouds lumber across the morning sky and amass like debris at the bend in a river.

He saw a young couple running down the road hand-in-hand, laughing. They paid him no mind as they slowed and came to a stop, battling the troublesome wind that buffeted her skirt and nearly stole his hat. They locked in a kiss, whereupon a feisty gust stole her scarf and sent it the Demon's way. With a little manipulation, he had the object catch in his waiting hand.

The lady immediately came to retrieve it, blushing in embarrassment. "Thank you," she told him, and her eyes caught his. She stared speechless until her partner called to her, breaking the trance. Then they were on their way, quieter than before. The Demon thought she had been rather pretty, with braided blonde hair and large blue eyes. She was probably his age, if not a little older. With a lingering sigh spurred by loneliness and even a hint of envy, he waited until they had gone before he resumed his mission.

When he came upon the old mill, he set to exploring all the shadowy niches and old tools left behind. The stream that had once powered the wheel was but a trickle, though a few small fish still darted through its current. The Demon unbound the cloth he had wrapped around his feet and rinsed the material while he numbed his toes in the icy water. He missed the warm weather, and while the winter had been mild thus far, the sky foretold of bitterness.

He retreated inside the dilapidated building and started a small fire with scraps of wood. He set his wrappings to dry on a couple of rocks he placed near the flames, stretched his feet out to absorb the warmth, and lay back on his pack. Eventually his eyes closed, but it was a fitful sleep that found him, and it was not quite an hour before he awoke to find he was no longer alone.

"I didn't want to wake you," Hawkwing said.

The Demon noticed he was without his hat. He could see the hints of silver in his brother's short-cropped hair as it came to match his frosted beard. "When'd y' get 'ere?" he asked.

"I haven't been here long," Hawkwing said. He looked at the pile of embers—all that remained of the Demon's fire. "We have a change in direction."

The Demon sat up and rewrapped his feet. "We riding?"

Hawkwing shook his head. "No. The horse is gone."

The Demon looked at him curiously.

"I gave it to a lucky fellow I met on the road. I sent him to Belorn with my hat."

"Right." The Demon studied him. "Y're worried 'bout something."

Hawkwing's golden gaze met his. "We're being followed."

"I didn' steal anything." The Demon smirked until he realized his brother's grim expression had not changed.

"Do you remember what I told you about the Watchers?"

There was a bout of silence before the Demon answered. "Y' think the other blokes found y'?"

"The Seroko, yes."

"What do they want with y'?"

Hawkwing tapped his temple. "They want to know what I know. The location of the Watchers' archives, for one." He did not mention his foremost concern: the Key. "So long as you're with me, you're in just as much danger."

The Demon's expression hardened. "'M not leaving."

Hawkwing patted his shoulder. "I'm not asking you to." He gave his brother a fleeting smile. "But we have a rough road ahead. If they fall for my ploy, we'll have a chance of losing them for a while. We'll quit the Link and travel north along the old mountain paths. Once we reach Mystland, we'll have the safety of the medori boundaries. We could be there within a week's time."

The Demon watched as his brother stood shakily. He did not express his concern aloud, but he did make it a point to shoulder the bulk of their supplies.

This did not go unnoticed. "You're forgetting something," the tracker said.

"What?" The Demon scanned the area for anything he had missed.

Hawkwing plucked the boots from his brother's shoulder, holding them before him with a trembling hand.

"I'll put them on later."

"I won't be the one to amputate your toes when you get frostbite."

"Whatzit 'amp-yoo-tate'?"

"When your toes freeze solid you'll need to cut them off to prevent infection."

The Demon gave him a strange look before reluctantly setting down his burdens to put on his boots.

"You may not thank me later, but I know you'll be grateful." Hawkwing smiled. He started to accumulate the supplies the Demon had set down.

"Leave me something," he grumbled. "'M stronger than I look."

"I know," Hawkwing said. *I'll need you to be strong for what's ahead of us.*

The two travelers left the Western Link of the Trader's Ring and headed into the foothills of the Chronleste Mountains. By late afternoon the remaining shards of sunlight had been swept away by blue-gray giants in the sky. The wind turned bitter, and with it the initial flakes of snow eddied against the mountainsides and swarmed around the brothers.

Hawkwing led the way with his hood drawn tightly, his great height shielding the slight form of his brother from the worst of the wind. Though they were careful in their ascent, the tracker stumbled more than once. When the sky darkened with undertones of violet, they found a niche among the rocky walls where they took shelter for the night. The winds subsided slightly, but the snowfall remained light and steady.

The Demon tended to the fire, violet flames consuming whatever brush and needled foliage he could find. The green wood hissed and popped, but the fragrance of pine was worth the attention it took to keep the fire burning. Meanwhile Hawkwing scrounged a meal from their provisions. He apportioned each of them some dried meat, biscuits, and cheese; he set a special costrel aside for their drink.

The Demon tried not to show how cold he was, but it was intentional that Hawkwing passed him the costrel first. "Take a sip. It'll warm you."

"Whatzit?"

The tracker did not reply but smiled as his brother took a swig. The Demon's face contorted as he swallowed, and Hawkwing's smile broadened. "Not too much, lest you lose your wits."

"'S enough!" The Demon readily handed the vessel back to him. Presently, he did feel a warmth spread from inside his chest up to his face and arms.

"Better?" Hawkwing asked.

The Demon nodded and tore a chunk of biscuit.

The tracker took a longer sip from the costrel and regarded his brother thoughtfully. "You've grown."

"What?" The Demon stared at him.

"You're not the same young man I met three years ago."

"Why? 'Cuz 'm taller?" He was trying to determine the reason for this topic. Hawkwing always had a point to what he said.

"Yes...and no." The tracker took a bite of his cheese. "You've matured...in several ways."

The Demon eyed him skeptically. "Don' start with that. Wasn' a kid when y' met me, an' I'm no diff'rent now."

"Ah, but you are. You speak better, you handle your anger better, and you've asserted your independence. You're ready to 'take the reins of your life,' so-to-speak."

"Stop it, Em'ri." Now it was evident to him what his brother was trying to impart, and the Demon would have none of it.

Hawkwing fell quiet.

After a while, the Demon felt the weight of his brother's silence and tried to resurrect conversation. "Met a girl t'day."

"What was her name?"

The Demon blushed, a hint of color rising to his white face. "Don' know. I didn' ask 'er."

"She was pretty?"

He nodded. "'Ad a bloke with 'er. 'E didn' seem like anything special."

"You think it takes something special to catch a lady's attention?" Hawkwing asked.

The Demon rubbed the back of his neck and stared at the flames. "Maybe. 'Ow else would she notice?"

"Circumstance. A conversation. A simple gesture." Hawkwing shrugged. "Women notice different things."

"White skin, sharp teeth, claws, wings..." The Demon kicked a rock into the flames.

"You don't look like that now—not in this form," Hawkwing said. "You're a handsome young man. I can tell you that comeliness runs in the family." He grinned.

The Demon forced a slight smile. "Doesn' really matter. 'M not like them."

"That is a curse and a blessing," the tracker said, passing the costrel back to his brother. "You can't live the way they do, but you'll have a life destined for other things. Greater things, perhaps."

The Demon looked at him. "'S what the Prophet said to me."

"Then he saw what I see. Only time will tell, Collin, but you will have your choices to make."

"An' y'll be there to make sure I don' mess up."

"You won't 'mess up.'" He watched the young man take a long drink. "And in one way or another, I'll be there with you."

The Demon wiped his mouth across his sleeve and gave a nod. "Good," he whispered. He suddenly felt very tired, his limbs heavy and awkward.

"Maybe we should try for some sleep," Hawkwing suggested.

"Bonzer." Already he felt he could fall back on his pack without a second thought. "Anyway," he added, his eyes half-closed, "I think she liked m' eyes."

Hawkwing smiled and draped an extra cloak over him.

Whatever had been in the costrel, it had allowed the Demon one of the most restful nights he had ever known. He rose with a restless sort of energy and an eagerness to be on their way. His bright humor, however, was diminished by the state of his brother. Hawkwing's pallor, while always present now, had shifted to a grayish hue. There was pain behind the tracker's eyes, and he was quiet this morning.

There were good days, and there were bad days, the Demon knew, and today would be trying. He knew better than to obviate Hawkwing's illness and immediately shouldered most of the load himself. However heavy it was, however his feet chaffed inside his boots, he could endure it. They had to get to Mystland, and the sooner they did, the sooner they could breathe easier.

The clouds lingered, and while the snow had stopped, a light layer now covered the trail. The travelers pressed onward after a light breakfast, penetrating deeper into the mountains. Footfalls grew heavier, and stops became more frequent. Neither brother would say a word; their ragged breathing spoke for them.

"Those bastards should be 'alfway to Belorn by now," the Demon said, breathless. He propped his back and the pack upon it against a ledge.

"I'd like to believe that," Hawkwing said, bent over his walking stick, "but I know them. The Seroko are as savvy as the Watchers, but they are driven by greed and power. That makes them relentless, and there are many who now follow their cause."

"But what do they want?" The Demon could not understand what would motivate anyone to hunt a man for years for what knowledge may or may not be inside his head.

Hawkwing studied him carefully. *Should I tell you? Should I tell you what they're truly after? The Key that was mine to bear has been passed on to you. No one knows of this but me, and perhaps it's best that the Key fade into obscurity. I would be willing to bear that responsibility to my death.*

"The Seroko would rule this world. Not through any emperor, not with legions of armed men, and not by seizing all the land they can take. They use the weaknesses of others to their advantage. They manipulate to reach their goals. They hide behind clever facades, and you are in their world without even knowing it. They can't be defeated because so many rely upon them." Hawkwing's expression tensed with a wave of pain. "We can't defeat them, so we must run from them."

"There aren't any Watchers left?" the Demon asked.

"They are few, scattered. The order has dissolved. I regret only that the Seroko survives them."

"Doesn' seem fair," the Demon muttered.

"What would be fair is if their empire collapses from within. I want to believe they will ultimately corrupt themselves, bring about their own ending." He gazed into the distance, his thoughts there too.

"Maybe we should stop for a bit," the Demon suggested. He watched as the tracker wiped his brow. "Snow's picking up."

"Soon but not yet," Hawkwing insisted. "There is a pass I'd like to reach before we're done for the day." He started walking again.

"'S not that much farther, right?" The Demon awaited a response, but when none came, his concerns deepened.

The trail grew treacherous as it skirted sheer cliffs and mountainsides. The snow became a blinding flurry, and it was all the travelers could do to keep sight of one another. The path narrowed and grew slick, and the Demon cursed the worthlessness of boots compared to claws.

That was when he fell.

They had just reached the steep summit of an overlook when the Demon shifted the weight of the heavy pack on his back. Too much, he lost his balance and scrambled to stay upright. His hands met with empty air as he careened backwards. He hit the ground hard and began to slide down the path and toward the ledge. His panic caused him to shift to his demon form, and he dug his claws into the frozen, rocky earth, feeling them tear as he desperately tried to slow his descent.

The grade of the slope steepened, and instinct drove him to his final option. Leathery wings tore through his clothes, ripped through the cloak. The Demon clenched his teeth, closed his eyes, and hoped his death would be quick and painless.

The ground beneath him vanished.

Nigqora!

Through the empty air he beat his wings furiously, praying for an updraft. Snow was everywhere: in his eyes, his mouth, his ears. His wings strained as they shoved down upon the air, but though his fall had slowed, he was still dropping. Just as his strength left him, an icy gale caught him like a kite and buffeted him backward. He slammed into something solid and dropped to the snowy ground, gasping for breath. Warm liquid ran down his face, and all he could hear was a deafening ringing in his ears. As he suffocated, the snow vanished, darkening into nothing but shadows.

~*~

His eyes met with his brother's hands as they cleaned the carcasses of two rabbits. He watched the knife's quick, deliberate strokes, and he wondered just how many times his brother had done this necessary task. The hands stopped working, and when they did, he watched them tremble: the mark of the Quake. The Demon wanted to turn away, but the fire in his head kept him still. He closed his eyes again, only to find that those unsteady hands were now carefully tucking another blanket around him.

This time when he opened his eyes, it was Hawkwing's careworn face that he saw. "Sorry," the Demon mumbled weakly.

"You were right," the tracker murmured, "we should have stopped. Forgive me."

The Demon sighed, feeling like a fool. It was not for his sake he had wanted to stop, but now their progress was at a standstill, and it was his fault. It angered him even more that Hawkwing should try to assume the blame. Deliberately he lifted himself upright.

His brother's large hands were there to support him, coupled by a regard of disapproval. "There is nothing worth losing you," he said, his normally even voice colored with emotion. "You don't know how close I was to losing the only family I have."

The Demon met Hawkwing's glassy gaze. Only now did he see the blood-soaked cloth by the fire, the bandaged tips of his own fingers. "'M sorry," he repeated, though he knew his brother's words were not meant to burden him with guilt.

Hawkwing gently squeezed his shoulder. "How are you feeling?"

"I'm alright," the Demon said, taking in the new landscape. The two of them were in a valley, shapes of the surrounding mountains darker than the night. His gaze returned to Hawkwing's trembling hands. *How are you feeling?* He wanted to ask but did not. It was another question that left his lips. "Where are we?"

Hawkwing pointed to a nearby silhouette. "The trail is above us."

The Demon frowned as he considered this. There was only one way his brother could have reached him, and that was by exerting his innate but sacred ability to change his form to that of an eagle. He had never seen the change, but he understood it was a meaningful sacrifice his brother had made for him. *Thank you.*

He touched the bandage tied around his forehead and tested his limbs. For all his scrapes and bruises, he had not broken anything. "We can start again in the morning. I'll be ready," he insisted.

"We'll see." Hawkwing glanced at the mountains. "We'll find another route; in the end, that may work to our advantage. I'll scout ahead in the morning." He looked evenly at his brother. "Nothing but rest 'til I get back."

Missing Pieces: The Hawk's Shadow

The Demon blinked and laid his throbbing head back on the rolled bundle. "Y' could've been m' father," he said in jest.

"Because your father would show just as much concern?"

"No. Because I kinda wish 'e 'ad." The Demon closed his eyes before he could see his reaction. In the aftermath of silence, he began to wonder if Hawkwing would respond at all. He half-opened one eye to find his brother gazing thoughtfully into the distance, the rabbits slack in his trembling hands.

"It's a difficult role to undertake," Hawkwing said quietly.

The Demon opened his eyes to regard him.

"You suffer through your children, live through their joys. They are so much a part of your life that you can't imagine a world without them."

"Maybe that's 'ow 'twas for y', but m' father was nothing like that." His words were thick.

"You never thought about what your father did after you ran away?" Hawkwing asked, meeting his gaze.

"I did. If 'e wasn' killed, then 'e went on the same without me." The Demon fell quiet upon seeing the sadness settle in the lines on his brother's face. The tracker looked far older than he should.

"If I had one wish for you, it would be that you find peace in your heart. What you carry with you will always keep you an arm's length from happiness. It's not easy to let go of the past, but you're too young to be looking behind you instead of focusing on the path ahead. You're bright, you're gifted, and you have a sound heart. Let those traits be what guide you."

"Y' think I really 'ave a future in Mystland?" The Demon was doubtful.

"If that's what you want." Hawkwing skewered a piece of meat and passed it to his brother. "I've arranged for you to study under a skilled wizard. Medoriate Raiskin has agreed to take you as an apprentice. He's a good man, and he will treat you well. You might even learn something from him." The tracker hinted a smile as he cooked his own dinner above the flames.

"I 'aven't met a good wizard yet," the Demon mumbled. "An' no one's been able to teach me anything. 'S like they've never seen a mage before." He turned the stick to cook the other side of the morsel. "They don' want to admit they don' know anything, so they try to show off an' prove they're better'n me. Treat me like a bloody kid."

"Admittedly, I don't think most of the wizards have seen a mage before. They're not sure what to do with you. Maybe you'll be the one to teach them. Wouldn't that be humbling?"

"The only reason they even looked at me was because y' were with me."

"I have no reputation in Mystland. Those I do know are people you can trust. Once you've grown with your magic, you can make the decision to stay or not. At least the medori will accept you as one of their kind. The world outside Mystland has its prejudices, and you have to be careful where you cast your gaze." Hawkwing withdrew the stick and gave the meat a moment to cool.

The Demon did the same. "Seems I don' 'ave many choices."

"Opportunities present themselves with time. You just need to be patient."

Matthew and Stefanie Verish

"I don' know that word," the Demon said stubbornly.

"Ah, good. You have time to learn it." Hawkwing winked and took a bite of his quarry.

The Demon cast him a wry smile and joined him in dinner.

~*~

Hawkwing was gone with the coming of dawn. His clothes were set aside in a neat bundle, and the Demon searched the sky for a glimpse of the eagle. The sun bled scarlet across the horizon, but he saw nothing but the jagged teeth of the mountains.

The Demon stretched and found the soreness had settled deeply in his muscles. He had suffered worse in his childhood squabbles, and trivial aches and pains would not deter him from his mission this morning: breakfast. He hoped to have it ready when Hawkwing returned. He dug through their bags and found more bread, but the cheese was nearly gone, and the costrels were almost empty.

He rebuilt the fire, packed the costrels with snow, and set them near the heat. Then he glimpsed Hawkwing's bow and quiver. If nothing else, he could try for something fresh this morning. He bundled his cloak around him, drew his hood, and slung the quiver and bow over his shoulder. He ignored the pain in his feet as he limped away from their camp and into the forested land to the south.

When he returned, he had a limp goose clutched in his frozen hand. He stumbled back to the dying fire. He was soaked and chilled to the bone, a state brought upon him by the half-frozen lake in which he had collected the bird. He had not intended to fall in; he had hoped the ice he had formed upon the water's surface had been thick enough to support him. It was a miscalculation he had come to regret.

It was all he could do to limp back to the camp, but if he could not rouse the fire soon, Hawkwing would have more to worry about than his breakfast. This upset the Demon more than anything else, for though his intentions had been noble, he had disobeyed his brother's order to stay put.

"It's the Shadow in you," Hawkwing had told him upon an occasion the Demon had been especially mischievous and ornery. Shadow or not, he never wanted to cause his brother grief. This hunting venture would earn him a lecture…if he survived long enough to hear it.

His numb feet and legs gave way a few feet from the fire. He lay there motionless, staring at the waning source of heat.

"Em'ri?" he gasped, but his brother had not yet returned.

The Demon reached for the flames and drew the heat toward him. It surrounded his shredded, outstretched fingers and spread along his arm, to his chest, then his neck, face, and the rest of his body. He tore at it greedily, feasting on the warmth that would save him. But the fire had died, and even the embers had gone cold and black.

With a grunt he forced himself up and gathered what brush he could find. He had to kindle the flames again—even at the cost of his waning energy. With a substantial pile of twigs, branches, and broken logs, he grudgingly concentrated his energy and watched the wood smolder. He started to shiver again as he nudged his magic a little more—just enough to give birth to a dancing flame. He nurtured it until it fed easily on its own, and then he collapsed again to bask in his creation. His body gave way to exhaustion, and he closed his eyes.

When he woke again, he was staring at a bird. Not merely the goose he had dragged back from the lake, but a very large bird with talons the size of his fists and a sharp, hooked beak. Arm's length from him, the giant raptor was tearing apart the carcass of the goose. It ripped at the flesh, scattered feathers everywhere.

The Demon stared, and as he overcame his initial shock, his mind started to reason through the scene before him. "Em'ri?" he whispered, not daring to move lest he spook the bird.

The golden eagle paid him no heed.

The Demon tried to look into its sun-gold eyes. "Em'ri?" he repeated, a little louder.

The eagle stopped feeding and cocked its head in his direction.

"'S me, Em'ri. Y'r brother." Slowly, painfully, he sat up. "Y' remember, right?"

The eagle took an awkward step toward him, its wild eyes sharp upon him.

"Awkwing," he tried again. "Em'ri. Won't y'—" As he reached out to the bird, it shied away, flapped its massive wings, and lighted in a nearby tree. The Demon swore.

He stumbled as he stood, nearly falling over as he reached for his brother's clothes. "Please," he spoke to the bird. "Please come back." He held up the clothes, feeling stupid but also feeling desperate.

Motionless, the bird stared at him.

"Please, Em'ri." He tried to remain calm, but his thoughts turned to the story his brother had told him about Snowfire, his wife. She had retained the form of a hawk for too long, and she had forgotten who she truly was. If he could not coax his brother to change back… Maybe it was already too late.

He set the clothes down and approached the remains of the goose. With a scowl he lifted the bloody remains. "C'mon. 'S y'r breakfast, eh? I didn't get to cook it, but I guess it doesn' matter." He approached the tree. "'Ere. 'S delicious."

The eagle did not move.

"What else y' want?" the Demon asked, losing his patience. "We can make it! We'll get to Mystland. I'll even wear my bloody boots 'til m' feet fall off!" He looked down at his feet and wished he had not. He stared at the bird for a long while, fighting the urge to cry. "This 'ow I'm going to lose y'?" he asked softly.

Dejected, the Demon tossed the goose to the ground and limped back toward the fire. He ran a hand through his hair and sat down, his expression vacant. *Maybe a wizard can change you back*, he thought, but his heart was not in his hope. "I wasn't ready to lose y' yet," he murmured, burying his head in his hands. He felt the bandage on his brow and tore it away in anger. When he finally looked at it, he found it was the golden bandana his brother always wore—a token of his people.

All right, he thought, wiping the water from his eyes. He glimpsed the eagle still perched in the tree. *For what it's worth, I'll keep going. But if you're testing me, I swear*

Missing Pieces: The Hawk's Shadow

I'll never forgive you.

He tossed snow on the fire and gathered their belongings. He tucked his brother's clothes in one of the packs and tied the bandana around his neck. He stared balefully at the boots before taking a deep breath and shoving each foot inside. His eyes watered at the pain, but with a wipe of his sleeve, he stood and slung one pack on his back. Then the second. Then the bow, the quiver, his saber and his brother's short sword... He took a step forward and nearly collapsed.

Nigqora.

He tore everything from him and emptied both packs. He took what belonged to Hawkwing, a few provisions, and their weapons, and he left the second bag behind. All he knew was that they were headed north, and eventually, they would have to cross the road to the west to reach Mystland. He trudged forward without questioning why, but with small consolation, he found the eagle following him overhead.

The day wore on, and the snow started again. Heavy wet flakes marked the onset of a storm. The Demon had found what he thought was an old trail, but it could just have well as been a deer path. He followed it anyway, and it carried him out of the valley and up into the rocky cliffs of the mountains again. He eventually lost sight of the eagle amidst the snow, but he did not stop to rest. If he stopped, he was afraid he would not have the strength to start again.

His diligence failed when he slipped a second time. Though there was no cliff to fall from, he hit the frozen ground flat on his belly, the weight of his pack crushing him from above. He lay there stunned and breathless and without the energy to pick himself up. Minutes passed as he strained for air, and he had all but passed out when his ears caught the sound of footsteps crunching through the snow behind him. He could not turn to see who it was, but he could tell by the gait that it was not his brother. And it was not just one person.

"That's not him," a hard voice said.

"Obviously. But he has been seen with a companion," said another.

"That still leaves the question of his whereabouts."

"I'd say we're about to find some answers."

The Demon found himself hoisted up by two brawny men. His pack was tossed aside, and he was pressed up against a dead tree. His hood was tossed from his face, and the point of a knife was lowered to his throat.

"He's just a kid!" one of the five in the group said.

"Not just a kid. Look at him." The bearded stranger with the knife stepped aside for the others to see.

"What is he?"

"Damned if I know."

"Jedinom's Grace, ask him!"

The bearded man returned his attention to the Demon. "Who or what are you?"

The Demon struggled to breathe. "Jus' a kid," he gasped with a hint of a smirk.

"That's cute. We know you were traveling with a man. Where is he?"

"'E flew away," the Demon replied, his expression now serious.

"He thinks he's being funny."

The man dropped the knife, drew the Demon away from the tree, and slammed him against the trunk. A renewal of blinding pain lanced the side of his head where he had hit it before. A fresh welling of blood sprang forth, and his world grew dim and fuzzy.

"So help me, if you kill him—!" Another one of the men stepped forward. "Let him down."

The Demon slumped to the ground, staring up at strangers surrounding him. The one who had stepped forward crouched in front of him. "We're not murderers," he began, drawing forth a handkerchief to dab at the Demon's wound, but the Demon turned away.

"We're looking for your companion. Hawkwing. All we want is information from him. The sooner we get it, the sooner you can go about your business."

"As I said," the Demon murmured, "'e's gone."

"Is he dead?" the man pressed.

"We found no body," said another.

"'E's not coming back," the Demon said. "So jus' go away." He heard a snort.

"You see, this is where we have a dilemma," the interrogator continued calmly. "What do I believe? Is Hawkwing dead? Or has he taken another route?" He eased back on his feet. "And then I wonder if you have any answers." He regarded the Demon thoughtfully.

"I don' care what y' believe." The Demon shrugged and closed his eyes.

"Bring me some rope," the interrogator said. "We'll have to take him with us." He turned back to the Demon. "Whoever you are to Hawkwing, I'm surprised he abandoned you. I'm disappointed, given his reputation. I suppose not all legends are as them seem." He bound the Demon's wrists. "You're fortunate we found you when we did."

The Demon opened his eyes but said nothing.

The man hoisted him up and was quick to brace him when he nearly fell.

"We won't get far with him like that," another said.

"We have plenty of time," the interrogator said. "I'll help him."

"He's your responsibility, Marksman," said the bearded man. "Let's move before the snow buries us. I don't want to be stuck on a mountain come nightfall."

They slowly picked their way along the cliffs until the light grew thin and the snow too thick to see. They made camp on an escarpment, near a stand of conifers. The Demon seemed all but forgotten as a fire was built, food was prepared, and primitive shelters were erected. He merely sat there quietly, tied to a tree, watching his captors race the pending darkness.

Finally the one known as the Marksman came to him with a bowl of steaming liquid and sat across from him. He soaked a piece of bread in the broth and offered it to the Demon. The Demon wanted to refuse it despite how hungry he was, but his brother had taught him patience. He needed to save his strength and his energy for the right moment—whatever that moment would be. With great restraint, he accepted the moistened bread and let it scrape down his throat like a rock.

"Who are you to him?" the Marksman asked. "You have traveled with him a distance, haven't you?"

The Demon merely stared.

"Where were you headed?" He held back the next piece, waiting for a response. He received none. "Somewhere we could not reach him, I would venture. There's only one place, really. Medori territory. You were heading to Mystland."

The Demon's expression betrayed nothing, but the Marksman smiled and nodded. "Perhaps he will meet you there." He gave him the bread. "I expect he has told you about us, judging by your silence. You have named us an enemy through the tinted perspective of a Gray Watcher, but being one of the Seroko, I can tell you that our methods are not so different from theirs. We value what they value: knowledge, culture, the very world in which we live...."

He gave the Demon a sip from the bowl. "If there is one distinction between the Seroko and the Watchers, it's that we have ambition. We believe in using the information we gain toward a greater good. Why keep secret a wealth of knowledge from which the world can benefit? Why not take the responsibility of shaping Secramore, helping those in need?

"That is why the archives we seek are so important. They should be used selflessly, effectively." He slipped in a question. "What do you know of the Key?"

This time the Demon's blank face derived from sincerity and not defiance. His brother had never mentioned anything about a key, and if Hawkwing had not spoken of it, he was less than concerned about it.

The Marksman gauged him and continued. "We are willing to be leaders. The Watchers have never shown any such inclination. Even through Hawkwing you can see they are evasive, secretive." The Marksman studied the Demon, trying to judge his reaction, but as before, the violet eyes were impassive. He was surprised, then, when the captive spoke.

"Sounds like y' 'ave a noble cause. All y' want is to do the right thing. 'Elp others."

"Yes," the Marksman said.

The Demon shook his head. "Sitting 'ere in the dark, tied to a tree..." He shrugged. "I jus' don' believe y'."

The Marksman frowned and turned to find one of his peers approaching. "Is he talking?" the bearded man asked.

The Marksman stood. "He doesn't know anything," he said, his voice now cold and flat. "Hawkwing is here somewhere or plans to meet with him. We need to head to Mystland."

"We can't cross their border."

"We may not have to." They started to walk away toward the fire, their conversation lost to the wind.

~*~

It was a race the Demon could not win. The cold was biting, and the snow had barely relented in the hours before dawn when he had made his escape. The Seroko had underestimated him, neglected to consider that he might possess magic. He had slipped his ropes easily, but he knew his pursuers would not make the same mistake twice. They would soon—if they had not already—realize he was gone, and they would be quick to his trail. They were going to catch him, but the true question was what he would do when they did.

He had stolen back his pack and weaponry out of necessity, but his burden was what slowed him, drained his energy. His aching, chaffed feet rubbed raw in his boots, making each step a painful one. The thick snow that now obscured the trail opposed his progress, and he kept his head low as the wind spattered fresh flakes into his face.

The Demon trudged onward, trying to keep his thoughts empty. Thinking of his brother would lead to despair, though it was because of Hawkwing he felt the need to succeed. Every now and then he would glance skyward and hope to see the giant silhouette of the eagle against the oppressive clouds, but there was only the wind and the snow.

He came upon a place where the flat surface of the trail seemed to split. One route continued along the mountain ridges; the other appeared to drop down into the valley below. It was hard to distinguish for certain where the paths led, as he could barely see a few paces in front of him. The Demon stood at the fork, shivering as he considered his options. He glanced up at the rocky walls and began to form an idea. He adjusted the pack on his back and started along the higher ground.

After less than an hour of travel, he stopped and set down his pack. Cautiously he crouched down to peer over the side of cliff at the valley below. The slope downward was steep but not sheer. The mountainside bordering the trail, however, was a vertical rise to the sky, and heavy snow drifts perched precariously along narrow ledges and rocky shelves. The Demon shoved the snow off a nearby rock, huddled atop it, and waited.

An hour had not passed when he heard the crunching of snow and muffled voices. The Demon stood and shoved the pack off the trail, watching it slide and tumble into the white obscurity below. He backtracked the way he had come until he glimpsed his pursuers. Then he pressed his back against the mountainside and drew a deep breath.

A shout indicated they had spotted him, and he fought the instinct to run. Instead he started to focus his thoughts and his energy upon his target. The Seroko were running toward him now, closing the distance. The Demon's magic responded sluggishly, as it always did when he tried to manipulate the earth. But once he had built enough momentum, there was no way of stopping the stubborn element from completing its course of action.

He could now distinguish the faces of the men approaching him. He closed his eyes and gave the mountain a magical shove. Nothing happened. Frantically he drew the energy toward himself, clutching and pulling as quickly as he could. It grew inside him like a tumor, pressure building painfully against his heart, his lungs. Whatever he had, he had to use it now; it had to be enough.

Missing Pieces: The Hawk's Shadow

He shoved the mountain again, but this time he did not relent. He pressed his hands against the rock and felt it shudder. The vibrations traveled up the rocky wall, and a sound like thunder roared in his ears and nearly toppled him to the ground. He pushed away from the mountain just as an onslaught of rock and snow raced down, a massive white monster devouring all in its path. He heard the men shout but did not look behind him as he tucked himself into a ball and propelled himself off the trail.

The Demon tumbled roughly down the slope, the sky and the earth becoming one as he smashed and scraped along the icy rocks. The debris from the avalanche caught him in a smothering torrent of heavy snow, suffocating him and burying him beneath several feet of pressure. All motion stopped, and he was entombed in silence.

It took a moment for him to realize his situation, the fact he could not move, could not breathe. Panic seized him, and he roused the heat from his body to radiate from him in a burst of energy. The snow liquefied, and he slowly felt the rigidity of his prison give way. He thrust his head into open air and gasped. He drew several deep breaths before he exerted the effort to free himself.

The Demon was utterly exhausted and overwhelmed by the cold. He stumbled down the changed landscape, and surveyed they valley. Of the Seroko there was no trace, but nor was there a clear sign of the trail he had sighted before. With a pained sigh he drew his damp cloak tighter and went in search of his pack.

He eventually found it near the edge of a half-frozen stream. Battered but not broken, the Demon found he was in much the same state. He changed his cloak for a drier one and ate a smashed piece of bread with cheese. The stream seemed just as likely a path to follow, and so he paralleled its bank until late afternoon. The snow storm had abated, and the thick clouds had broken enough to allow the amber sunlight to touch the ground in scattered beams.

The shadows were lengthening, and the day would fade quickly. With the skies clearing, the night would be especially cold. The Demon suppressed a shiver and looked for a suitable place for shelter. He inspected a stand of pines, and while peering past their bare bottom branches, something in the distance caught his attention. Up in the cliffs were strange-shaped shadows, and he went on to investigate.

His eyes widened when he discovered that carved into the cliff's side was an entire village. Sheltered from the snow beneath the rocky eave, the simple stone structures shone orange in the sunset. Open doors and windows were cast in purple shadows, but there was no movement—not a trace of life to be found. He picked his way along the snowy path that wound its way up the rocks and to the village, his curiosity dominating his weariness.

Falquirian, the Demon thought, walking through the empty streets. *They all left or...* He shuddered at what he hoped not to find, but the village was completely vacant. He peered inside one of the structures and drew a single flame around his finger like a candle. The main room had a woven rug upon the floor and a pit with a hole in the roof for a fire. There were clay pots along the walls, a grinding stone near the fire pit. The adjoining room was bare except for a ladder that led to a man-sized hole in the ceiling.

The Demon left his pack below and ascended to the roof, finding other rooms had been built upon the flat surface. The longer he stood still, the more intensely his feet throbbed, and he climbed back down to the room with the fire pit. He gathered some of the dried grasses that had been strewn across the floor and shoved them into the pit. They would not burn long, but they might give him enough time to find something better to feed the flames.

Hawkwing had packed a bag full of magical sand, anticipating a time when the self-sustaining flames of Wizard's Fire would remedy a dire situation. The Demon discovered the bag in his pack and cast a handful amongst the grasses. He lit the fire with barely a thought, and the blue-violet flames grew and crackled. They would last until dawn if he was lucky.

He sat on the rug near the fire and pried the boots from his feet. His blisters had broken twice over, and pale pink flesh burned in the cold air where his skin had rubbed away. He warmed them near the fire, watching the grasses blacken and flare as the fire spoke to him. It was poor company.

His thoughts drifted to the avalanche, the Seroko he had buried—probably killed, and his brother. Hawkwing was gone, and the realization that he would not return struck the Demon hard. He was truly alone. Hot tears welled and spilled before he even knew they were there.

He untied his brother's bandana from his neck, finding it stained with his own blood where Hawkwing had tied it over the wound on his temple. He stared at it a long while, wishing he could bring him back with his thoughts. In a fit of grief he crushed the material in his hand and cast it into the flames. He watched in regret as it caught fire and slowly turned to ash. *Nothing left.*

The Demon sank down again, his head resting upon his knees. His eyes closed, and he succumbed to an uneasy sleep. He did not know for how long he had slept when he awoke suddenly, startled by a sound. The noise could have been part of his dreams, but when he heard it a second time, his senses snapped to attention. The unmindful fire was unchanged, a sure beacon to his presence. If someone or something was there, it was well aware of him.

Should he try to hide? Wait for the inevitable encounter? Or should he swallow his fear and investigate? Surely it could not be the Seroko....

Without a sound he rose and crept to the doorway. The stars were holes in the black velvet sky, light shining through them and the sliver of a moon that had been cut with a sharp blade. The blue snow and dusky mountains were cast in a pale, ethereal light. His vision was excellent in the dark, but there was nothing for him to see when he peered outside the structure.

He drew back inside, his demon form asserting itself. Sharp ears listened attentively, and they perceived a faint sound—akin to rustling or soft footfalls. The sound grew more persistent, closer, until he could hear someone's irregular breathing.

The Demon's heart quickened as he waited, his senses growing wild as the breathing came from just outside the door. He drew back into the shadows and blended with them, though his eyes never left the door. A dark shape passed before it and hesitated. A hand gripped the frame and braced the looming figure from falling.

Missing Pieces: The Hawk's Shadow

The Demon's large eyes widened in disbelief, and he stepped free of the shadows to meet his brother. "Em'ri!"

It was his brother—naked and trembling with cold. His golden eyes held a distant look, and when they met with the Demon, they searched him in confusion.

The Demon was quick to shed his cloak and drape it around the gaunt man's shoulders. He eased Hawkwing down near the fire and dragged the pack to him. He searched for his brother's clothes, and Hawkwing began to speak.

"I know you," he whispered though bluish lips. "You...."

"'Collin,'" the Demon said, pausing to gaze at him fully. "Y'r brother."

Hawkwing's brow furrowed as he sought to remember. "Yes," he murmured at last. "Collin." His narrow face broadened into a smile. "My brother."

The Demon saw recognition in the golden eyes and sighed. "I thought y' were gone." He presented Hawkwing a bundle of clothes and turned away.

"I nearly was." Weakly he began to dress. "I went to scout ahead, and I saw..." He paused, recalling what he witnessed. "The Seroko," he said urgently. "They aren't far behind—"

"We met," the Demon said. "They won't be following us anymore."

Hawkwing looked at him questioningly.

"The snow an' rocks came down," he said.

"An avalanche," Hawkwing supplied. "You—" His eyes swept over him in concern, noting the dark, recessed circles around the Demon's eyes, the dried blood upon his face, the condition of his feet.

"'M alright," he said.

"Collin, I'm so sorry. I never meant to leave you like this. I meant to return and tell you—"

"I know," the Demon said softly. "Y're 'ere now." He gave his brother a rare smile. "An' we don' 'ave to worry anymore."

Hawkwing nodded.

The Demon pulled a small pot from the pack and poured into it water from his costrel. He sprinkled a packet of spices into the pot and set it near the flames for their dinner. "What's this place? Falquirian?"

A wash of sorrow swept over Hawkwing's features. "It was. It was the sight of this village that called to me, helped me to remember." He glanced around the room. "Many villages were abandoned as the plague took hold. They sought out other survivors, formed new communities. The mountains grow empty."

"We can go back to the road now," the Demon said, determined to make light of their improved situation. "No worries."

Hawkwing smiled and gripped his brother's hand. "No worries."

The fair weather held for the next couple days until they were out of the mountains. They traveled at a leisurely pace, and upon reaching the Western Link of the Traders' Ring, they celebrated their hard-earned survival with a night's stay at a reputable inn. A warm bath, fresh clothes, and a hot, filling meal aided in their recovery. Though the feather mattresses and clean linen sheets were enticing, they did not bed down until late. Much of the night was spent in conversation and telling tales. It was, for the both of them, one of the most memorable times in their lives.

After a light breakfast, they traveled north along the Link to a town called Sirotel. It was there that the Demon made a reluctant announcement. "'M not going to make it."

Hawkwing studied him with concern. "We're less than a day from Mystland's border. What troubles you?"

"'S just it," the Demon said, gesturing to the darkening clouds in the sky as they walked. "I can feel the magic as we get closer, an' it's building inside me." He ignored the cramps in his stomach, though walking upright was becoming difficult.

"A welling?" Hawkwing asked.

The Demon nodded, frustrated that he should have an episode before they could reach their destination. They quit the road and ventured a distance into the forest. They stopped at a clearing, and the Demon sat down, breathless.

"How can I help you?" Hawkwing asked, though he already knew the answer.

"Y' got to go," the Demon said. "Cross the border, an' I'll meet y' there…when 'tis over."

Hawkwing hesitated.

"Y' 'ave to, Em'ri. I'll be alright. I'll find y'." He folded his arms tightly and crouched forward.

Hawkwing emptied some of their provisions and a map and bundled them in a spare cloak. "Just follow the edge of the forest. When you come to the lake, you'll be close. There is a gate—"

"I know. I remember. I promise I'll find y'." He purposely met his brother's gaze.

"I can leave you my bow…."

The Demon shook his head. "Y' better go." He winced.

Hawkwing squeezed his shoulder. "I'll be waiting for you."

The Demon nodded and watched him disappear among the trees. He could feel the energy building around him and inside him. The heavens rumbled a long, deep reverberation that shook even the earth. It would not be long now.

"Been a while since we had a storm like this," the guard said, marveling at the deluge outside. The cabin creaked and whistled in the wind.

Hawkwing did not respond, staring fixedly out the window at the dark world beyond.

"You all right, sir?" the guard asked, regarding the tall man's untouched food.

The tracker glanced at him. "Yes, thank you." He had reached Mystland's gate by sunset and took a room at the nearby inn. The off-duty guard was looking for company and joined him at his table. He was a talkative fellow, and while Hawkwing was normally an attentive audience, his thoughts were elsewhere this night.

"You seem kind of anxious," the guard said, not ready to abandon the one-sided conversation.

Hawkwing turned to face him. "I'm expecting someone."

Missing Pieces: The Hawk's Shadow

"No one will travel in this weather. Your friend won't get here tonight." He patted the tracker's shoulder. "Wait for morning, when all this blows over." Then, seeing Hawkwing's troubled expression, he said, "I'll tell you what: I work the morning shift. Find me at the gate, and I'll let you know if I've seen him...or her...."

"He answers to 'Collin' or even 'Hawkshadow,'" Hawkwing said, remembering his brother's acquired nickname in Mystland.

"And what does he look like?"

Hawkwing smiled slightly. "Very pale. Violet eyes."

"Anything else?" the guard asked, confused by the vague description.

"I promise you won't miss him."

The man nodded and shortly went on his way, leaving Hawkwing to his thoughts.

The night was a long one, and Hawkwing slept little—even after the storm had abated. He went out early and found the guard at his post, but his brother had not yet arrived. The tracker waited until early afternoon before he checked again, but still there was no word of the Demon's arrival. As the sun waned, Hawkwing decided to risk missing their rendezvous, and he ventured outside the border to find his missing brother.

The Demon was always weak after his wellings, and this one had seemed especially potent. It was entirely possible that his brother was on his way; they might even cross paths if fortune was in their favor. Hawkwing tried to remain optimistic, but instinct or habit found him traveling armed.

Walking briskly along the forest edge, he found no immediate trace that anyone had traveled that way. Much of the snow had melted in the rain, but what remained upon the ground had turned to crunchy ice, and where there was no ice, there was mud. Any footprints would register in the aftermath of the storm. But if his brother had not followed his instructions...if he had traveled deeper through the woods, Hawkwing might miss his tracks completely. He could only hope the Demon had heeded his words.

As he neared the place where he had initially left his brother, he found—not surprisingly—that several trees had been felled by lightning or by wind. In the clearing were footprints—not just the small ones belonging to his brother, but several sets that surrounded his. The story unfolded in a tale of horror that he read upon the ground: the trampled and muddied earth, broken branches, and darker stains that mingled in the cloudy puddles. Hawkwing felt a knot twist inside him.

There was one path that had been taken both to and from the clearing, and with a growing sense of dread, he followed it. He caught the scent of smoke in the air and slowed. With the setting sun on the horizon, the eerie orange light of dusk streamed through the trees and painted deepening shadows among the trunks and upon the forest floor. He heard branches snap and leaves rustle as a group of silhouettes manifested several yards away.

"Twice you've abandoned your companion," said a voice. "Twice you did not save him."

When he could better distinguish their features, Hawkwing stopped. He could discern his brother's small frame among them, supported by one of the men. A cold fury stirred in his heart.

"I am the Marksman."

"I know who you are," Hawkwing said, his voice hard. "And your purpose means nothing to me." He gestured to his brother. "Let him go. He's not part of this."

"He is now. We want the location of the archives, and we want the Key."

Hawkwing stared. "After all this time, the Seroko is still incapable of understanding."

"That is why you were sought." The Marksman was calm. "We want you to enlighten us."

Hawkwing sighed. "Then you will be disappointed." He took a step forward. As the sun slipped lower, he could finally see his brother. There was blood covering the side of the Demon's strained face, and he was held upright by the bearded man behind him. A luminous rope bound him—doubtless a work of magic to keep him restrained. Hawkwing stared hard at his offenders.

"It matters not what you think of our cause," the Marksman said. "All that matters is what you know and will give to us."

"One condition," Hawkwing said, his attention solely upon the Demon. "I willingly take his place, and you let him go."

"I think not. There will be no bargains. That opportunity was lost beneath the avalanche."

Hawkwing shook his head. "Do you truly know what it is you seek?"

"The Key...."

The tracker watched the knife poise at the Demon's side. "It's not a key."

The Marksman stared, considering. "I don't believe you."

Hawkwing watched the Marksman raise his arm and begin to signal to the man restraining the Demon. He took a desperate step forward. "If he dies, you will never have the Key."

The Marksman clenched his fists. "Your fate will be decided soon enough."

"No. You fail to understand."

"No, it is you who fails to understand!" the Marksman shouted, his patience lost. "You will give me the Key and the location of the archives, or he dies!" He spun and pointed toward the Demon to find that his prisoner had faded to shadow and slipped his bindings. The Demon's silhouetted form staggered a couple paces and fell before he materialized again.

Hawkwing was already charging at his opponents, his short sword cutting down two of the Seroko before they realized what had happened. The bearded man who had been holding the Demon drew his own sword but was outmatched by the tracker. Just as Hawkwing withdrew his blade from the man's chest, he felt the sword enter through his back.

The Marksman did not bother to withdraw his weapon, for the Demon was struggling toward him, encompassed by violet flames. The remaining member of the Seroko fled into the darkness of the forest.

The Demon's flames extinguished when he dropped next to where Hawkwing had fallen. "Em'ri," he mouthed, unable to find his voice. He pulled the sword from him and flung it away. He met his brother's clouded gaze and gripped his hand tightly. Hawkwing slipped away in silence.

~*~

The Demon stared out the window as freezing rain assailed the road below, his thoughts consumed by the pain of his recent loss. Would it always be this way? Others making sacrifices on his account? First his mother, then the Prophet, and now his brother—the only family and friend he had remaining. He had abandoned his homeland hoping to find Hawkwing, hoping to escape a future of violence and death. Now his brother was dead—murdered—because he had been a liability. Perhaps "the Demon" was just that—a demon and nothing more.

He did not turn when the servant girl rapped softly on the door and entered the room. "How are you feeling?" she asked, approaching the bed with a fresh tray of food. She noticed with a frown that his previous meal was untouched.

Though he did not answer, she continued to talk to him. "You should try to eat something," she coaxed. "It will help you feel better."

I don't want to feel better, he thought, grief-stricken.

She lit the candle on the stand beside his bed. "A little light," she said with a smile. "It's so gloomy outside." She reached to draw the shade, but he gently stayed her hand. "No? All right, I'll leave it open." She studied him a moment before turning to go. "I'll be around if you need anything."

The Demon glanced at her and turned back toward the window. He heard her close the door, but she had evidently discovered someone in the hall.

"Oh, you must be his friend! He's awake now and doing much better, though he won't eat anything."

The second voice—a woman's—was softer and more difficult to discern. "How did you find him?"

"One of the villagers found him on the main road. He was just laying there, covered in blood. He must have been attacked, as he was in a bad state. We weren't sure he would make it. He was brought here, and we've tended to him. Word must have spread, because you're here...."

"Whatever he needs, I'll take care of it," the familiar voice spoke. There was a pause. "He was found alone?"

"Alone, milady."

"Thank you for all you've done. May I see him?"

"I can't promise much; he hasn't said a word. Just stares out the window."

"That's all right. I'd like to talk to him."

The Demon tensed, for though he was less than eager for company, a glimmer of curiosity had him wondering who this "friend" could be. All his friends were gone.

As he heard the door click, he extinguished the candle, leaving the room dark with shadows. From the corner of his eye he caught sight of the petite hooded figure standing in the doorway. She took a hesitant step forward.

"Collin?"

Matthew and Stefanie Verish

About the Authors

Matthew and Stefanie Verish are co-authors as well as husband and wife. They knew they were destined for marriage when they could write together without killing each other. Their writing partnership has rewarded them with wonderful journeys into the realm of fantasy, culminating in the epic tale, Raven's Heart. The couple shares a love of nature and art and lives in Northeast Ohio with their large family of cavies.

Hemingway's Challenge

Invented the scythe before the plow.

-Todd Austin Hunt

About the Story

"At the Expense of Kings" opens up the possibility of a new world.

At the Expense of Kings
By
Todd Austin Hunt

The five hundred Groundkids ambled their way to the enemy's troops at LeFaux's command. Their heavy footsteps splashed mud onto perpetually dirty faces never more than four feet high. With vacant smiles, they waved blunt weapons in the air: clubs and chains and pipes and granite fists heavy and dark.

At the bottom of the hill, just yards from the waiting foe, the Groundkids stopped. A score at the front made happy, yarping noises to the cloaked enemy, but offered no attempt to advance. Equally bizarre was the stillness of the adversary.

Mounted on his molehog, LeFaux overlooked the Groundkids' halted approach from the hilltop by the Counselor's tent. He clutched the chain around his neck, that which held the Groundkids in his thrall. Through clenched teeth, he hissed, "Attack! I have commanded you to attack! In the name of my vanished brother, the King!"

A few of the Groundkids at the rear of the scattered formation turned his way and grinned, waving their hands and weapons at him, but all disobeyed his orders, and merely stared curiously at the sparse assailants.

Impatient and furious, LeFaux shouted to his generals, "If they will not heed their master . . . ." With a slow twist, he tore the chain from around his neck, pulling it from the contact of his skin.

The effect was immediate. All five hundred Groundkids twisted and grew rigid, facing LeFaux. The sound of heavy weapons falling was a low rumble. Each rough hand drifted up to a broad, youthful face, past a smile fallen and forgotten and a red, wet nose to the chain that connected the iron plugs in the eye sockets. Each link in the chain was a perfect eight of green metal. Simultaneously, the Groundkids yanked out the plugs. They swayed and shortly wept before their bodies unraveled in blood and mud, leaving nothing but twenty-five score crimson and brown puddles.

A few gasps sounded behind LeFaux, but were quickly stifled.

LeFaux removed a leather thong from his coat and thread it through the chain, tying it around his neck once again. He dismounted his beast and rushed through the flaps of his Counselor's tent.

Missing Pieces: At the Expense of Kings

~*~

"We haven't enough strength to overcome them, milord! Their ranks are boiling with a power I've not seen before," Renard shouted, grasping the other man's wrist.

A freezing wind ripped through the flaps of the war tent, spraying a crystallized mist on the two men standing face to face over battle plans. Dying candlelight lit LeFaux's blue eyes and noble brow, twisted in anger and contempt. He pulled himself away from Renard's grip, his fingers resting on the hilt of his sword

"So you have finally shown to be a coward, Counselor?" LeFaux gestured to the tent's exit. "We outnumber the enemy a hundredfold."

Renard bent his head, placing his slender hands on the strategic maps. "You have not listened to me." He gazed straight at his liege. "They wield the weight of the heavens, a sorcery far beyond my paltry magicks. The edge of your broadsword and a hundred thousand others is nothing to it. I beg you; we must surrender. Either way, I cannot lend myself to this mass suicide." Renard paused. "It would be one cruel slaughter too many."

"I will not suffer a coward," LeFaux said. With liquid grace and speed, he unsheathed his sword and cleaved Renard's head from his body. The Counselor's black blood fountained, spattering the detailed battlegrounds as his head landed on the table and rolled onto the ground.

LeFaux whirled through the tent's threshold into the cold and wet morning. False dawn illuminated the sky, and thin clouds raced over the night's last stars. His generals encircled the tent, all mounted on bristling molehogs. If any noticed the blood on his sword, he did not speak. He mounted his molehog, which grunted and ground its clawed hooves in the dirt.

With his sword, he pointed to the multitude of warriors waiting for his word above and below him. He then turned his beast toward the enemy far below, a scurvy band of shadows, a creek next to his ocean. The enemy open and vulnerable.

"ForWARD!" he screamed and then was enveloped in the bloodlust clamor of his army as they roared down to crush the enemy, swords raised and molehogs gnashing razor teeth.

In this horde of violent noise, the soft whispers were not heard, nor the breeze from the lips to the heavens felt.

LeFaux was the first to near the enemy. The sky flashed and his molehog bit into a thin, cloaked figure. The form merely fluttered and reformed, unscathed. The molehog reared and squealed, throwing LeFaux onto his back. He bit his tongue, tasting blood as he watched green fire form the figure of eight behind the scrim of clouds above.

Black rain fell from the sky and the valley was flooded with thousands of mad lunatic wails of agonized soul-ripping.

LeFaux joined the chorus.

~*~

The enemy had vanished from the battlefield, leaving a thousand corpses splayed and torn across its expanse. The bodies were indistinguishable from human form, eviscerated from the inside out by souls plucked out like treats. Down on the bloodied earth, the cavalry's molehogs scuffled and snorted about, enjoying a greedy feast of their masters' remains; while in the sky above the soil, the souls of the LeFaux's army clashed in the air, screeching and clawing futilely at one another.

Two figures walked freely through the carnage. One cloaked and tall and narrow, the other short and broad and cheerful. A Groundkid. They wandered from corpse to mutilated corpse, searching.

The cloaked figure pointed a finger ahead. A molehog crouched over a wailing shape. Fine boots were twitching visibly from beneath the beast's wiry hindquarters, while a shade's head flickered above the animal's lowered, snuffling head.

"Colby," said the cloaked one. "Will you please remove that foul thing?"

The Groundkid nodded and smiled. "That I do, Ardo."

Colby closed in on the crouching beast, looking ridiculously small in comparison. He closed his thick hands around its hind leg. The molehog squealed as Colby swung the beast into the air like a small bag of stones; it sailed through the air and crashed against the ground hundreds of yards away, squeal halted.

Bending over the form, Colby said, "He not letting go, this one."

Ardo joined the Groundkid. "It's the Duke. LeFaux."

LeFaux's body was split from crotch to throat. His soul clattered and wailed above LeFaux, dancing like a black flame struggling to be free. The Duke's jaws were clenched; his teeth clamped onto the soul, restraining it from escape. His turquoise eyes pulsed.

"He is salvageable," said Ardo from within his cowl. "But I must encage his spirit before we get him to the Machine. Which means you must carry him. I will not touch him."

Colby nodded, the chain on his face rattling.

Ardo raised his arms in a V. Splaying the fingers of both hands, his lips moved and he lowered his hands. A translucent, violet web formed in the air and pressed down against LeFaux's frantic soul, confining the shade, pushing it down into the Duke's torn body. The soul's screeching reached a violent pitch as the cage learned the shape of LeFaux's corporeal form, fitting tight as skin. Ardo snapped his fingers into a fist and the cage sealed shut with a snap. The soul desperately sought for windows of escape, bulging in and out of the web's miniscule openings around LeFaux's face, but it was securely trapped.

Colby picked up the Duke and slung him effortlessly around his shoulders. LeFaux was a tall man; his hands and feet dragged against the ground. Although the man's soul bubbled along the web, LeFaux was in too much pain to protest against the handling; he could only stare at the soil.

Ardo turned and walked toward the base of a hill. Again he whispered, and a seam appeared in the bloodied earth, opening with a hiss. An enormous mound of obsidian rose up, at the front of which was a twin doorway sealed by the emerald figure of eight.

Ardo glanced at Colby and gestured at the doorway. The Groundkid approached and pressed his forehead against the symbol, causing the mound to tremble. The doors fell inward into a dimly lit stairwell that descended into unimaginable darkness. Colby started down the stairs with Ardo following, carrying the Duke as if he had never had a burden. The green chain connecting Colby's socket plugs shone strong in the dark. When the deep black swallowed them, the doors shut as the obsidian hillock sank below the earth.

~*~

Hours later they stepped down on a landing, facing an identical doorway. This time, Ardo reached out and touched the symbol with his palm. These doors opened outward, and a pale but strong light lit the landing.

LeFaux's struggling soul was still for a moment, shrinking into the recesses of his body. He moved his head to stare up as Colby followed Ardo into a vast, high-ceilinged chamber. Strange and foreign light poured through windows in a perfect semi-circle where the walls met the vaulting. The outer walls of the chamber were rounded. At the center of the room stood a base, but solid throne which faced a raised platform. Stairs ridged each side of the platform. A great, green loop emerged from the flat, central wall at a 45 degree angle over the platform. The twin bands of the loop joined and began to cross at the point where they met the wall. Below the loop another door stood at the front of the platform, at the center of which was the figure of eight.

Colby lifted the Duke from his shoulders to cradle him in his arms, like a baby. LeFaux glared up at the Groundkid, and with great effort, he spoke, "Is this my palace? Your touch revolts me! Put me down!"

The Duke's revulsion had no effect on Colby. The Groundkid gently placed LeFaux in the throne and backed away to a single door to the left of the platform.

Ardo touched Colby's shoulder and walked to LeFaux. "Although this is not your palace, it is a palace. We have brought you here to make you whole again."

The encaged soul passed over LeFaux's face like a dark cloud before he was able to reply. "Who are you?"

Ardo bowed his head, still enshrouded in its hood. "We are your servants." He turned to Colby. "Allow your brothers ingress, Colby."

Colby opened the small door and immediately three Groundkids lurched through. The chamber quickly filled with their stink, that of neglect, sewage, constant toil and despair. Their small, stocky bodies were filthy and hands bloodied from overwork. Despite this, their faces were youthful and each grinned at LeFaux.

"Duke, Duke, Duke," they clamored.

"Children," Ardo said. "Mount the platform."

They obliged without question, ascending the stairs to stand in a semi-circle behind the flare of the loop. Their socket chains began to twitch and rattle in the proximity of the emerald loop. Ardo went to the door in the platform and raised his hand to touch the symbol. His hand inches away from the symbol, he sang in a low voice:

> "Without the Spirit's blessing
> They bound youth to their will
> To break the bones of the Earth
> To live in demon's swill
>
> Thus joy became a privilege
> Of men sprung from fathers high
> While the forever children
> Would suffer until they die
>
> By this symbol of time's chasm
> A chain held in hands of thieves
> I give wonder and relief
> From what the master grieves."

Ardo touched the symbol and the light from the windows ceased. The loop bulged and hummed, and an iridescent red light raced from within, around the circle and back though the crossed section to reappear moments later. The green band increased in size, and it pulled the Groundkids forward. The band dissolved the socketchains of each Groundkid as the crimson light entered every ear and coursed out one socket and into the other, finally flowing out the other ear.

The band and its light enthralled them.

Images floated in and out of the air above their heads. Beautiful visions of love and joy. A regal woman in cascading robes holding a baby close to her lovely face. A father and son hunting alone in the forest at twilight. Long tables piled high with dishes and food from all over the known world, a birthday feast with an army of friends and family in attendance. A lean, young man teaching his younger brother swordplay.

LeFaux cried out, "Morgan?"

The images swam and overlapped while the Groundkids smiled and laughed and wept from jubilation heretofore unknown to them. The captivated Groundkids began to stoop. Ears and noses and feet grew larger while teeth fell from loose, gray gums. Spots and wrinkles appeared all over their skin and muscles sagged in accelerated time.

Threads of jade energy coalesced at the edge of the loop, growing and growing in power. The energy cracked forward, engulfing LeFaux on the throne. His body became erect and straight. His restless soul calmed, retreated into a condensed form deep within his chest as the awful wounds closed up, leaving fresh, new skin. The soul-cage evaporated in the fading light of the loop's power, along with the green chain hanging from around his neck.

Missing Pieces: At the Expense of Kings

LeFaux stood and stretched, laughed in glee at his returned health. "I am whole again!"

Upon the platform, the loop became still, releasing the now-ancient Groundkids. Where the green socket plugs had been were glowing embers of malachite. They rocked on feet for a moment, faces awash with bliss, before light once again cascaded through the windows, igniting their bodies into motes of dust.

"I am happy to see that you are well again, milord," said Ardo. After flourishing his hands, the door at the front of the platform opened. "You have much work to do. Your throne waits ahead."

LeFaux examined the enrobed figure's back as he followed him through the threshold down a short flight of stairs. "You will be rewarded richly for this, Counselor."

Colby walked close behind the Duke. The door slid shut at his back. At the foot of stairs was another door, embossed again with the figure of eight. They passed through, emerging into another lyceum almost identical to the one from they had come. The windows above were black with a thick night. Another loop emerged from the wall, the other half of the figure of eight. This loop pointed down toward the chamber floor.

A marvelous throne rested in the center of the jade loop. A king's throne. A crown was visible from the back of the authority.

LeFaux stopped. "What is this?"

"Colby," Ardo said.

The Groundkid grabbed LeFaux's left wrist with crushing strength. The Duke reached up for his master's chain, but found nothing. Colby encircled his waist and carried him to the throne. It was not empty.

"Morgan! My brother!" LeFaux screamed.

The scrawny black remains of the King sat in the chair. The corpse appeared charred, however Morgan's facial structure was intact, but starved and all over the color of pitch. The ornate crown rose from his brow, and the band of the loop was embedded in his head, keeping his sagging form from falling to the stone floor.

Ardo touched the loop and it became momentarily insubstantial, allowing Morgan to collapse out of the chair into a small mound of LeFaux's royal ancestors' remains. Colby lifted the Duke and pressed him into the newly-vacant throne. The ephemeral loop made a shimmering sound in his ears.

"Counselor!" LeFaux roared. "Slave! I command you to release me!"

Colby held him down without cease, grinning. The Groundkid's socketchains brushed against the Duke's nose.

Ardo removed his hooded cowl, revealing a neck with rapidly healing scars. He absently touched the scars with delicate hands.

LeFaux sucked in through his teeth. "Counselor Renard?"

"That is Ardo," Colby agreed.

"Yours is a killing family," Renard said. "I learned long ago to make precautions." He gestured to the black mound below. "Several of your grandfathers have afflicted me worse. Now, young Duke LeFaux, how would you define a great King?"

"A great King is Master and Ruler, every word and whim law," LeFaux spat. "It is damnation to oppose the King! Release me or earn that damnation!"

"No, milord. A great King is a servant to his people, to those weak and suffering." Renard nodded to Colby. "Some filthy magick embedded the livelihood of his kind into the vile hands of your family in a memory long before mine. To free them is beyond my power, yet I conceived a path using that magick to give these children some surcease from your wickedness. What you see of King Morgan is all the selfishness, all the squalid hatred and murder in his heart. All that is left."

Renard picked up the crown and placed it upon LeFaux's head.

"King Duke," Colby spluttered in his face.

"Because of your family," Renard said. "They have lost their will and intelligence. All beauty and rapture stolen from their present and future. I say that is a foul sin."

Renard tapped the green loop and it solidified, buzzing through LeFaux's head, searching and probing for those gorgeous bits of love and pleasure, the gratification of being alive and free. Colby released him. He convulsed as the infinity loop took and took and took.

"So I give them whatever shreds of happiness I can give," Renard said. "At the expense of Kings."

About the Author

Educated at University of Kentucky (B.A.) and Eastern Kentucky University (M.A.), Todd Austin Hunt has been publishing short stories since 2003. His love for fantastic fiction developed at a young age, heightened and secured by a reading of Stephen King's Misery at age thirteen. He won an Honorable Mention in the 2003 Annual Ray Bradbury Writing Contest and was nominated for The Pushcart Prize in 2007. Todd lives in a tree house along the Wando River in Charleston, South Carolina.

Todd Austin Hunt

Hemingway's Challenge

The funeral was a wonderful party.

-Dylan Birtolo

About the Story

This short story tells the tale of two of the more interesting characters from my second novel, *The Bringer of War*. Cameron is an apparently ruthless second-in-command of the Shadows, the organization of shape shifters that opposes Darien. Yet, despite his cold efficiency, Cameron has a special caring relationship with Lisa, another member of the Shadows. This piece explores their early history.

Decisions
By
Dylan Birtolo

The wind whipped hard enough to make the rain come down in slanted sheets. The drops pounded against the metal frame of the car with an almost deafening cacophony. Cameron paid no attention to the sound; all of his attention was focused on the one-story house across the street from his parked vehicle. He stared at the single lit window with a predatory gaze. His right hand slid from the steering wheel to touch the gun concealed underneath his jacket. When the light switched off, he started to count. When he reached three hundred, he opened the door and stepped out to face the full rage of the storm.

His clothes were completely soaked through before he even crossed the street. He hunched over, scrambling forward as he crossed the front yard. He stopped when he reached the corner next to the previously-lit window. Closing his eyes, he flattened himself against the wall and took a few deep breaths, slowing each subsequent breath. His body faded into the empty air, replaced by a small millipede clinging to the wall.

The creature crawled up the slick surface and crossed the wooden windowsill. He found a small crack underneath the bottom of the window where it was not completely sealed. He crawled into the opening and made his way inside the house. Once he was on the other side, he dropped down to the floor without a sound. Within a matter of seconds, Cameron was standing in the room as a human once again. He reached into his jacket and pulled out his gun.

He was standing inside a home office. A large desk sat near the window he just entered. Several papers and photographs rested on the desk, as well as a lamp that was still warm from recent use. A couple of bookcases stood against the wall on the other side of the room. Cameron walked around to stand behind the desk and look at the papers. He reached out with his left hand and moved them around, searching in the limited light filtering through the window. There were several sequential pictures of people disappearing and being replaced with animals. The sequences proved the existence of shape shifters.

Missing Pieces: Decisions

Cameron took the pictures and the notes, stacking them up and stuffing them inside the pocket of his coat. Once he was satisfied that he recovered all of the incriminating evidence, he opened the drawers of the desk, pilfering through them in search of the negatives. His search proved fruitful as he found all of the negatives on the bottom of one of the drawers underneath a large pile of folders. He stuffed those into his coat as well.

Once he was finished recovering information, he walked across the room. He knew the bedroom was to the right, just outside the office. He slid across the floor, inching his way towards the bedroom. Stopping at the edge of the door he peered around it and saw his quarry sleeping in a queen sized bed. The man was on his stomach with his arm draped over the edge of the bed. Cameron watched for a while, making sure that the man's breaths were slow and even, before he crept into the bedroom. He stopped when he was even with the man's head, but made sure he was more than an arm's reach away. Caution was always prudent.

"Wake up, Mr. Erickson."

The man stirred, rolling over onto his back. He rubbed the back of his hand across his eyes and turned his head to face the intruder. It was a few seconds before his eyes focused and he was aware of the situation.

"Who are you?" Mr. Erickson shouted as he shot up to a sitting position and pushed himself away until his back was against the wall.

Cameron patted the air with his gun and his empty hand. "Calm down, Mr. Erickson. I could have killed you in your sleep if that was why I came. I needed to speak with you."

"What do you want? You can take it all. Please, just let me live."

"Pleading will not accomplish anything save to make me impatient. I need information."

"I'll tell you anything."

"I need to know if you told anyone about the shifters."

"What are you talking about?" The man asked, glancing out the door and avoiding eye contact.

Cameron grabbed his gun in both hands and aimed it at his quarry's head. "Don't insult my intelligence. You know what I am talking about and I promise you, I'm not known for my patience. I advise you not to try it."

Mr. Erickson bit his bottom lip and glanced around the room. Cameron stood still, keeping his weapon aimed at the man. "I..." the man began, and then stopped. He looked at Cameron and met his stare. "I tried to tell a few people, but no one would listen. People don't believe me."

"You should not believe it either. Perhaps you were seeing things. Hallucinating."

"Yes, that could be." The man's voice was soft and instantly agreeable.

"Did anyone believe you?"

The man shook his head back and forth. Cameron smiled in response. "Good." Then he pulled the trigger.

~*~

Cameron sat in his kitchen after returning to the conclave from his successful mission. He looked around his condo as he sat straight in his chair. He had been living here for three years, ever since the Shadows found him and explained the unusual circumstances going on in his life and what they meant. One corner of his mouth crept up into a smile as he thought back to three years ago. He thought he was going mad at the time, having all-too-realistic dreams of being an animal. Instead, it turned out to be reality, and there were others like him. They gave him this home, and all they asked in return was that he helped keep their existence a secret, kept their society working beyond the eyes of mortal men. It was a good arrangement. But, more than that, it was where he wanted to be.

A knock at his door startled him out of his thoughts. As he was going to answer it, the messenger spoke through the closed portal.

"The Dark wants to see you immediately, Cameron."

His steps paused for a moment at those words. Then he continued to the door and opened it. "I'll be right down," he said to the young woman standing in the hallway. She gave a nod and walked off.

As Cameron made his way to the central meeting hall, his mind wandered to thoughts about the Dark. What could he want with Cameron? His last mission was executed flawlessly, or so he thought. Did he miss some important detail? Did he fail to recover all of the evidence and it was in a greater spotlight now because of a murder investigation? He had never been to see the Dark before; he always received orders from subordinates who relayed the messages. His hand shook as he knocked on the double doors leading into the main meeting hall. Yet by the time they opened, his hands were motionless at his sides and his chin was up. He strode into the room without hesitation.

The room was large and circular with only two visible pieces of furniture: a single chair in the middle of the room and a desk across from it. The Dark sat in shadows behind the desk; only his hands could be discerned. The rest of his shape was a silhouette. Standing in front of the desk and facing the door was Cameron's superior and the Dark's primary agent – Stacy McVale. The Dark waved his hand, gesturing for Cameron to come forward. Cameron stopped when he was standing next to the chair. He gave a slight bow before speaking.

"I am here at your request. How can I be of service?"

While he couldn't see it, Cameron could hear the smile in the Dark's tone. It was much lighter than he expected. "I believe you have already been of excellent service, which is the reason that I have requested your presence. Stacy just completed reciting the details of your latest adventure, and I was impressed at your attention to detail. I have also received reports from our agents on the police force that classifying such a case as unsolvable due to lack of evidence will be a trivial matter. We all appreciate your dedication to the tasks at hand."

"Thank you, sir." Cameron gave another slight bow and noticed that while the Dark's tone was light, Stacy's face was drawn tight and her eyes narrowed.

Missing Pieces: Decisions

"It also seems that such performance has been a trend for you. Your career over the last few years has been exemplary and continues to exceed expectations with each passing year. It has been quite fortuitous for our entire family that we found you and rescued you."

"I couldn't agree more, sir. It's nice to have a home."

"I am glad to hear that, Cameron. I believe that you will escalate through our ranks and soon find yourself in a position of authority. In fact, that is the ulterior reason why I requested your presence at this moment. I wish to present an opportunity to you. There is another person who poses a threat to our organization and must be dealt with. However, this would be a mission that would require the teamwork of multiple agents; it is not a solitary mission."

"Who would you like me to work with?"

"That will be your decision. The purpose of this task is to present you with the opportunity to choose your own team, arrange the mission as you see fit, and then carry it to completion. I expect that I will be hearing of your success in the near future."

After those words, Stacy stepped forward to escort Cameron out of the room. He gave one final bow, uttered a quick statement of gratitude, then turned around and walked with his superior out of the room. Once the doors were closed and they were walking down the hall, she gave him the details.

"Your target is a public official looking into matters dealing with the local police department. He is starting to investigate what he calls 'shoddy police work'. Considering your recent activities, I trust you can see why this may be an issue. If he happened to find any of our agents or noticed the extra bonuses some officers receive..." she let the sentence trail off.

Cameron saw no need to respond. He waited for her to continue. Glancing out of the corner of his eye, he noticed that Stacy did not look at him and kept her attention focused down the hallway ahead of them both. After a few steps, she continued.

"You have two weeks to do your research and eliminate him. You need to make it look like an accident. If his death is even slightly suspect, this will be too public to cover up in our usual manner. How you go about it is up to you."

"I understand. I won't let you down."

"You should know, this mission was not originally you responsibility."

"Whose was it?"

Stacy paused to turn and face her subordinate. Her eyes were narrowed a small amount. "Mine."

Cameron took half a step back, but said nothing. Stacy turned away and continued her journey down the hall. She turned her head enough to talk over her shoulder. "Just remember your place, insect. No one encroaches on my territory. I'd be all too glad to remind you of your place."

Cameron stood there, watching her go. Only when she turned a corner did he resume his trip to his place and start planning the forthcoming venture.

Dylan Birtolo

~*~

Once again, Cameron found himself in his car, watching a house and waiting for the last light to go out. He was waiting along with two other Shadows to begin their operation. They were in a car just in front of him. He didn't know either of them personally, but they both had records that showed they had no compunction against killing. In fact, one of them seemed to enjoy the task. They were well suited for this mission, even if they bristled at taking orders from a younger Shadow.

Cameron glanced at the fenced back yard. Six dogs were kenneled in that area, and they were large breeds – Dobermans and German Shepherds. The other two Shadows had the ability to shape-shift into dogs. The plan was to have the Shadows attack the target as dogs and maul him to death. Then, they would force the gate to the kennel open and start a fight amongst the animals inside. With any luck, it would look like the animals had gotten loose and killed their master. It was not a foolproof plan by any stretch of the imagination, but it was believable – and that was the important part. A believable story could be sold through their connections, even if it was improbable.

After the last light was extinguished, Cameron waited for several minutes. He could see his two companions turning and looking at him, but Cameron shook his head and held his hand up. When he was satisfied that enough time had passed, he got out of the car and walked across the street. He stopped on the sidewalk, waiting for his companions to join him. When they were all together, Cameron went over their plan briefly. They nodded their assent and then looked around for observers. Not seeing anyone, they approached the house and crouched down behind the bushes. Away from prying eyes, they changed their shapes. The two dogs waited as Cameron crawled up the side of the building, looking for an opening near a window.

Finding what he was looking for, Cameron entered the house and took a look around before resuming his human form. He walked on the balls of his feet towards the front door, making almost no sound as he searched for the alarm console. Once he found it, he entered the code that he purchased from a disillusioned security installer. The indicator light turned green, letting him know the alarm was disabled. With a barely suppressed smile, he opened the front door so the dogs could come into the home.

The two other Shadows followed Cameron as he led them up to the second floor. Cameron directed them to their target's door and looked through the keyhole. It was completely dark in the room beyond. He turned the handle and pushed it open a few feet. Then he stepped back, letting the dogs take the lead. He had no need to observe the carnage that was to follow. He made his way downstairs to open the back door and prepare the second part of their plan.

From the bedroom, he heard a scream start but get cut short with a wet gurgle. While the man may be already dead, they still needed to illustrate the scene. Cameron had just unlocked the back door when he heard a second scream, this one much higher pitch, echo down the stairs. It shot down his spine and made him leap into action. He drew his gun before he was halfway up the stairs. Just on the top of the landing he saw a young girl – no more than six – backed into a corner and crying as she tried to backpedal away from the dog growling at her with blood dripping from its jaw.

"No! She is not the target!" Cameron shouted as he ran up the stairs. The dog turned to him and grinned, licking his lips. He turned back to the girl and lunged at her.

Cameron hurdled the last three steps and slammed into the dog with his right shoulder, driving the animal into the wall. It yelped in response then turned and snapped at Cameron, but he rolled away. Cameron stood up, putting himself between the dog and the little girl. The animal narrowed his eyes and growled at Cameron again. It tried to maneuver around to the side, but Cameron pushed the girl so she stayed behind him, turning to face the animal.

"She is not the target," Cameron repeated.

The words had no effect on the dog. It growled and took a step forward, with its lips pulled back over its teeth. It made another lunge for the girl but Cameron reached out and got his arm in the path of the dog. The animal chomped down on his arm, but let go immediately and tried to jump back out of range. Cameron snarled and brought the gun around like a club, whipping the dog with it in the head. The dog backed off and Cameron picked the girl up with his injured arm, holding her on his hip. He walked to the stairs and backed down them, keeping his gun leveled at the animal. The dog shook his head back and forth then turned to face Cameron, advancing slowly.

"Leave us alone," he said, holding the girl closer to him as she sobbed into his shoulder.

The dog continued to stalk them as Cameron made his way backwards down the stairs. He never let his gun drop from his target. In the upstairs bedroom, he could still hear the other Shadow dog finishing the illusion of an animal massacre. Yet this Shadow still pursued him. The dog lurched forward, snapping at the girl once again. Cameron twisted, pulling the girl away from the jaws and placing his body between the two of them. He had the muzzle of his gun almost against the dog's front shoulder when he pulled the trigger. The dog yipped in pain as he hit the ground and slid away from the force of the shot. His eyes were tightly shut and he whined. The girl sobbed even harder, clutching tightly against Cameron's shirt.

"Finish the job, and do it right." Cameron said before turning around and walking out of the house. He jogged over to his car, opening the back door and trying to get the girl to go into the back seat, but she wouldn't let go. She slid her arms up around his neck and latched her wrists together. Cameron eventually conceded and sat in the front seat with her still curled around his neck and half-sitting in his lap. Cameron gave the house a final glance, then turned on his car and drove off.

~*~

"Where is the girl?" Stacy snarled at Cameron as he stood in front of the single chair in the main meeting room. He refused to sit and continued to hold his chin up despite the admonishment of both the Dark and his superior. He had been called into attendance immediately after his return, to explain why one of his agents needed to be treated for a gunshot wound to the front shoulder.

Stacy stepped up to him from the front and twisted her hands in his shirt to pull him close. "You would dare to shoot one of your own kind for the sake of a normal human? How do you even try to justify that?" She pulled tight enough on his shirt to make Cameron lean forward beneath her eye level. He did not meet her gaze, looking just past the side of her face to the rest of the room beyond.

"She was not the target. The target was eliminated."

"It doesn't matter. She would just be a casualty of war. One more or less is irrelevant."

Cameron turned his attention to match her stare. "She was innocent, too young to know about any of us. She did not deserve to die."

"You shot a Shadow! For that alone you deserve to die."

"Enough!" The Dark said, slamming the flat of both of his hands on the desk. "That is not for you to decide, Stacy. The punishment that you propose far exceeds that of the crime committed. Our brother has not been killed, merely injured. You would escalate the punishment for your own personal vendetta."

Stacy let go of Cameron, enabling him to stand up straight and lift his gaze into the darkness beyond the Dark. She turned to face the Dark and held her hands out to either side. "But, sir, we need to consider the fact that what he did was treasonous. It's not just that he hurt someone in our organization; he betrayed one of his own kind and can't be trusted! This is a very serious matter!"

Cameron clenched his jaw, forcing himself to keep from commenting. The Dark spoke in his place. "It is my position to decide the punishment for his crime. He had reasons that are understandable for his course of action, even if that fails to justify his course. An execution would be excessive and inappropriate for punishment."

"Then have him turn the child over. Show him that no one ranks above the other members of our organization. Allow us to deal with her as we decide would be appropriate."

"She is innocent. She has done nothing wrong." Cameron said, unable to hold his tongue any longer. "I will not tell you where I hid her."

"See?" Stacy said, the grin audible in her tone. "He has become attached to the child. It divides his loyalties. Eliminating her will serve as punishment and guarantee he stays focused."

Cameron dropped his gaze to stare at the back of Stacy's head. "That's not fair to the child!"

"I rest my case," Stacy said, turning to smile at Cameron over her shoulder. He glared at her but said nothing.

They stood there for a few minutes as they waited for the Dark to respond. Stacy turned around to face the Dark after a couple of breaths. He sighed once and then spoke. "Stacy, leave us."

She opened her mouth and started to respond, but the Dark held up his hand to stop her. "I will handle the matter. He will be punished. I will speak to you after I have finished with him."

Stacy nodded and dropped her head. "As you wish. I will be waiting outside." She turned around and walked towards the exit. As she passed Cameron she paused long enough to whisper to him. "I will find the girl." Then she continued on her way out. When the door closed, Cameron's shoulders slumped, the tension easing noticeably.

"Your actions must be punished, Cameron. There is no way around that simple fact."

"I am aware, sir. I will abide by anything you see fit."

"And if I dictate that you should turn over the girl to Stacy to do as she wishes?"

Cameron's response was immediate. "I would not. She is not the target and she does not deserve to suffer."

"Even if that was against my mandate?"

"I trust your wisdom and sense of justice more than that."

The silence in the room stretched on. Cameron stood up straight, sticking his chest out and holding that position, but this time it lacked the tension in his shoulders that existed with Stacy's presence.

"She will not stop searching for the child as long as you are within our domain."

Cameron tilted his head to the side for a moment. It was a while before he spoke. When he did, he straightened his position and said, "I understand. Thank you." Without another response, he turned around and walked out the door after his superior. Stacy waited just on the other side for him.

Before she went into the room, she sneered at Cameron. "I told you I would be here when you made your mistake."

~*~

Cameron pulled into the hotel parking lot and parked near the front entrance. All of his belongings that he cared to take with him were stashed in the two suitcases in the backseat. He parked the car and entered the hotel, going up to the third floor where he had a room. He unlocked the door and walked in, peering around the corner from the entry hall. The girl was sitting on the bed with her legs curled up to her chest and her arms wrapped around them. When she saw Cameron, she ran over towards him. He got down on one knee so that she could wrap her arms around his neck. He allowed her to hold on for a few seconds and then stood up with a hand wrapped underneath her backside to hold her in place.

"We're going to take a trip. Would you like that?"

The girl nodded, and sniffled.

"What's your name?" he asked while he was carrying her out the room.

"Lisa," she said.

"My name's Cameron. We're going to take a trip down to Texas. Have you ever been there?"

She shook her head.

"Me neither, but hopefully that's far enough."

The hotel door slammed shut behind him as he walked down the hall towards the elevator.

Missing Pieces: Decisions

About the Author

Dylan Birtolo is a writer, a gamer, and a professional sword-swinger. He pays for his passions by being a technical writer, but the evenings are filled with shape shifters, Japanese demons, and epic battles. He has two fantasy novels and a couple of short stories published. Recently, he has also been testing the waters of writing short pieces for game companies in their worlds. He trains with the Seattle Knights, an acting troop that focuses on stage combat, and has been in live shows and video shoots. In addition he teaches the academy for new and upcoming acting combatants. He has had the honor of jousting, and yes, the armor is real - it weighs over 120 pounds.

Dylan Birtolo

Hemingway's Challenge

They met. They played. They wrote.

-Tracy R. Chowdhury

About the Story

A Simple Twist of Fate is a story that fits in between my first duology (Shadow Over Shandahar) and the second one (Dark Mists of Ansalar). In the second book of the first duology, the heroine goes back into time, and while there, inadvertently alters it. Sydonnia is one of the men she meets while there, a man who she knows in her time (the future) as uncle to her fiancé, Sirion Timberlyn. In the future Sydonnia was shirwemic (werewolf), an evil abomination who has wreaked havoc within Elvandahar for many years, recently slain by his own nephew. But when she meets him in the past, it is at a time predating his terrible transformation. In spite of her efforts to have no influence, Adrianna's friendship with Sydonnia changes him forever, altering the future as she knows it. And as it also turns out, Sydonnia's relation to Sirion is not what everyone once thought.

A Simple Twist of Fate
By
Tracy R. Chowdhury

Massacre at the Terrestra River
32 Thaliren CY543

Evening was approaching, and the forest had become eerily quiet. Sydonnia's breath plumed into the chilly air as he turned in place, his faelin eyes straining to see into the trees surrounding him. The ragged sound of his breathing was harsh to his ears, and his heart seemed intent upon beating out of his chest. He could no longer hear the sounds of the battle he left behind, a battle that had not the noises one would customarily hear: the hiss of metal sliding out of scabbard, the twang of arrows leaving the bow, the ring of sword upon armor, and the shouts of men fighting one another. Instead he heard only the sickening sound of claw upon flesh, the thud of body against ground or tree, the pop of breaking bone, and the tormented screams of men fighting a terror they had never known before.

With the sleeve of his studded leather tunic, Sydonnia wiped at the sweat threatening to run into his eyes. He held his longsword before him, an uncharacteristic weapon for a hinterlean ranger, and one for which Servial teased him mercilessly. But Sydonnia was no ordinary hinterlean, so why should he carry an ordinary blade? And who was Servial to be the ultimate knowledge upon which weapon a ranger should or should not make his primary?

Sydonnia couldn't help but feel resentment. Before their assignment, he had confronted his brother about Lilandria during the latter part of a journey they were making together. Servial downplayed the accusation. In the ensuing argument, his brother had made Sy out to be the fool, a lovesick pup who couldn't understand the depth of feeling that had arisen between Servial and the lady. And then Servial had asked Sydonnia how he ever could imagine Lily feeling anything but pity for a man who had delusions of reality.

It wasn't the first time Servial had taken interest in a woman to whom Sydonnia felt an attraction. With her long fiery red hair and golden complexion, Lilandria of Kleyshes was quite a lovely woman. Yet, Sydonnia didn't just find her to be attractive in the physical sense. She was witty and humorous, yet quiet and gentle. Everything about her was perfect. He had come to realize that he was in love with her, and to see her with Servial was heart-wrenching. Sydonnia had rather hoped she would begin to have romantic feelings for him, but it was painfully easy to see that she had fallen for the charms of his philandering brother.

As children the brothers had always been close, and they grew into adulthood as boon companions. Yet in spite of their kinship, Servial felt the urge to compete, for it was simply in his nature. Most likely, Servial probably didn't even realize it. And Sy knew his brother well. As soon as Servial was certain he had her affections, the handsome ranger would leave Lilandria behind, just as he had the multitudes of other women in which he found temporary interest.

Once hearing what his brother had to say when Sy made his accusation, the depth of anger he felt had never before been achieved within his lifetime. He struggled to keep from smashing his fist into Servial's face, for he was sure he would have broken it. The strength it took for him to simply turn and walk away was extraordinary, and he knew he would never be able to achieve the same feat again. The remainder of their journey was intensely strained, and it was a good thing the end was near. Sydonnia had only to suffer the presence of his brother for two more days before they reached the silvery forest realm of Elvandahar, and then each man took his own path back home.

Once reaching the tree-top village of Merithyn, Sydonnia immediately became aware of something amiss. The rangers had all been called to meet at the home daladin of the Hamzin of Filopar, and the king's regent, prince Thalios, was in attendance along with the Hamzin of Kleyshes. Sy went to his own daladin to briefly unload his travel pack and extra equipment before rushing to the gathering. Many of the men had brought their families, most of whom would await them in the courtyard for the duration. His chest ached when he caught a glimpse of Lilandria, for he had a very sinking feeling for whom she would be waiting when the meeting was adjourned.

The next morning, the rangers of the domains of Filopar and Kleyshes left the sanctuary of their families and daladins to answer the call of protective duty to the realm of Elvandahar. The information they had been given in regards to the menace was paltry to say the least. When they met the enemy at the Terrestra River at the border of their domains, the rangers were woefully unprepared.

They were monsters. Standing at least seven or eight feet tall, they bore a strange resemblance to three of the most potentially dangerous animals in the forest: alothere, wemic, and kyrrean. Armed with tooth and claw, they were unnaturally strong and agile, with an ability to withstand ordinary weaponry that was phenomenal. It was painfully obvious they had once been faelin, and that somehow they had become twisted, despicable beings that seemed to harbor no regret with murdering those who had once been their brethren.

Once more, Sydonnia's breath took shape in the chilly air. He stood alone among the trees, the crackle of dried leaves beneath his boots intermingling with the sound of his harsh breaths. It wasn't his intention to abandon his comrades, but he had felt oddly compelled to make his way deeper into the wood. Strangely, in the fore of his mind was the anger he felt towards Servial. The intensity of his emotions swept over him, and Sydonnia heard a voice emanating from the trees behind him. It was deep, and spoke in barely a whisper.

"I can feel your anger."

Sydonnia swung around, brandishing his blade before him. From out of the forest stepped a figure cloaked entirely within the folds of a dark robe. Even the face was hidden within a deep hood.

"I can feel your hate."

Sydonnia swallowed heavily and stepped backward as the figure advanced towards him. A chuckle emerged from within the hood, and the voice spoke with a strange sibilant quality. "I chossse you, Sssydonnia Timberlyn. You are everything I want, everything I *need* to complete what I ssset out to accomplish."

Sydonnia shook his head and pulled his brows into a frown, somehow finding the courage to make a reply. "Who the Hells are you? How do you know my name?" he asked petulantly.

The figure stopped. Sydonnia could sense that the face hidden within the depths of the hood was smiling. "I am Gaknar, the Mehta of the Daemundai. Already you have met sssome of my petsss. But *they* are nothing compared to what *you* will be."

Sydonnia swallowed past the sudden lump in his throat. He shook his head again, keeping his increasing trepidation under control. "I want nothing from you. Go find somebody else, someone who might actually give a damn."

He spoke with forced bravado in the hopes it would be a deterrent. Once again, he heard a faint chuckle from within the folds of the dark hood. "I think not. I know you, Sssydonnia. Whether you want it or not, I am your dessstiny."

Sydonnia nervously tightened his grip on the hilt of his sword. His hand was sweaty inside the leather glove he wore, and he was glad he had donned it that morning, for the weapon would surely have slipped from his palm by now. Once more the figure began to slowly advance. Sydonnia held his ground, keeping his sword between them. From within the voluminous folds of the cloak, a misshapen hand with wickedly curved claws appeared. Sydonnia felt his eyes widen, but when he tried to retreat, he found himself held in place by some unseen force. He fought to control a surge of fear, knowing that if he allowed it to overwhelm him, the enemy would certainly persevere.

"Even now I can feel it," he hissed. "Your anger isss consssuming you. Give in to your hate, for it can show you a new path."

Sydonnia stoically watched the cloaked figure approach, a yellowish fluid dripping from the claws. Strangely, he felt the anger within him stirring. He wondered about it for a moment, for it should be the last thing on his mind in his present situation. But it seemed as though the cloaked man was bringing it out in him. And until now, Sydonnia had never really realized there was a part of him that actually *hated* his brother. The question was, would he ever consider acting upon that hate?

Suddenly the robed figure was before him. Sydonnia had no time to react as the claws swept towards him. He caught a glimpse of the visage within the depths of the hood as they met his vulnerable throat. If he had the inclination, he would have recognized the hideousness of it. Instead, Sydonnia grasped at the deep wounds at his neck, struggling to keep his life's blood from soaking the front of his tunic.

Missing Pieces: A Simple Twist of Fate

Time seemed to slow down for a moment as he felt himself fall heavily to his knees. Shifting and wavering around him, the world had a strange quality to it. *So this is what it is like to die.*

He slumped onto his side, his eyes staring vaguely into the space before him. The blood flowed heavily from between his gloved fingers to moisten the ground beneath. All of a sudden, Sydonnia felt something sweep through him, something strangely invigorating. Then the pain came, and he screamed...

1 Decaren CY544

Sydonnia swept through the trees towards the scent of his brother. More than seven moon cycles had passed since Servial and the other surviving rangers had conducted their agonizingly brief search for him the morning after the massacre. Hidden among the forest brush, Sydonnia had looked on as Servial cut the search short, claiming that he had seen Sydonnia being dragged into the forest by one of the attacking monstrosities. It was a lie, for Sydonnia had walked calmly into the forest of his own accord. Servial had then staged the impression that he was extremely upset over Sydonnia's loss, and that they should return to the capitol city of Alcrostat as quickly as possible in order to report to the king.

Sydonnia knew he could have chosen that moment to enter the scene. Maybe he should have. He thought more of the idea now simply because, at the time, he had very little understanding of what had befallen him. Standing there within the shadows, he had been afraid of what happened and bore very little understanding of what he had become. Not only had he felt betrayed by his brother, but he felt feel himself an outcast. He had changed in more ways than just the physical. It was mental as well.

Sydonnia had abandoned his comrades, much as they abandoned him. At first he remained in denial. He was loathe to face the monster he had turned into, but the intense satisfaction he derived from the chase as he brought down his victims was something that he could not disavow. And then there was the pleasure he felt in the killing, and the fact that he looked forward to the day his prey would be more than just a simple animal.

Sydonnia remained obscure within the depths offered by the silver wood. He encountered other men, and the first was torn into bits within barely the space of several moments. The next time he was somewhat more restrained. After a while he came to the realization that if he allowed a man to live after delivering his bite, a strange thing happened. The person became fevered and tormented. He writhed about in his unconscious state until a transformation overtook him. When the man awakened, he was no longer the simple faelin he once was. Sydonnia had forged into being a new monstrosity, *fathered* him. And the newly changed man was his *family*.

It wasn't long before Sydonnia and his pack had begun to wreak havoc wherever they went. Their hunger was insatiable. The small villages became their feeding grounds, and Sydonnia saw that not everyone transformed after sustaining his bite. These rare people suffered through the fever and sickness through to the next day, upon which they awakened and began to recover from their ordeal, unchanged. He couldn't understand why they were able to withstand the transformation, but it bothered him very little. Many of these he simply killed once he realized they would not change.

And such was the way it went until the need to see Lilandria struck him, followed closely by his desire to exact revenge upon his brother for the wrongs Sy felt had been done. First Servial had taken Lilandria away from him, and then made him feel the fool when Sydonnia confronted him. Then Servial had lied about Sydonnia being taken into the forest. Finally, his brother had abandoned him to an enemy that had destroyed an entire contingent of rangers within the short space of time it took Shandahar's second moon to join her sister in the evening sky. Why? Was it all because of Lilandria? Or was it that Servial simply couldn't accept that Sydonnia might be able to accomplish something that he could not?

Sydonnia had easily found his brother. It wasn't difficult, for he had trained his senses to hone wholly upon Servial. He had been waiting quite a while for this moment to arrive, biding his time until he felt it was right. All the while he kept Lilandria in his thoughts, remembering the wonderful friendship they had once shared, and the love he knew that lay somewhere deep within her.

Love she felt for him.

Sydonnia stopped a farlo or two from his brother. The area was open, almost devoid of the silver oak trees that comprised the majority in Elvandahar. As of yet, Servial had not sensed him, and Sydonnia smiled in anticipation. Stupid fool. Servial thought himself so lofty that he ceased to extend his senses outward, one of the first things one learned in order to become a good ranger. Sy's grin widened. Obviously Servial was not a good ranger.

Sydonnia stepped out from the concealment of the trees. Servial was instantly aware, finally sensing the predator in his midst. When his gaze settled upon Sydonnia, his eyes widened with shock. Adjusting quickly, Servial schooled his face into an expression of joy.

"Sydonnia, where in the Hells have you been? We thought you were dead!" Servial rushed over to him. He stopped when he was but an arms-length away. "We searched and searched to no avail. Brother, where were you?"

Servial's expression had turned from one of astonishment and joy, to confusion and a small degree of dismay. Sydonnia remained impassive despite the temptation to fall into Servial's trap. His brother hoped to use his charming manner and show of caring in order to draw him in. Sydonnia refused to allow it.

"Did you?" Sydonnia spoke in a deep monotone. It was one of the many things about him that changed since the transformation. His voice had always been rather deep, but now... "Did you really search for me, *Brother*?" He emphasized the last word, spoke it as though it was an expletive. He watched as his Servial's eyes became shuttered and his lips pulled taut. Servial quickly surmised that Sydonnia somehow knew full well the events that had taken place.

"Of course, *Brother*. Why wouldn't I?" Servial's voice had an edge to it as well, and his eyes narrowed slightly.

Sydonnia shrugged his broad shoulders. "I don't know. Why don't you *enlighten* me?"

Servial's eyes narrowed even further. Sydonnia could see the interplay within Servial's mind in spite of his attempts to conceal it. He wasn't accustomed to the Sydonnia who stood before him now, the one who used fancy words and sported a voice as deep as the darkest Silverwood. He wasn't used to the Sydonnia who would stand up to him in defiance as he did now.

"You are a deserter. You could be tried by the hinterlean crown and determined a traitor. You could be banished, and even worse, killed. I doubt you want that, Sydonnia."

Sydonnia smiled widely, baring his sharp canines. "Ah Brother, you think you know me so well. You even think they could capture me." He laughed then, a full throated one that seemed to reverberate off the trees that circled the clearing. "They have no chance."

Grim understanding seemed to dawn upon Servial then. His body stiffened almost imperceptibly, and the pupils of his eyes widened in response to an instinctual reaction that was suddenly brought to the fore. It was the sensation associated with the presence of a predator and that danger was near.

Servial swallowed convulsively. "You don't frighten me, Sydonnia. I know what you are and I know why you have come. You will not have her. Lilandria is mine, and always will be." Servial lowered his voice into a hiss. "You are a fool to have come here."

Sydonnia growled deep in his throat. "You forget how well I know you. You will use Lily just as you do all the women in your acquaintance. After a while you will tire of her and cast her aside just like all the others." Sydonnia cocked his head. "As I recall, one of them even bore you a child. You refused to acknowledge her as your bastard, claiming the mother slept with another man. You have a daughter that you have never seen. I wonder what she must think of you."

Servial shook his head slowly and grinned. "What are you going to do about it big brother? Are you going to be her champion? As I recall it, Lilandria chose me over you."

"Yes, but she didn't know the dung-eaten calotebas that you really are, and that you left your own brother to die in the forest." Sydonnia grinned in return. "And yes, I am going to be her champion..."

Sydonnia's sentence was cut short as Servial chose that moment to rush at him. The extra long blade of the hinterlean-style dagger reflected briefly before it was plunged into Sydonnia's unprotected abdomen. It sunk in deep, and with a savage twist, Servial drove it deeper. Damn, it was disheartening to know that one's own brother would so easily attempt to murder him. Of course, Sydonnia had thought to do the same. But Servial had acted first, and he wasn't even the monster.

Sydonnia felt it begin almost instantly. It was the change that took him from a man into something in between, half man and half beast. It was where he could use the best of both worlds, and in this hybrid form, he was also the most powerful. As his fingernails lengthened into claws, he gripped Servial by the front of his vest and pulled the man up off the ground. With his increasing strength, he then threw Servial into the nearest tree. He was gratified to hear the impact of flesh upon wood. As Servial struggled to rise, Sydonnia strode towards him, picked him up once more, and then called out. Just like before, it emerged as a howl, one that told the others of his pack that the hunt was over and the prey taken down.

Sydonnia felt Servial shudder beneath his grip and smiled malevolently. He was so tempted to bite his brother and then leave him to the same fate he now endured. But he knew the impulse was a foolhardy one. Once in possession of the same strengths that Sydonnia now possessed, Servial would surely thwart him. The two would always be at odds with one another, and Sydonnia would see no end until the other man was dead. Yet, despite the darkness that he knew had overtaken his soul, he didn't have the heart to kill his brother. He couldn't help recalling the games they had played together as boys, their plans to raise their families together as one, and the promises they had made to always stand by one another.

Sydonnia angrily cast his brother from him. Servial hit the ground with a resounding thud and Sydonnia barely glanced at his still form before turning away. Servial was right about one thing. Sydonnia was indeed a fool to have come. He should have gone immediately to Lilandria, for he may have had more luck with her. He completed his transformation and swiftly left the area. He could hardly wait to see her.

Seven moon-cycles after the massacre
2 Decaren CY544

Lilandria turned to look behind her for the third time since arriving at the path that would take her to the heated springs. The pools were a boon to the people of Alcrostat and Merithyn, for none like them existed elsewhere within the realm. Usually she had no problem with the walk it took in order to reach them. But today she couldn't shake the feeling that she was being followed, and she was beginning to feel nervous.

Several moon cycles had passed since Servial and a small contingent of surviving rangers returned from the banks of the Terrestra River. She had been distraught to find that Sydonnia was not with them. He was proclaimed missing, for his body had never been found. She lamented the loss of her friend, for they had become quite close during the months leading up to that fateful mission. The details were kept from her and the others who awaited the return of their loved ones. Three fourths of those people never returned. It was a historical moment for all of Elvandahar, and the mourning was long and sorrowful.

But at least Servial had returned from the ill-fated assignment. He had yet to say much about his brother, but she knew that it was only a matter of time before he would confide in her. In spite of her own feelings of loss, she knew that Servial's were so much greater, and she vowed to be his bastion of support when he finally broke down. She was initially taken aback by his lack of emotion concerning Sydonnia, but in the end realized it was simply his way of coping with the loss. She respected that, and she would be there for Servial when he finally came around.

Finally Lilandria reached the springs. Within the center of each of the four heated pools, water bubbled up from within the ground and mist rose into the air. It was the perfect place for people to get together and mingle whilst they bathed. More often, women visited in the mornings while men did so in the evenings after a long day. Even though she had arrived closer towards mid-day, she was surprised to find herself alone. It was an uncommon occurrence, and it took her slightly aback. This day would have been a good one to have companionship.

Lilandria slowly set her pack upon the ground next to one of the flat rocks situated around the pools. She had always wondered if they were placed there by natural whimsy or faelin inspiration. She hesitated to begin removing the gown she customarily wore to the springs and then admonished herself. By the gods, she was being so silly. What had gotten into her? She would have known if someone were indeed following her. And why would anyone do such a thing anyways? It simply wasn't civilized.

It was only a moment later that her skin began to prickle, and Lilandria immediately felt the unmistakable presence of another person. She would have loved to believe it was someone whom had come to bathe, someone much like herself who had a late start to their day. But she instinctively knew it wasn't the truth, for her body reacted as though imperiled. She sensed *danger* emanating from the presence behind her.

Lilandria slowly turned in place. She fought her inclination to close her eyes, an immature reaction to stress. If it can't be seen, it must not really be there. Then she saw him standing at the tree-line, a man she had thought deceased. *Sydonnia*.

She mouthed his name without speaking, her eyes widening with disbelief. She then put a hand to her chest in a subconscious attempt to stop her racing heart. Lilandria thought she must surely be dreaming, but her physical response to his presence was definitely not imaginary. He then stepped towards her with hands outstretched, and she rushed to him without considering her body's earlier warning of danger.

"By the gods, is it really you?" She breathlessly spoke the words so low they were almost a whisper. The feel of his arms around her was not like she remembered, the embrace seeming stronger somehow, more powerful. Yet, the scent of him was familiar in spite of the musky undertone.

"Did you miss me?"

His deep voice carried a bantering quality, and she thought the question a strange one, especially from one who had been considered lost in battle. She pulled back, and through the tears in her eyes Lilandria took in the ruggedly handsome face. It was much the same as it had always been: the cut of jaw, the shape of his lips, and the arch of his thick brows. But something was different, something she couldn't quite place.

"Sydonnia, where have you been? They went out looking for you, but..."

He placed a forefinger to her lips and she stopped. Lilandria felt a slight shift in his demeanor, and once more her skin prickled. "Sssh. It doesn't matter. I am here now," he said solemnly.

Missing Pieces: A Simple Twist of Fate

His voice was so deep, deeper than she recalled it to be. Her breath caught in her throat; *what was happening?* He had disregarded her inquiry without a shred of care or thought. She shook her head. "It *does* matter! I thought you were dead!"

He grinned disarmingly. "Well now you know that I'm not."

Lilandria frowned and took a step back, struggling to discern the slight changes she noticed had taken place. "Sydonnia, that's not good enough. I need to know what happened." She paused and then continued. "Does Servial know you are here?"

Lilandria sensed it immediately. It was a shift in the very air surrounding them. His brown eyes focused piercingly upon her, eyes that seemed almost feral. She thought it strange that particular word popped to mind, and she slowly began to feel a pervading sensation of peril.

Sydonnia regarded her with a frown. "I suppose the two of you have become rather close in my absence. I guess I can't blame you since you thought me deceased," he said gruffly.

Lilandria shook her head and drew her brows together. "Sy, what's gotten into you? Servial and I...what...*how* does our relationship bear any consequence to your whereabouts for all of this time?" she stuttered.

"It has everything to do with it!" he growled. "You think you know my brother." Sydonnia shook his head. "You know nothing! He knew I loved you, but he focused his attentions upon you anyways." Sydonnia paused and then continued. "Don't look so surprised, my dear. You had to have known my attraction to you, an attraction I continue to harbor. And somewhere deep inside, I know you have a similar feeling for me. Only now, Servial's charm has blinded you to it."

Lilandria shook her head once more. "Sydonnia, what are you talking about? This attraction...what has it to do with where you have been? I don't understand!"

Sydonnia closed the gap between them and grabbed her by the arms. "Don't you see? He knew that your attraction was more than just simple friendship. That is why he stopped the search. *Servial never wanted me to be found!*"

Lilandria instinctively tried to pull back from his grip. "By the gods, Sydonnia. Listen to yourself! Do you honestly believe what you are saying? Servial loves you. He would never have left the river knowing you were still there. Hells, he thought you were dead!"

Sydonnia shook his head vehemently. "No! He knew how I felt about you and feared I would take you away from him, much as he had taken you away from me. Before the assignment we had a fight. It was about you. We never reconciled! He left me, Lily! I was there, hiding in the trees, when he stopped the other rangers from continuing the search for me!"

Lilandria regarded him incredulously. "By the gods, this is craziness! This attraction you keep talking about... Sy, it was never there for me, not the way you think!" Lilandria paused and then continued. "You are wrong to believe Servial purposefully left you at the river! He would never have done that! He had nothing to fear because I was never in love with you!"

Sydonnia suddenly became still. She winced as he tightened his grip upon her arms and her senses screamed to her of imminent danger. It seemed that he then began to change before her very eyes. His canines began to elongate, the hair around his face thickened, and his stature broadened. Fear swept through her like a scythe, and despite the discomfort she redoubled her efforts to escape his grip.

"My brother has poisoned your mind," he hissed savagely. "Just look deep within and you will find I speak the truth. I felt it between us, still feel it, a connection that can't be denied," he continued. "Come away with me, Lilandria. I can give you everything you have ever wanted. Before I was weak, but now I have strength I never could have imagined!"

"Sydonnia, please. Let me go." She struggled to keep her voice from wavering. "I don't want any of this."

Sydonnia pulled her close to him, placing his lips near her ear. "You don't know what you are saying. I know that you want me; you have only to look past the shroud my brother has placed over your mind."

The fear became overwhelming, and Lilandria was suddenly aware of what he had become. He was one of those whom everyone spoke so much about, one of the monsters that wreaked havoc upon the outlying villages and towns all across Kleyshes and Filopar. A lycanthrope. By the gods, the innocent people that had been killed already. And the children...

Her breathing accelerated, but she somehow found it difficult to get air. Her heart felt as though it might beat from her chest at any moment. Lilandria felt herself becoming faint, but she resisted it. She looked up at Sydonnia, into the face that she had once found so comforting. All she saw now was a terrible beast. Lilandria began to struggle against him. "I don't want anything to do with you. Get away from me!" she shouted.

The impact of Sydonnia's hand across her face was enough to make her head snap around on her neck. Tears sprang to her eyes, and as her consciousness began to waver, Lilandria felt herself being forced to the ground. Struggling feebly, she vaguely felt her clothing being torn away. Then a sudden penetrating pain overwhelmed her senses, and her world shifted to dark.

Almost 28 years after the massacre...
29 Jicaren CY571

The shadows lengthened as the sun set upon the darkening horizon. Sirion looked down at the length of the young corubis curled around him, light from the nearby fire reflecting off of the dappled tawny fur. The animal was a gift, one bestowed upon him by his father several moon cycles ago. They had waited for the litter to be born, and then they waited even longer until the pups were old enough to be weaned from their mother's milk. It was the day that Sirion was allowed to meet the pups for the very first time, to see if any of the weanlings would single him out from any of the other young faelin men and women who were also present for the auspicious occasion. It was always a special day when a corubis litter was ready for *imprinting*. And Sirion had been one of the lucky ones chosen.

His name was Dramati. Sirion had chosen it from a long list of hinterlean words that were no longer in use by the general populace. It meant "loyal, steadfast companion" in the ancient texts, and Sirion knew the animal would be just that. It would be good to have Dramati for his next run, one that his father told him would be rather long and arduous. Sirion would be developing even more of the hand-to-hand combat techniques he had at his behest, as well as some additional skill with the blade he would develop from an elite swordsman his father had met many years ago. It didn't feel like much time had elapsed since he left his mother and sister behind in Merithyn, but the passage of the moon cycles was testimony to that. Not to mention, the accomplishments he had made under the tutelage of some of the most renowned masters upon all of western Ansalar.

Sirion glanced up at the fire that his father had built for the evening. Within the pot hanging precipitously over the flames, a stew of ptarmigan and leeks was slowly cooking. They would eat well this night, and Sirion was proud of the contribution he had made to the stew-pot. The game had been difficult to spot within the thick foliage, but he had persevered thanks to the help of Dramati. The long-legged canine was a good hunter despite his young age. His father started to smile at him from the other side of the fire, but stopped when they suddenly heard a resounding howl emanate from the trees around them.

Servial was suddenly at the alert. He stood from his position at the fire as he drew his hinterlean dagger from its sheath strapped to the belt around his waist. Sirion could sense the tension emanating from his father and knew that something was seriously amiss. It was then that he smelled it, a musky odor often associated with a predator. Dramati stirred in his lap, and Sirion knew that he sensed it too. Sirion heard a faint sound coming from the wood, the light trod of a hunter stalking his prey. And it was coming straight towards them.

Sirion froze in place, suddenly recognizing the presence of danger. Dramati sensed it as well, and Sirion felt a low growl begin to emanate from deep within the corubis' body as Dramati took a more defensive position. They both startled when a man walked out of the shadows of the surrounding wood and into the light offered by the fire. He was quite large for a faelin, standing a few hands higher than Servial, and at least two or three hands broader. He walked nonchalantly into their encampment, almost as though he belonged there, and he wore a wide smile on his stubbly face.

"Well, well, well. Who have I come across this time?" he drawled. "Oh, it's my faithful brother, mayhap coming to give me a visit as he passes through the Sheldomar Forest." His thick brows suddenly pulled down into a frown. "Hells, but he never bothered to before." He then cupped a hand beneath his chin in mock thoughtfulness. "Hmm, I suppose I need to remind him of the importance of *family*."

Sirion remained still. He had heard the stories of his father's brother, a man who had died in the fight against the lycanthrope menace almost two decades ago. He had no recollection of another brother. Silence reigned for a moment before his father spoke. "What do you want, Sydonnia?"

Sirion's thoughts began to race when he heard the name, and he gripped at the thick fur circling Dramati's neck. *Sydonnia was the name of his father's dead brother.*

Sydonnia simply shrugged his wide shoulders. "It's been so long, but I vividly recall when last we met. I stood as victor at the end of our little skirmish." He paused for a moment and then continued. "Oh, and so sorry about the leg, Brother. Sometimes I don't know my own strength." Sydonnia smiled again, his canines shining brightly white in the firelight. Sirion swallowed heavily as feral eyes came to rest upon him in spite of efforts to be invisible. The gaze was coldly calculating, and it almost seemed as though Sydonnia touched the outer fringes of his soul with the intensity of his stare.

"I see you have brought your whelp," he said in a monotone. "It surprises me that you would place him at risk knowing that me and mine are loose within these forests. You are a fool, Servial." Sydonnia growled the last, swinging his gaze back towards his father.

Servial shook his head and curled his lips. "You are only jealous because Lilandria bore my son and not yours," he sneered. "Your life is pathetic, Sydonnia. You have accomplished nothing, and no one cares about you. I *almost* feel sorry for you."

Sirion felt it immediately, a sudden change in the surrounding air. Sydonnia's stature increased, and his voice deepened. "No. You are the pathetic one, Servial. You left her, just as I knew you would. One day, your son will discover the truth about you, and he will come to despise you. Unfortunately, you won't be there." Sydonnia paused and then continued. "You asked me what I wanted, and now I will tell you. I have come to kill you, Brother, much as you left me to die all those many years ago at the Terrestra River."

Servial had barely enough time to raise his dagger before Sydonnia was upon him. The man was monstrous to behold, standing at least two hands higher than he did when first entering the encampment. His body was now covered with hair, and his face strangely elongated. The most terrifying changes were the wickedly clawed hands and sharp canines protruding from the upper jaw. Sirion could only hunker there in abject fear, terrified to the very core of his being.

With unnatural grace and power, Sydonnia leaped at Servial. As their two bodies collided, Sydonnia wrapped his arms around his brother and sunk his sharp claws deep into Servial's back. At such close range, the studded leather offered only minimal resistance. Sydonnia raked them around to the sides and then savagely thrust Servial away from him.

Servial landed upon the ground with a heavy thud. Blood had already begun to stain the tan vest, surrounding the huge tears at the sides and back. Sirion finally found the courage to rush to his feet. He drew his own dagger and without thinking, he sprung towards the enemy with Dramati following beside. With the greatest of ease, Sydonnia blocked the attack. With one hand he took Sirion by the throat, and with the other he swept at Dramati. The corubis flew through the air. Sirion heard a heavy thud followed by a sharp yelp as the animal landed about a farlo away.

Sirion scraped at the hand closed around his throat, desperate to free himself. He looked into the chaotic gaze of his uncle, saw the madness brimming just below the surface. Suddenly remembering he still had the dagger in his hand, Sirion plunged it into Sydonnia's unprotected abdomen. The man gave a vicious growl and then retaliated. Sirion felt the wicked claws slice across him, starting at his shoulder and ending just above his navel. He then felt the crushing power of the hand around his throat, squeezing...squeezing...until he began to see a smattering of bright pin-points in the periphery of his vision. Sirion abruptly found himself airborne for a moment, but then his face was scraping against the debris of the forest floor as he suffered a brutal landing.

Unable to move, Sirion slowly opened one of his eyes to a narrow crack. The terrible scene he witnessed would be burned into his memory forever. Servial stood in the middle of the encampment, his blood-drenched tunic and vest hanging in shreds around him. He wore an expression of deep sadness, almost as though remembering something he had once lost. A huge white wemic entered Sirion's line of vision. He knew that the animal was the completely altered form of Sydonnia, *and that all vestiges of reason were gone.*

The wemic attacked Servial where he stood. The man offered no resistance, for he knew it would be futile. The massive jaws closed around Servial's neck and then Sydonnia savagely shook the limp body back and forth. Sirion could hear the sickening sound of cracking bone; blood spraying onto the thick pale fur of Sydonnia's neck. The wemic flung the broken form away from him and then followed to the place where it fell. Sydonnia then proceeded to ravage the lifeless body of his brother until it was barely discernible.

Sydonnia stood over the bloody remains for a moment. He then curled his stained lips into a snarl and slowly turned in Sirion's direction. He could do nothing as the animal padded noiselessly towards him. The feral eyes bore into him, eyes that Sirion could only vaguely sense contained the soul of a man. His heart felt as though it would beat out of his chest, and just as his father had done, Sirion gave himself up to Sydonnia. He knew there was nothing he could do to stop the inevitable. From the massive wounds across his chest, he could feel his life's blood seeping through the fabric of his tunic and into the ground beneath. His vision wavered. The horrific visage of his uncle appeared before him, crimson red lips baring long white teeth. Yet, there was an eerie beauty about the beast.

Sirion had never heard of a white wemic...

51 years after the massacre . . .
7 Decaren CY594

Adrianna had heard the story. It was told to her in bits and pieces over the course of time she was getting to know Sirion. Parts of it were related to her as the Wildrunners journeyed back to Elvandahar after their battle against the deathmage, Aasarak. Yet, most of it had been told much earlier than that: before she and her sister defeated Lord Thane in the Ratik Mountain Pass, before she went into training within Master Tallachienan's citadel, and before she met her dragon bond-mate. Sydonnia had allowed Sirion his life that evening so long ago in the Sheldomar Forest. Inasmuch, Adria thought it such a tragedy that someone could be driven to murder his own brother, and that the brother's son would, in turn, be fated to return the favor many years later. Such was the basic premise of the story of Servial and Sydonnia Timberlyn, two men who once would have laid down his life for the other.

Adrianna glanced about her as the group rode astride the lloryk and larian that had carried them so far. The silver canopy of Elvandahar's forest loomed overhead, so thick it blocked out most of the sunlight that sought to venture through. It hadn't really been that long since the Wildrunners last saw the beauty belonging to the realm of the hinterlean faelin. Yet, that visit had ended with the tragedy of Sydonnia's death at the hands of his nephew. She was certain Sirion still suffered the aftershock.

Adrianna sighed and swept a hand through the strands of pale blond hair that escaped from its customary plait. The strain of the knowledge she carried weighed heavily upon her, and she fervently wished she could divulge all of it to Sirion. Truth be told, she had already returned to Elvandahar within the interim of this visit and the last. Her visit was one that made quite an interesting tale, one that matched the one she heard told about Servial and Sydonnia before. It was a continuation of it, actually, one which she had the opportunity to experience first-hand.

It had happened as an accident one day whilst in training. She had been worn down by the intensity of her studies, and her misery was perpetuated by an overbearing master. Adria had sought only to escape the confines of Tallachienan and his dark citadel for a time, to visit the place she knew as her childhood home: the city of Sangrilak. She had succeeded in sending herself to a place vastly different from what she remembered.

Adrianna had been shocked when she met Sydonnia outside the limits of a much smaller Sangrilak. Accompanying him was another man, one she had never met. When she noticed the similarity to Sirion, and then discovered that his name was Servial Timberlyn, she made the difficult realization that she existed in a different Time. Hells, how could she have known that the master had taken her into the past in order to meet her training requirements in the present? Knowing she was trapped until Master Tallachienan came to retrieve her, Adrianna found herself in a situation she could not escape without bringing too much attention to herself. Forced into proximity with Sirion's father and uncle, she was given the opportunity to see the story first hand, for she had suddenly become a part of it.

Adrianna found herself pulled away from her thoughts when she felt her larian slowing to a halt. Glancing towards the head of the procession, she saw Sirion standing there, looking into the trees before him. It was then that she noticed it, a familiar musky odor tinged with a predatory undertone. The hairs at the back of her neck immediately began to rise in response to the danger, and by the look of his stance, she knew that Sirion felt it too. However, instead of reaching for his weapon as he ordinarily would, Sirion stepped forward with his hands at his sides, saying something she couldn't quite decipher despite her excellent faelin hearing. And then, when she saw the individual who stepped out to greet him, her heart almost stopped in her chest. The man had died several moon cycles ago at Sirion's hand. It was Sydonnia Timberlyn.

Missing Pieces: A Simple Twist of Fate

In shock, Adrianna almost slipped from the back of her larian. The breath caught in her chest and her heart seemed to become still for a moment. No. This wasn't possible. Hells, what was happening? Had she somehow traveled through Time yet again? Or was this some type of terrible dream from which she had a difficult time awakening? She thought back on all of the conversations she and Sirion had shared since her return to the group after her training, and with a blow she realized that not once did Sirion mention the death of his uncle. She hadn't noticed it because there was no reason to state the obvious. The man was dead, so why say it aloud? It was for that reason Adria had forbore to mention it as well.

By the gods, what had she done?

In the past, Adrianna had developed a camaraderie with the man she would later know as a monster. Within the time she spent in his company, Sydonnia had become more than just Sirion's deranged uncle, but a good friend and fierce protector. She had balked at the course of events that would eventually take place, and even more that she could do nothing to stop it. Right from the start, she knew that any changes made in the past would affect the future as she remembered it. She had realized she couldn't take the risk of those changes affecting her relationship with Sirion, for it was their union that most likely influenced the joining of the original Wildrunners with the younger individuals who would one day carry their name. Not to mention that without the merger, Aasarak may never have been defeated.

And the world would still be repeating itself.

A few days after the massacre at the Terrestra River
3 Chanteren CY543

Sydonnia slowly opened his eyes, immediately aware of the chill in the air. Where he lay upon his back, he could see the silvery canopy above, interrupted by widening swaths of blue sky beyond. He moved one leg, and then the other, cringing with the pain the movement caused. The memories of what he endured returned in bits and pieces, and by the time he made it to his feet, it had all come back to him.

He remembered the hideous dark-robed priest, the wickedly curved claws, the feeling of himself beginning to die, and then the terrible pain. The torment had swept over him in an agonizing wave, taking away thought and reason until barely anything was left. His body had writhed upon the ground, muscle tearing and bones snapping until everything had rearranged itself to fit the description of something other than faelin. He had become something more, something much, much more. He just didn't know exactly what that was.

He then began to feel it. It was overpowering in its intensity, a sensation of hunger he had never experienced before. Overcome by the demands of his transformed body, Sydonnia hunted under the pale light of the moons. The urge to kill was strong, and he satisfied it with the life of a young leschera. Sydonnia was surprised with the ease it took for him to bring down the deer-like animal, especially by himself. The pleasure he derived by sinking his elongated canines into the throat of the beast was astounding, and when he felt the heart cease beating, he had already begun to feed. Imagining what the animal might be feeling those last few moments of life was invigorating, and as the leschera died beneath his hands, Sydonnia lifted his head and cried out with ecstasy. The sound that emerged from his throat was a howl, a sound he had often heard from the wemic packs that set their territories along the ground beneath his home village of Merithyn. It was then that his full awareness began to return, and he became truly cognizant of the creature he had become.

And then he remembered his brother and the contingent of rangers whom he had accompanied to the Terrestra River.

As the moons began to wane, Sydonnia made his way back to the banks of the Terrestra. The carnage he passed was gut wrenching, for each of the bodies he passed was someone he knew: childhood friends, comrades in arms, respected citizens of the domains of Kleyshes and Filopar. All of them unceremoniously ripped to shreds, torn apart by beasts such as the one he had become. Then, as the sun began to crest the horizon, he found the survivors. It was easy, for his sense of smell had become so keen. He stood hidden within the trees as they searched for him, afraid to come out lest they see that something was changed about him and mayhap realize what he had become. He struggled to work up the courage to step forward. Yet, he found he hadn't the time. The sun had barely begun its rise into the sky when they were gone. At the behest of his own brother, the rangers cut their search short and abandoned Sydonnia to whatever grisly fate awaited him.

And now he was alone, with nothing but his memories and his lust to kill...

Sydonnia let the anger come, let it envelop him like a shroud. His thoughts returned to a time several moon cycles before ago, when he had first begun to notice the attention Servial was starting to pay Lilandria, a woman whom Sydonnia had begun to develop deep affection. Servial had a propensity for always getting his way with the female population, no matter who might stand in his way. Obviously that included Sydonnia as well. He had every intention of confronting his brother about the situation on their return trip from a journey they were making to the town of Sangrilak on business. But as fate would have it, they came across a lone woman just outside the town limits.

Keilah Laremion was an enigma to them. She was quite attractive, and it was so uncommon to see a faelin of her coloration and appearance in that part of Ansalar. She refused to divulge much about herself, and at first seemed somewhat disoriented. All she would tell them was that her brother would be coming for her. Nevertheless, they took her under their protective wing, unable to simply leave her without a proper escort. A lone female out in the middle of nowhere was unheard of. On the way back to Elvandahar, Sydonnia found a strong rapport with her that turned into friendship. The discussion he wanted to have with Servial about Lilandria was pushed to the background, for somehow Keilah's presence had affected the two brothers and they had started to rediscover the intense bond they had shared since childhood.

Yet, when they had arrived in Merithyn, all of that began to change. Servial started to bestow upon Keilah the type of attention he had shown Lilandria before their business in Sangrilak. All of the negative emotions came rushing back to Sydonnia, but with the added realization that Lily would be hurt when she saw Servial giving his affections to another woman. Interestingly, Keilah seemed virtually immune to Servial's charm, and it served to increase Sydonnia's respect for her.

Just as Keilah began to get settled into life in Elvandahar, the brothers had received a summons for a call to arms. It was agreed that in two days, the rangers of the domains of Filopar and Kleyshes would leave the sanctuary of their families and daladins to answer the call of protective duty to the realm. The information they had been given in regards to the menace was only that the situation was dire, and that people were dying. As the two domains prepared to face the threat, the brother that Keilah had always claimed would come for her finally arrived. Bravin and Keilah stayed the night and early the next morning, Sydonnia felt his heart ache as she embraced him for the last time. He could see a similar ache also reflecting in her eyes before she finally stepped back. As he watched her walk away, he couldn't help but feel that something momentous had happened, and that it would not be the last time he saw her.

Later the same morning, the rangers had met in the city of Alcrostat. There were well over two score, and many of them had corubis companions in accompaniment. Sydonnia was disgusted to see Lilandria in Servial's arms once more, despite what she had seen of his pursuit of Keilah. He must have downplayed it, making her believe that what she saw was nothing but simple friendship and that he had feelings only for her. It wasn't long after that they were leaving the city, and that evening when camp was set, Sydonnia finally confronted his brother.

Of course Servial had trivialized the accusation, and then made Sy out to be a besotted fool. An argument ensued, but before he became too angry to think rationally, Sydonnia walked away. It was one of the most difficult things had had ever done, for all he wanted to do was smash his fist into Servial's sneering face. Subsequently, the remainder of their journey to the Terrestra River was intensely strained. Fortunately, Sydonnia found himself preoccupied with the coming battle and the mysterious threat. But when the group of rangers met the enemy, they were woefully unprepared. A massacre ensued. Sydonnia was lured into the wood.

And now he was a monster.

Yet, in spite of the wrong his brother had committed against him, there was a part of Sydonnia that wanted to return home. Perhaps he would go to see one of the hinterlean wise-men. The nivorlan would know what to do to help Sydonnia, and he would once more be an ordinary man. He would go to Lilandria, make her realize the scoundrel that Servial really was. Sydonnia would tell her...

Sydonnia suddenly took a deep breath, flaring his nostrils He could smell it so clearly, a leschera that slowly approached in the wood beside him. He realized he hadn't eaten for a couple of days now, and he was hungry for the kill.

Tracy R. Chowdhury

Seven moon-cycles after the massacre
2 Decaren CY544

Sydonnia watched as the young woman slowly set her pack down upon one of the flat rocks situated around the thermal pools. Even after all that had happened, he still thought her to be the most beautiful woman in the world. While Servial's desertion of him after their failed mission at the Terrestra made him feel as though he died a second death, thoughts of Lilandria had brought Sydonnia back to life. Now, after the passage of almost seven moon-cycles, he made the decision to return to Merithyn, not only to have closure with his brother, but to see her again.

Abandoned, and fueled by anger and betrayal, Sydonnia had turned away from the civilized world, immersing himself in a journey of self-discovery. Instead of remaining in denial, he embraced what he had become. With his venomous bite, he gave others the terrible disease people began to call lycanthropy. With those he transformed, Sydonnia once more had a family. And as the pack grew, so did their insatiable hunger.

The beasts had wreaked havoc upon the nearest villages. They killed the men, ravaged the women, and even began to torment the children. Some people Sydonnia gave the opportunity for transformation, others he did not. Only a rare few of those he transformed carried the 'ability' to transform others. And strangely, not everyone who suffered the bite went through the change. Sydonnia had very little understanding of this, but he really didn't care. All that mattered was the pack he had fathered

Every once in a while he would have dreams of the home he had left behind, the friends he had once known. Many of them had met their demise at the Terrestra River. Then he would think of Keilah. And Lilandria.

Once deciding to return to Merithyn, he had gone to see his brother first. Visions of revenge were prominent in his mind. Yet there was a part of him, albeit a small one, that hoped Servial would prove him wrong, and that he had never meant to desert Sydonnia in the enemy-infested forest. But just as he thought it would be, the meeting was a vast disappointment. He only confirmed that he was right to believe his brother was a traitor. The meeting ended in a fight, but Sydonnia derived very little pleasure from walking away the victor. In a way, he would have much preferred for his brother to finish the job he began by abandoning him at the Terrestra. But then he wouldn't have been able to see Lilandria...

Now, Sydonnia couldn't help but smile when he noticed her hesitation to begin removing her gown. He knew it was because she sensed his presence. Lily had always been very intelligent and perceptive, and those abilities had drawn him to her right away. Deciding to make his identity known, Sydonnia stepped from out of the shadows of the trees. Lilandria slowly turned in place, and when she saw him standing there at the tree-line, her eyes widened with disbelief. Then she mouthed his name without speaking....*Sydonnia.*

He stepped towards her as she rushed to him. "By the gods, is it really you?" She spoke the words so low they were almost a whisper. The feel of her within his arms was just as he remembered, and he reveled in the scent of her after so long.

Missing Pieces: A Simple Twist of Fate

"Did you miss me?"

The words slipped out before he could stop them. He gave his voice a bantering quality, his way of diffusing the intensity of the inquiry, of arming himself should he receive the answer he feared. But he immediately realized how strange the question sounded, and barely a moment later her tear dampened eyes reflected the same sentiment.

Pulling back, she regarded him in near astonishment. "Sydonnia, where have you been? They went out looking for you, but..."

He placed his fingertips at her lips and she stopped. "Sssh. It doesn't matter. I am here now," he said solemnly.

She shook her head. "It *does* matter! I thought you were dead!"

Sydonnia regarded her solemnly, felt the intensity of her emotion. She was right, it *did* matter where he had been. While certain other things probably didn't matter, some of those were details he felt strongly tempted to tell her. Yet he refrained, somehow knowing that they would be more of a burden than an enlightenment. Unfortunately, the answer would deserve an explanation...

He grinned disarmingly. "Well now you know that I'm not."

Lilandria frowned and took a step back from him. "Sydonnia, that's not good enough. I need to know what happened." She paused and then continued. "Does Servial know you are here?"

Sydonnia inhaled sharply and felt his hackles rise. He could see that she felt it immediately, a shift in the very air surrounding them. He focused his eyes piercingly upon her, felt the animal within him beginning to emerge. She had unwittingly brought forth thoughts of his brother he would sooner have left alone. He hated to be a prisoner to them, and one day he hoped to break free. But not this day.

Calming himself, Sydonnia bit back a caustic retort and shook his head. "No. And it might very well be better this way," he said in a low voice.

Lilandria shook her head and drew her brows together into a slight frown. "Sy, what's wrong with you? Servial is your brother and deserves to know! He has missed you so much these past..."

Sydonnia interrupted her. "No. My presence here is only between you and me." Sydonnia shook his head. "You *must* promise me, Lily."

Lilandria stood still before him. Sydonnia regarded her intently and awaited her response. The air crackled between them, testimony to the energy lying there. He had suddenly become so attuned to her, knew it when she came to the realization that he would be long gone before she had any opportunity to tell Servial of his presence. And he knew when she simply accepted his presence there as a gift...

Sydonnia closed the gap between them and took her by the arms. "Don't you see? It doesn't matter where I've been, only that I am here now." He paused and then continued softly, "I am not the same man I was when I left."

Lilandria nodded slowly, her head lowered. "I know. By the gods, Sydonnia, I can feel it," she said in a near whisper.

"But I still want you the same as I always have. My feelings for you have never subsided."

Lilandria looked up at him, her brows pulling together into a frown. "What are you saying? I never knew..."

Sydonnia placed his fingertips at her lips, once again interrupting her. "You *did* know. You just didn't recognize it. But now I'm *telling* you. Don't be afraid to accept the truth, Lilandria."

She was suddenly still for a moment. He held his breath and waited. He knew that she needed to make the connection on her own. Any pushing on his part would simply make her run away. He remembered a conversation he had once shared with Keilah. Many things were said, but there was one line in particular that came to his mind. He hadn't really understood was she was saying then, but now... *"Sometimes you simply have to let something go so that it can make the decision to come back to you."*

Sydonnia felt it when Lily's barriers finally came crashing down. He could feel that she wanted him, wanted him with the same passion and intensity he felt for her. Sydonnia kissed her for the first time, tasted a sweetness of which he had before only dreamed. Her scent overwhelmed him as he gently lay her down upon the mossy ground, a scent that beckoned to him of what was to come. And he would not have been able to resist it, even had he wanted to.

Eleven moon-cycles after the massacre
15 Cisceren CY544

Ending his patrol for the evening, Servial did one last check before heading back into Alcrostat. Another ranger would meet him on the way, the one who would be replacing him for the night. Sensing nothing amiss, Servial increased his pace to an easy jog. It wasn't long before his leg began to ache, the one that was broken when Sydonnia came to him that day more than four moon-cycles ago. Servial had been rendered unconscious in their struggle, but when he finally came to, he found that his brother had left the area without a trace.

Or should he say, the *monster* that had once been his brother.

Despite the discomfort, Servial kept the pace. Lilandria was waiting for him at her daladin, and he was looking forward to spending the evening with her. His interest in her had become revitalized when, just a few days ago, she had confided her pregnancy. He had always wanted children, and Lilandria would make a good mother. Of course, he had one child already. He had never realized that Sydonnia knew about the girl.

Servial decided to slow down to a walk. Now that his thoughts were centered upon Sydonnia, he suddenly wasn't in such a hurry to get home. It had been a shock to see the image of his brother step out of the trees that day, and even more, that Sydonnia fully realized the crime Servial had committed against him. There was a part of Servial that felt regret for the transgression against his brother, but an even larger part that cared only to serve himself. And it was just as well, for Sydonnia was now nothing but a monster. Servial refused to believe he had any part in making Sydonnia into such a hideous beast.

Missing Pieces: A Simple Twist of Fate

And then there was Lilandria. She didn't know that Sydonnia still lived and that he had come to the city in search of his brother. It was better that way, for she wouldn't think to yearn for him. And now that she was pregnant, he wouldn't want to burden her with information that might upset her. Sydonnia was a lycanthrope, a threat against hinterlean society. One day, the disease would spread beyond Elvandahar to infect other realms. Servial knew it was his destiny to prevent this from happening. He would one day rid Shandahar of the menace and kill Sydonnia. It was only a matter of time.

Almost 50 years after the massacre
18 Brinaren CY593

Lilandria looked upon her son for the first time in so many years. At one point, she had feared him dead, murdered at the hands of his own father. Once discovering Sirion still lived from his ordeal, she only found herself devastated again several years later when she heard he had been killed in battle against the dreaded Daemundai. To see him standing before her now was nothing short of miraculous.

Despite her best efforts, Lilandria couldn't stop the tears. By the gods, he looked so much like Servial. It was the more subtle features that he inherited from Sydonnia. Sirion quickly crossed the room, and within moments she was ensconced within her son's embrace. "Mother, I have come to tell you I am well. I know that Anya has been here to tell you otherwise, but she does not yet know that I survived," he said softly.

Lilandria felt herself begin to tremble. She would never forget the day, several moons ago, when her daughter came to tell her that Sirion had died. For the second time, Anya had lost a brother, and she a son. Then, only two days ago, when the scouts came to tell her that Sirion still lived, she felt her heart almost leap from her chest. The memories came rushing back to her, memories of his childhood, his birth, and then his conception.

That long ago tryst at the heated pool was the last time she saw Sydonnia. Not much later, Lilandria knew she was pregnant. Counting back the days, she knew the precise time that the child was conceived. She never told Servial about Sydonnia's visit, even when she made the realization that Sydonnia had been to see his brother before he came to her. Servial had suffered a plethora of wounds from their meeting, including one that never properly healed. With time, she came to recognize it as yet another reason for Servial to hate his brother. And she slowly began to wonder exactly what had happed on that failed mission to the Terrestra River.

However, Servial never had a reason to believe Sirion was not his son. And when the boy came of age, Servial took Sirion away from her and never returned. It was the first time she thought Sirion was dead when she discovered that Servial had met his demise at the hand of the same perpetrator. After all Servial's years of tracking down the beast, it was Sydonnia who found Servial. And then Sydonnia killed him. Yet, for some reason he had left young Sirion alive. Lilandria liked to believe it was because something deep within Sydonnia realized the boy was his own flesh and blood.

Lilandria spoke into the silence, finally recovering enough to take control of her voice. "When the scouts came to me two days ago, bearing the tale that you lived, I refused to let myself believe them, afraid that I would get my hopes up for nothing. But here you are, holding me in your arms like I dreamed you would."

Lilandria felt his arms tighten around her. "I will never leave you again," he whispered.

She felt a wave of joy sweep through her. "I believe you." Lilandria wrapped her arms around his neck and kissed his cheek. Finally they stepped apart.

Sirion continued to hold her hands, somehow knowing his mother didn't want him to let her go. "I am also here to serve the realm," he said solemnly. "I am here to aid in the removal of the lycanthrope threat."

Lilandria looked up at him, deep into his eyes. "My son, you *are* the realm."

51 years after the massacre
7 Decaren CY594

Sydonnia's gaze swept over the procession standing behind his nephew. Over the years, the younger man had made a name for himself, and he had proven himself a leader. Hells, Sydonnia couldn't be prouder had Sirion been his own son. But it was then he saw her. She stood among those who made up the small band of people who called themselves the Wildrunners. He could tell she recognized him, the expression upon her beautiful face was adequate testimony. In spite of her disbelief, Keilah Laremion stepped away from the group and slowly began to make her way towards him. Equally astonished, Sydonnia watched his old friend walk out from the confines of his past and into his present.

Adrianna had known the moment he recognized her. His eyes flashed, and his body became still. By the gods, this man was the friend she had left behind no more than several fortnights ago; the friend who would attest more than fifty years had passed since seeing her last. He was the friend who she thought had died by Sirion's hand, the one whom she still cared for very much.

Adrianna didn't stop until she stood before Sydonnia. He was large, his frame carrying much more mass than the man she met in the past. She remembered those arms around her, gentle arms that protected her. Yet, they were the same arms that hurt her when Sydonnia captured her as a way of getting to Sirion.

However, that scenario had obviously not taken place. It was plainly obvious this was the first time Sydonnia had seen her since she left Merithyn all those years ago. In spite of her efforts to be careful, something must have happened during her time spent in the past, some simple twist of fate that had brought into play a new reality.

Adrianna's mind warred with the complexity of the concepts thrust upon her. Her mind was a vortex of mixed emotions, both negative and positive. But the positive ones came to the fore, because she found herself holding back a tentative smile. She knew that Sydonnia was not the same being she once knew in the past. He was a monster who had wreaked havoc throughout Elvandahar for decades. But he was still *Sydonnia*, and she couldn't believe that not even a small part of the man she remembered still resided within.

Missing Pieces: A Simple Twist of Fate

Sydonnia regarded her intently as she approached. By the gods, she hadn't aged a day since he saw her last. She was still just as beautiful as the day she had left. He vaguely registered the surprise written upon his nephew's face as she passed by him, and Sydonnia wondered what might be between them. Considering it for a moment, he thought the match would be a good one.

"I always knew I would see you again," he said solemnly.

Silence rang throughout the area for a moment before she made her reply. "I thought you were dead."

Once more there was silence. Then, "This isn't the first time you have been erroneously informed."

He saw the corners of her mouth curve slightly upward. "Yes, I think you are right. It's about time I sent my advisor away. Besides, for someone who doesn't know very much, *he is so expensive!*"

She gave him a smile, one he knew was meant solely for him. It suddenly didn't matter where she was from and what he had become, only that they were both there now, standing before one another after so long. Sydonnia didn't understand it, but all those years ago she had changed him in ways he would never know. Within the short span of time they spent within one another's company, they had shared experiences that would last a lifetime. But that was another story.

Sydonnia closed the short distance between them, took her gently in his embrace and whispered in her ear. *"I have missed you my friend..."*

Tracy R. Chowdhury

About the Author

In 1975 I was born in the small town of Tunkhannock Pennsylvnia. I was the oldest of five children, the remaining of whom are all brothers. I spent much of my childhood in imaginary play, always fascinated by the possibility of magic and intrigued by dragons, fairies, unicorns and other mystical things.

As I got a little older and learned how to read and write, I began to write my own little stories. Mostly they were about love and friendship, the characters in a fantasy-world setting. As I continued to grow up, they became more complex, and the scenarios had more depth. But I never really became serious about writing a novel until I was in my later teens.

In 1998 I graduated from Miami University in Oxford, Ohio with a bachelor's degree in Zoology. Later in the same year I got married to my husband, Abdul Gaffar. It was then that I entered an AD&D campaign with a friend of mine by the name of Ted Mark Crim. I began to write down the details of his campaign, and thus how I began to write my first novel.

Currently I have four children, one girl and three boys. I live in Cincinnati, Ohio with my family and with the help of my co-author, Ted, I am in the midst of writing the fourth book of the Chronicles of Shandahar. The release date is planned to be by March 2011. After that, I hope on starting work on a novelization of the events taking place before the chronicles began, my first manuscript that will not have origins in an AD&D campaign.

Hemingway's Challenge

Her smile. Her knife. Rape unforgiven.

-V. J. Waks

About the Story

HUNGER, the tale of a research expedition that finds more than it bargained for, actually had its origins in a dreadful nightmare I had had; writing helped make it easier to get to sleep and recover from that sense of dread when you finally turn out the bedroom lights. But it is also useful as it's formatted fairly well into a three act structure, even with its diminutive size. Those interested in exploring structure issues might find it a good read for this reason alone.

Hunger
By
V. J. Waks

We're scared now, Tom and me, so scared we don't dare leave each other alone, not even for a second.

Scared enough to have to keep the lights on all night, even in just our little set of rooms, as low as they are, flickering like they're ready to quit forever, risking bringing the whole system down. Both of us scared because we no longer wonder which one of us is going to go out to it, we know which of us will stand up, all simple, uncaring, completely calm and at ease. And walk out to it. To whatever it is that's out there, in the compound itself. In the dark. Whatever it is that's been slowly killing us.

That was four days ago, it started. There were five of us then, all good men. Sound. Not a crazy one among us. Close, like guys get, working together, living almost in each other shoes because in jungle this thick, you don't take chances. You lean on the guy next to you. He leans on you. That's the way you stay alive. And it was working real fine; we were almost done with it, done with the heat and the sweat and that feeling of being all closed in, even when you stepped outside the tents. All closed in, especially then. All ready to pack up our gear. And go home.

Four days ago. Out of nowhere. Nick, the tall guy, as good on a computer as he was on a baseball diamond. Team leader, triple degrees in AniSci, Plant Biotech and Evo. You couldn't touch him, he was as hard as a plank of white oak. He went first, four days ago.

It was midnight. We'd all just finished the last test run on the new water samples we'd pulled. He just stood up, calm as you please, like he was going to take a walk in the jungle, all wild, loud green, like every jungle is, even in the dark, like he was going out to take a leak. Easy and relaxed. He ran his big hands through that thick, blond hair of his and smiled, like he wasn't as tired as the rest of us, with the last week of round the clock tests.

"Well," he said. "That's enough for me. Time to eat."

He stood up, six some-odd feet of him, the ironman, and started for the door of our makeshift lab. Robbie, our Exobiologist from Houston, all bright, brown eyes and twitchy limbs like spider, he actually laughed at him.

"Where you going? You hungry again? ... we just ate, what,...like an hour ago."

Nick's cool Nordic gaze clouded over a moment and he stared at Robbie like he didn't know him, as though Robbie had called him back from a place where only he stood, way apart from the rest of us, miles away from where he stood now.

"What?" he said.

"Where you going, man?"

"Dinner," Nick answered, and his forehead was all puckered, his voice soft and strange. "It's time. Time to eat..."

What a joke, we thought. And as we laughed at him, not really seeing it, not thinking, he walked out the door into the night. We should have known somehow, somehow we should have guessed, when we saw that look in those usually clear-blue-lake eyes, when a man we knew as solid, uncompromising genius suddenly started acting like half his mind was gone.

We never saw him again. Oh, we looked, not realising the danger we were in even looking, if we had stumbled on it out there in the night. Next morning, we found his clothes. They were torn to pieces. Shredded and nearly pulverised into a damp powder, they were nothing but a slick paste of gummy fabric and something else. Wetter than they should have been even with last night's light rain.

But no Nick. We took his stuff in and it was Stan who thought to run some biochem on them, Stan, our top Physio man, one of the best rugby players at Cornell, who later that night called us all together, standing there looking at him like a bunch of disbelieving owls, while he told us what he'd found or thought he'd found, impossible as it seemed. That the stuff on Nick's clothes wasn't water, wasn't sweat, not even blood, at least not blood from a man or any other animal or plant he knew before.

And that night, the sounds of the jungle around us stopped. That noise you'd get used to hearing all around you, night and day, all the time. It came to a still, breathless halt outside the compound itself, stopped dead, like you'd cut off the voice and heart of every damn living thing within ten clicks of here. Like suddenly nothing was out there now, nothing was in the jungle but us. And something else. And that night, Stan walked out to meet it.

It was late again. We were all sitting together, moody, edgy, thinking about Nick, wondering, some of us, me even, plain worried. The silence was thick enough to taste. Like a warm, heavy blanket over us, dark and uncanny. That and something else. It was the feeling that there was something there. Something in the dark. Somewhere close by, maybe even in one of the buildings nearby, we only had three real buildings, none of them big. And the refuse and storage areas, they were always so cluttered and hard to sort through even when we knew what we were looking for, even when we weren't scared -- anything could have been in there, waiting. Something that moved, if it moved at all, so quietly. Like the dry creak of an otherwise well-oiled door, always moving just before you touched it, making a sound always just beyond the edge of hearing. And it took Stan next.

He got up from the mess table and walked to the window, looking out at the supply crates and storage tanks, all tumbled together, not fifty feet away. The lights were working reliably then, but dim, like they always were at night to save power. You couldn't see much out there that night, not even on those nights when the light from a full moon would somehow pierce the canopy and get down to us here in the valley.

But we could see he was looking at those crates like he could see something there among them, something darker than the shadows. But he didn't say a word, not a frown on that rugged face. And next to me Tom laughed, a little weakly because he was drinking again, what with Nick gone and what the hell to do about that stuff on those clothes.

"Now don't you tell us you're going out to take a walk, too?"

And Stan turned and stared at him, stared through him. He looked back at all of us like he was looking at television, eyes dull, glazed, calm as you want.

"Yeah. I think I will..."

What do I know? Me, I'm just the numbers guy, the resident Stat nerd. I don't know what I was thinking, what any of us were thinking. But as I watched him I could feel the fear starting to rise in me like nausea, cold and unstoppable. Stan was a firecracker; I'd never seen him like this, almost dazed, his mind a mile away. Tom stood up and I jumped up.

"Don't go out there, Stan..."

"Why not? It's time. Time to eat. Hungry...It's time."

And he walked right out the door.

For a second, Tom, Robbie and me, we were simply thunderstruck. We just stared at the door, then at each other. Then we ran after him. He was gone. Nowhere. And we went out, staying together, our voices too loud in that terrible stillness, now afraid of the dark outside our dimly lit, silent little island. Afraid of what was out there. In here with us.

What could we have done? What could anyone have done, there was no way to understand it, to even guess what might happen next. There was never any time -- it never gave us time to think. Stuff was coming too fast.

Too fast. Now it was Robbie; he's the one who trashed the radio and comm system. It was next day and totally without any warning at all. One minute he stood there at the table, his bright eyes gone all dim and flat, looking at the radio, just staring down at it like he'd asked it a question and was waiting for it to answer. Seconds later, with both Tom and me practically at his throat, he was still swearing he hadn't done it, even though we'd watched him, frozen in disbelief, as he'd pulled the unit to pieces almost in front of us. He swore he hadn't done it and his eyes were stony, unblinking, almost unseeing the whole time. Just like Nick's had been. Just like Stan's.

So we locked him up. We didn't have to lay a hand on him. Quiet, unresponsive, walking like a clockwork creature, he followed us like a lamb into the ready room and that's where we left him, calm and still, locked behind closed doors.

While Tom and me, armed to the teeth, went through the whole place together, with a fine tooth comb, looking for god knows what.

We didn't find a thing. No, I mean it -- we found nothing at all. No insects, no birds, not a single living thing. Nothing but hot, green, jungle, here where the animal species count was in the thousands, the most densely populated spot in the whole damn delta.

Again the eerie silence. But now -- horrible, even thicker, like something alive, right in your face -- silence now in the full light of day.

And we both felt it now, both of us without even having to say a word.

There was something there, something growing out there, all around us, growing like a plant with a rich, new, food source, growing as fast as any plant, as hungry as any animal. That's why the other creatures left, they knew something was there, too. They had the sense to leave.

It was already late day when we finally realised that we were losing the generators, they were going on us and we were damned if we could figure out why. Tom worked for hours on the system and all we knew for sure was that we'd have lights that night but not really for sure and maybe not all where we needed them. And when we finished, tired, the fear starting to grow in us again, even as the daylight slipped away, we looked back into the conference room to check on Robbie.

There he stood, all pissed. He was laughing, as sane as either one of us, demanding to know what the hell had happened, why we'd locked him up in there alone. And when Tom told him, his face was utter astonishment, like we were telling him a story, describing crazy events and even crazier actions that had happened to someone else.

So we let him out, and started praying, not just for him, but for all of us, hoping we could get through another night all in one piece. So we could make a run for it. But by that time, it was already dark....

Like every time before, it was real late. We were all in the mess tent again, staying close to one another, trying not to look at the windows, trying not to look at anything but each other, jittery. Listening for the next silent call. Because it seemed too unbelievable that it wouldn't come, that whatever was out there in the dark would let any of us get away.

"We have to get out of here. While we still can. I don't think we have a choice," I said. But Robbie looked at me kind of strangely. It was only a quick glance, then he looked away. And Tom and I locked eyes. And waited.

"What...what are you thinking, Robbie? Huh?.. tell me, man.." said Tom, and his voice was casual, so smooth, not showing a shred of the fear I knew was growing in him, like it was growing in me, a cold, hard knot.

"Oh, I don't know. I just think...I don't think we should leave. Why should we leave?..."

And he looked at us with those brown eyes suddenly glazed, as cold and empty as a fish's.

This time it was much worse. Because both Tom and I were watching him, we were waiting for it, waiting for Robbie to straighten suddenly, slowly, almost imperceptibly stiffening in his chair. His head came up and in a heartbeat he was a stranger; rigid, straining in his seat.

He seemed to be listening for something only he could hear, while outside, the silence did something impossible, something silence couldn't do in any normal world, not in any sane universe, not in any universe we knew.

Because outside the tent, it actually seemed to get quieter; quieter and quieter until it was so still that the silence seemed like something alive, palpable, solid. The silence spoke and Robbie was the only one who could understand the words in that horrible speech.

And with the lights beginning to flicker, so dim we could hardly see, both Tom and I were on our feet long before he started to rise, slowly and mechanically, to his. We grabbed him, yanking hard on the man who, eyes staring ahead, staring at nothing, was ready to move to the door, to walk through the door to where that unknown, impossible silence called, hungering for yet one more of us. And so strong was that call that even with the two of us hanging on him, terrified, desperately calling his name like two panicked kids, tearing at him as hard as we could, he pulled us along with him, dragged us to the very brink of the door that led beyond into some kind of voracious, incomprehensible hell. We fought him, fought with every ounce of our strength to hold him, and still he dragged us with him.

I don't know what god it was that stopped him, there before the door. It sure as hell wasn't us. It was with empty, sightless eyes that he was now staring through the window, exactly like the others had stared before him. He turned to us, all gentle, mild as milk, and he spoke to us and his voice was as low and as hollow as a corpse's.

"I'll be going now. It's time to eat. Have to...come out. Come...come out..."

And in a sudden icy fear, I looked out the window, following the line of those cold, unblinking eyes -- to the storage areas just across the way, into the doorway which led beyond to the little tarp- covered holding area.

I looked out to see something there that shouldn't have been there, that wasn't there, not in any normal sense of the word. And I was so frozen with fear, me, a fucking man of science, rock stable in any world of wonder, I was so afraid that when I finally spoke, I could barely get out a whisper. But Tom heard me.

" The door...look at the door. Tom...do you see it, Tom?!"

It took an eternity of two seconds before he could get out his answer and his voice was hoarse and horrible and I knew he felt what I did at the sight, at the impossible sight of that unhallowed thing in the shadows under the tarp.

"Yeah. Yeah, I see it..."

And Robbie stood there at the door, Tom and me beside him, with our fists white-knuckled and knotted in his clothes. And we all looked out to the doorway under the tarp, with

The lights flickering on and off, as the generator caught and choked, to where something darker than the shadows stood. Rounded, low to the ground, like a figure but not a figure of anything I knew, short, dense, unmoving. And even though none of us could see them, there were eyes in that dark mass, watching us, aware, still. Hungry. And all of us knew that whatever we were looking at was not a man, not a figure of anything we knew at all, and whatever it was, it was still growing, growing as fast as a plant, as hungry as any animal.

"Don't you see it, Robbie? You can't go out there... my god, Robbie !! "

And in some kind of desperate fury, I lost it. I hit him, hit him hard, hard enough to hurt him. I know I hurt him. I heard him gasp, once, hard, his breath like a shot in tent. The lights in the compound actually flashed, flashed and stayed on; once, real fast, like a really bad stage joke. And incredibly, Robbie roused a moment. For just one split second I thought we had him back, I thought we had him.

Then he was gone. He looked at us again, placid, once more calm, unruffled. And without blinking an eye, he grabbed the gun from my belt, raised it and pointed it straight at us as we drew back, away from him, drew back in horror from the man who would have killed us if we tried to save him from the thing standing out there, waiting for him, darker than the shadows. We kept backing until there was some twenty feet of room between us when the lights failed utterly and in the total terrifying darkness, I heard the gun hit the floor and the sound of the door opening and closing. And I flew to it, to that sound of the door closing, stumbling blindly forward into the hard chairs, shoving them out of my way, fighting to get to the door, to get out there into the dark after him.

Tom caught me just as I reached the door. By now, the entire compound was out, totally in darkness now. No moon that night, no stars through the thick canopy.

So black was it that there was no sign of the tarp or the thing under it and I fought him, struggling against Tom's grip that was keeping me inside, his voice loud, like thunder in my ears next to that horrible, knowing silence.

"No! You can't save him, not that way! It's too late! He's gone!"

"Let me go! Let go of me, you son of a bitch!"

And I hit at him, fought him as hard as I could, trying to get out that door as, without warning, the lights came on again, came on full and bright, blinding us both. My last sight was of Tom's fist coming straight at me, right into my face and I dropped, senseless, not even feeling it when I hit the floor.

It was just beginning to get light when I finally came to, came to propped up against the wall of the mess tent, neck cramped, my head splitting.

And I could hear Tom beside me. He was talking in a low whisper, his voice so soft, so strange, that it took me a few moments of hard listening before I could make out what he was saying. At first I thought he was talking to me. Then I thought it was himself. I was wrong.

"..where are you going? ... where do you go ..where do you wait -- before you come to get us? It's getting light now. It's getting too light for you, isn't it? You can't take it yet. Not yet. But soon...maybe after you've had another one of us....Come back! you can hear me, I know you can! Come back, you son of a bitch, I'm gonna get you. I know how, now I know how to get you! I'm the one who's gonna get you for good..."

Then he stopped talking because he could see I was watching him.

"You can hear it now, can't you," I said. "Like the others did. In your mind. It's there in your mind now, too, isn't it..."

A full minute went by while he stared back at me without saying a word and the look on his face never changed. I looked into his red, tired eyes, looked at his drawn, white face. He looked like hell. I knew only then that he hadn't closed an eye all night. Then he glanced down and I saw that he still had the gun in his hand. When he finally spoke, he was still staring at that gun, staring at it as though it were a crucifix, never taking his eyes off it.

"I'm next..."

He wouldn't tell me how he knew, how alone out of all of us, he was the only one who could hear it before the call actually came. Before it got dark. I don't think now that he actually knew the answers himself or even how he seemed to know with such absolute certainty what he needed to do now.

But he did know and as the day went by, the more I watched him, the more scared I got. I could feel it, as plain as you can feel the winter's cold, the teeth of an icy, hungry wind all around you, picking away at your clothes, trying to get inside.

Something terrible was going to happen. It would happen very soon and it would be something much more horrible than our losing all these men, one after the other, losing them in silence and some kind of dreadful, killing calm. And this thing was something that Tom intended to do himself.

Because that was what it was -- the calm, at least that was a big part of it, from the pieces I got from him, the hints that he let himself tell me, stuff that made me sick to hear it.

It needs us to be calm, it can't take it when we 'feel' anything. Not yet anyway. And the dark -- it still needs that, too. It makes the dark. The lights -- you remember the way they dim, ... when it's out there, waiting? And how bright they got when you hit him, when you fought with Robbie...just before...It needs us to be still. No anger, no fear, to be almost dead inside...otherwise....

And he wouldn't say any more. I tried, pushing him as far as I dared; all day long, my mind frantic to think of what I could possibly do, to help him, to stop him, to save him. What could I possibly do now at all... At the end, all I could do was follow him around and watch him while he walked back and forth across the compound, like he was pacing the distance between the mess door and some spot just before the storage areas. And I saw he never passed a certain point -- he always stopped before that doorway, where we'd seen it -- and he wouldn't let me near the place at all. He stood there, just before the door, and he put out his hand, like he could feel something in the fabric of the air itself. And his hand would freeze like that; all his fingers outstretched, still, reaching, until his hand finally dropped to his side. And it trembled.

But he wouldn't tell me. It was as though telling me might somehow expose me, let that thing get closer to me before he could be ready. Because the door in his head swung both ways, I saw that even then. And I saw it was taking everything he had to just get himself ready, to protect me and still not let that thing know what he had in his mind, what he was now ready to do. As it started to finally, inevitably --- get dark.

Because it did start to get dark. That hungry, knowing darkness crept up and over us like it had before, but now it was just Tom and me left. And finally here we were together, both scared, all the lights on, knowing that we could only keep them on so long, that they wouldn't stay that way, that eventually that thing out there was going to suck the light out of our pitiful little rooms like it had ripped the life out of four good, strong men.

My nerves were so hair-trigger raw by then that you'd think I'd have been ready for anything. And I thought I was ready; at the first sign, I was ready to move, I wasn't going to wait.

Missing Pieces: Hunger

But neither was that thing out there. Before we could even light the hurricanes, vainly trying to stave off that darkness, to outsmart it -- Tom cried out.

He dropped his lamp, and his hand went to his forehead, like he was in pain. And the lights, they were dimming even as he screamed, his eyes staring out, one second glazed and the next lucid, as he fought that thing that was calling to him. I ran to him; all I could think was to keep him inside but he threw me off, struggling with me as I fought to hold him, as he started laughing and the lights began to flash on again. In another second he'd shoved me backward and I saw the knife in his hand, the one he always wore, his big bowie, and its blade glittered in the dim glow of the one lamp we'd managed to light.

He glared at me, and frozen with horror I watched as he pulled the blade of that knife across his own arm, the bare skin opening, the blood rising bright and red even while the lights began to flash horribly, angrily, even stronger than before.

And the echo of that stillness outside -- famished and reaching -- it suddenly rose to a roar of silence and I could hear the loud pop of sparks discharging out under the tarp, like some kind of mad lightning had suddenly touched down.

Tom's eyes glazed over again; he was fighting with every bit of his strength and as the blood ran down his arm, he gave a shout of triumph. He was moving to the door as I grabbed him again and when he tossed me backward this time, it left me crumpled up against the wall. He'd thrown me off him with the strength of many men, like with that one act he was saving my life and his own soul. Even with the blood running into my eyes, I could see the lights dim as he tore through the door.

He was running as hard as he could out into the night and I could hear his feet pounding. He was shouting as he ran and they were shouts of rage and a wild mad joy and a lust to kill that thing that was waiting for him. I stumbled to my feet just as he reached the far side of the compound. And once more, that horrible silence was coming alive.

But this time was different. This time that thick, cloaking stillness had started to vibrate and hum. With no sound at all, the heavy dark air was throbbing with it, the air that was pulling itself out of my chest while the very thoughts in my head were humming with awful jarring pulses, one after the other. And the space in doorway under the tarp crackled and roared like some kind of fabric was ripping apart and tearing itself open.

I heard him scream. That's how I knew he'd done it. None of the others, not Nick or Stan or even Robbie -- none of them had been able to scream.

It was a scream of not just fear or pain but of real triumph that I heard and that's how I knew. And I was ready to run to him, to run out there into the dark, but I couldn't. I just stood there, just outside the door, holding onto it, trying to stay upright, trying to keep from screaming myself.

Because of what I heard after that long, last terrible cry from Tom. Because from out of the dark where I was going to run, even as Tom's voice died away, there came another roar. It was like a wind that grew and grew until all the air was throbbing with it, a sound of hate and despair and a terrible hunger, like a great starving mouth had opened into hell and all these voices came out, all starving, all screaming at once.

And I stood there, shaking and crying because my ears hurt so bad, my skin was on fire, because it seemed that something unstoppable, a thing made of blackness and some terrible cold fire was eating into my mind. I stood there in agony, hardly able to stand, and suddenly -- it was gone. Like a dark, cold, tearing wind that just hits you and then passes you by, and you look out, still standing, at a world gone mad, now quiet, now still. Like a door had opened and let damnation look out. And just as suddenly closed.

The lights were on again, blazing brightly all over the place when I finally stumbled forward, crawling almost on hands and knees until I found Tom.

He'd made it as far as the doorway under the tarp. That was where I found him, lying on the ground, face up, sightless eyes staring up at the trees over us.

He'd gutted himself. He was sprawled just before the door, his white hands still on the hilt of the hunting knife sticking up out of his split rib cage and his flesh and abdomen gaped open almost to his groin, still bleeding, still warm. Somehow he'd had the strength to open himself up, to take that thing with him as he died. There were burn marks all over him, like he'd stood in flames or some kind of terrible heat and his body had been burned, almost charred by it. And he'd been right; there was a smile on his face to light up even the deepest corner of any real hell, however dark.

And there, not five feet away from him -- what was left of it. A pile of something blacker than any midnight sky, black but bleeding redly, bleeding blood that was not its own.

And I stood there crying like a child and watched it collapse inward, folding into itself, the blackness and blood shot with light that had no colour at all, wasn't light from any place I'd ever seen or dreamed, I watched as that blackness flickered and moved with light from some nightmare place where real light and human feeling was the enemy.

I breathed twice. And whatever was left of the thing under the tarp was gone.

And the whole jungle was getting light now and then I heard something that finally brought me to my knees, sobbing, not able to breathe with the sobs that came out of me.

It was the song of a bird. A bird, singing high up in the canopy. And it sang until the sun rose full up, it sang as if its heart were breaking with joy and pain, just like mine was. And its voice rose and soared, until all I could hear was that pure, clear voice and the voice of thousands of other living things once again. And the whole jungle was once more filled to overflowing with clean, wholesome, earthly light.

About the Author

A fomer New Yorker, V.J. WAKS now lives in a haunted carriage house in Los Angeles, where she is hammering out sci fi novels (HAMMERSPACE, Book Two in the TAU4 series is just about ready to launch) and a screenplay or two, just for fun.

V.J. Waks

Hemingway's Challenge

In the beginning; death. The end.

-C. E. Rocco

About the Story

"Bringer of Bedlam" details a realm bathed in constant shadow. The world is tidally locked, so the sun always faces one side of the planet and the other is constantly shrouded in darkness. The most hospitable section is where the light and dark meet--in the shadows. Bringer of Bedlam offers a look into the past and a glimpse into some of the characters in the future Wizards at War series.

Bringer of Bedlam
By
C. E. Rocco

BEFORE TIME REMEMBERED
Tsavin hung his head at his impending fate, more so because the ceiling was too low to stand erect than any emotional indifference to his imminent death.

Carefully Tsavin twisted in the confined room as a distant explosion rocked the building. His head slammed into the ceiling and he only just managed to catch his footing to avoid falling on the cold, hard stone floor. His cell was barely the width of a man and hardly twice that in length. Had the room been occupied by a human it would have been barely tall enough to stand with a stooped head; Tsavin was not of the *slave races* and the ceiling prohibited him from standing even remotely upright; his sore head was a constant reminder.

The faint glow of the runes, invisible until touched, slowly died into the darkness once he regained his footing. The runes of entrapment prohibited him from using his gifts to escape an otherwise miserably cold and wet prison. He ignored the pain they caused. Pain was something he understood and something he could control.

Until the assault on the Ziggurat had begun, Tsavin had been the Carrion Inquisitionor. In this capacity he was third only to Hunden Gǿr, the Grand Imperial Legate, and Tsavik, the Supreme Commander of the Kāori. During the eternal struggle between the Kāori and the Nazari, Tsavin's ability to inflict unbearable suffering to extract information, and more importantly mana, from the nearly dead made him an invaluable tool. Unfortunately for Tsavin, Tsavik had other plans for him which did not include his living to tell of the secrets he gleaned from excruciation.

His preferred method of torture was impaling the victim. After slow agonizing months of torment and inquisition, Tsavin would drag his victims to the woods bound and gagged. There he would present them with the option; cut and sharpen the stake for their impaling or face the alternative. The Home Guard would find a limb of suitable size, leaving the bark and small limbs in place, making the impaling worse. The thought of the added pain of the impurity of bark and branches formed a twisted and terrifying logic within those soon to die. As if the cleaner stake would bring about a cleaner death, almost everyone opted for crafting their own stake.

Whatever the choice, he would have the victims dig a hole for the stake themselves and secure the stake to the ground. Then, he would pick them up with his massive strength and impale them from anus to clavicle in one deft move; his years of skill preventing the rupture of vital organs. Those who opted to craft their own instruments of death screamed in pain, feet barely able to touch the ground, their life force taking days to slip from their battered bodies. As they slowly died the mana gradually bled from the confines of their mortal souls. Those who opted for the alternative found death much longer in coming and more agonizing; Tsavin saw to that.

Now he waited for his own impending impaling once Tsavik returned from his final conflict with the Nazari. *I wonder who will do the honor*, he thought, for no other Kāori matched his capacity for brutality.

The sounds of battle raged for most of the day.

The explosions of magic and clashes of thunder filled the sunlit hours; the reverberation of the final conflict sounding off like a symphony of destruction. Then, for the longest time, silence.

Tsavin resigned himself to death.

A sudden white radiance blinded him. The concussion of the subsequent blast threw him forward. He jerked his arms up as the guardian runes flared red and pain seared through him. He spiraled into unconsciousness.

Tsavin awoke with a ringing in his ears and the pain of the guardian runes prodding him to consciousness. The whole right side of his body was in agony from being slammed into the wall. He tried to brace himself with powerful arms, but his right arm failed and he crashed onto the cold stone floor.

Tsavin knew that something had gone horribly wrong. He could feel a disturbance in the Æther. For something to disturb the Æthereal so vastly could not be good. He turned lengthwise in the small room, cursing himself for crafting such a fine prison. He crossed his legs, being very careful not to provoke the guardian runes again. He closed his eyes and drew within himself; tapping his gift on a primal level, he searched the Æther for some cause of the disturbance. The whole of his right side burned through his concentration. He forced himself to keep pushing down the pain and tried again.

Nothing.

The door to the cell opened on creaking hinges and slammed into the wall from the howl of a gale wind. A shaft of light split the darkness and illuminated the swirling of dust and debris. He raised his hand to cover his eyes and instinctively stood only to crack his head again on the low ceiling. How many times had he been on the other end of the door greeting those about to die? The irony of his predicament was not lost on him, he was simply indifferent.

It was the Kāori way. One mind, one body, one goal. The Supreme Commander had ordered his death, had ordered the need for his mana, the need for his knowledge; the only Kāori to attain that knowledge, he was only too happy to oblige. As the white spots in his vision faded, he resigned himself to his impending death and with head held high he stood as upright as he could manage and presented his hands to be bound. Death would not make him a coward.

A flash of lightning and crash of thunder filled the sky. The wind drove the rain and hair into his face.

Nothing.

Tsavin turned his head to avoid another gust of wind. Blinking his eyes to clear his vision he saw the imperial guards on one knee with heads bowed low and fists to hearts. Yyamin held her robes gathered loosely in her right hand with her head also bowed in reverence. Her left hand held a thick chain attached to the collar of a Nazari prisoner. Tsavin knew this prisoner. Ðruñe was Tsavin's equivalent within the Narazi nation. He was battered and bloody, but alive.

"What word?" queried Tsavin in a calm deep voice of unmistakable authority. He limped a step forward, nearly losing his balance in the wind. His confidence and commanding presence had not lessoned with impending death. If anything, his plight had made him more arrogant.

Silence was his only answer.

"Let's get on with it then," he commanded. His vision was finally free of white spots. *Good*, he thought, *I want to see clearly for my own death.*

"Carrion Inquisitionor Tsavin," said Yyamin from the doorway. She addressed him with reverence, yet there was an underlying hint of loathing.

He cut her off.

"That is no longer my title, so Tsavik has decreed."

"My lord, Tsavik has fallen, our glorious leader is dead."

"Long may he live in our hearts and dreams," the congregation said as one, as was customary. Tsavin's face instantly went pale, his always stoic features twisting in dismay. He could feel the grief of the Kãori nation through his bond to them. He thought he saw a slight smirk of satisfaction from Ðruñe.

"This cannot be," he whispered in abject horror. It is not as I have foreseen."

"My lord," said Yyamin from the doorway as she snapped her fingers before Tsavin's eyes to attract his attention and break the spell of disbelief. "Carrion Inquisitionor Tsavin, Tsavik is no more and his command falls to you."

"No," he said, presenting his hands again. "Command falls to Hunden Gǿr."

"My lord, the Grand Imperial Legate has also fallen," she said nervously.

"Impossible!"

"Improbable," she corrected. "My lord, their link to the Æthereal has been severed after the black out." She paused to see if he understood. Tsavin's silence indicated that he did.

Tsavin closed his eyes and connected his gift to the Æther flow. The air, for those who knew how to seek it, was thick with the unrestrained power of the two fallen Kãori leaders. Their mortal coils no longer confining the flow of their power; it had been returned to the Æther. Tsavin, in his capacity as the Carrion Inquisitionor, was able to capture this raw mana and make use of it in ways no other Kãori could. However, he could only do so from the very recently dead. It had to be before the mana drained from its former host and there was only one way to gather that power for use. The successors had to be quickly named to those posts lest the mana be returned to the Æthers for all time.

Yyamin, the Devout Hierophant of the Kãori, was one of a few who could transfer the power from one Kãori to another. The ritual was simple, named and recognized to the new post and accepted by the nation, the authority and power stopped being drawn from the dead and released back into the Æthers and instead flowed into its new host. In times of peace a ceremony was customary, even if brief. In times of war however, all formality bowed to necessity.

"Carrion Inquisitionor Tsavin, you are now the Grand Imperial Legate." As Yyamin formally named him the Imperial Guard saluted with fists to hearts. Tsavin felt the Legates power slam into him, adding to his own formidable strength. Tsavin, the first and only Carrion Inquisitionor, was chosen because of his unique indifference to emotion; no other Kāori held the capacity to match the brutality of the Nazari. Because such brutality was not in the Kāori nature, Tsavin's people could not understand his methods though did realize the need. Yyamin's hint of loathing for Tsavin was not for fear of his doing what had to be done, but because of what anyone might do with this much power and no conscious. As the power flowed into Tsavin she watch his wounds heal and saw the raw mana of the Legate swimming in his eyes. Never before had one Nazari held both positions of power. With reservation she continued with what had to be done.

"Tsavin, Carrion Inquisitionor and Grand Imperial Legate, you are now the Supreme Commander." Yyamin led the way and fists were raised to hearts to acknowledge the transference of power. Again, Tsavin felt the power slam into him, adding to his own and the newly gained power from the Grand Imperial Legate. But this time it felt different, as if not all of the mana was given to him.

Perhaps Tsavik had used more than I have foreseen? he thought.

"My lord, you are now the Carrion Inquisitionor, the Grand Imperial Legate and the Supreme Commander. What are your orders?"

Unable to shake the feeling that not all of the mana transfer was complete he asked her, "Where is the Supreme Commander's body?"

"My lord?"

"Tsavik's body, where is it now?"

"In the Ziggurat where he fell my lord. None have touched his body."

She hesitated and whispered, "None can get close."

"Of course," he said in a whisper of sudden realization. "That is to be expected. Yyamin, open the Æther corridors for teleportation, no restriction."

Whatever reservations Yyamin had regarding Tsavin paled in comparison to the alternative so she did not hesitate to follow his orders. Failure to do so could prove deadly. Sparks of magic ignited from Yyamin's fingers and a jolt of pain crippled the Nazari attached to her chain. Defeated, the Nazari prisoner also complied, silently unblocking the protective shields surrounding the Nazari nation. These shields prevented anyone from invading the Nazari Ziggurat by way of traveling the corridors of magic. With these shields down Tsavin felt the Æthers and knew without question that, should he wish it, he could teleport from this location to the Nazari Ziggurat unhindered.

"Assemble the Home Guard and the Legates. We leave for the Ziggurat as soon as they amass." In a swirl of mist and smoke three of the guards rose from the ground and disappeared, teleporting to locations unknown, spreading the command.

"Set commands to round up the slave leaders and present them to the elemental nodes," Tsavin commanded as he turned his attention to address a group of five guards to his left. They too vanished with a fist to heart. He stepped through the narrow opening into the daylight, standing erect for the first time in days. He turned his attention to a group of guards to his right.

"I will need the Elementalists gathered near the monolith at Breckhaven."

Again with a fist to heart they obediently followed the command, and as the others had before them, vanished in the air. As they disappeared on the winds of the Æthers one of the first guards to leave and gather the Home Guard rematerialized. Bent on one knee with his head bowed, he indicated the deed had been done as requested. Already the Legates and Home Guard began materializing as well.

Tsavin turned his attention to the bloody field before him. His province was death and this was his killing ground. Lightning filled the sky revealing thousands of bodies. They were impaled on the visible hills in various states of dying or death. The low moans and occasional gurgling screams filled the day's failing light.

Tsavin's work.

Yyamin turned her head from the grisly scene as did many of the other Kāori. They were an empathic race, Tsavin was an oddity.

Strange, Tsavin thought, *night should be upon us.*

"We are in need of mana. I will hasten them to that end."

PRESENT DAY

"Hurry or we will be late," said Asil as she gathered her thick robes in one hand and Jarik's hand in the other. The two classmates had been thick as thieves ever since they had come to the Wizarding Academy and often lost track of time, deeply engaged in the discussion of magical theory and its various applications.

"For what? The presentation of your thesis is not until last. Afraid that we might miss Drogan's presentation? I hear tell that he is presenting a paper on the mastery of his own ego," he mocked. It resulted in an unexpected punch to his shoulder. He groaned in pain; she hit hard for a girl.

"Take that back! I told you he meant nothing and your continual jealously over the matter is disturbing. He is a dog with the ego of a cat. Why, if he were here right now I would tell him as much. I could care less about him."

Jarik stopped, and Asil soon followed when his arm did not.

"So, you could care about him," he argued rubbing his sore shoulder.

"I told you I don't," she fumed.

"No, you told me you could; could care less that is. Could care less is caring, if only a little. Not caring at all is a different matter altogether." He flinched and turned his body to protect his shoulder when it looked like she would hit him again.

"I-could-not-care-less," she grunted through gritted teeth, punctuating each syllable with a punch to the shoulder, "and if he were here I would tell him as much." She raised her hand again, but held her fist. When he flinched, she punched him twice more, a wry smile escaping her tender lips, "and two for flinching."

"Caring hurts," he commented, rubbing his sore shoulder and quickly running ahead of her new assault and ducked around the nearest corner.

The two ran smack into Drogan as they rounded the corner. Asil instantly regretted her previous proclamation, not because she was unwilling to tell him off, but rather because she loathed speaking to him on any level. Drogan and his ilk had been pushing Kindle around in a circle, teasing him and holding his thesis above his head, passing it from person to person whenever Kindle would get too close to retrieving it.

"Yeah, here's your chance." A dirty look that only a woman could muster silenced Jarik further.

Dropping her robes, Asil waved her hand, connected with the flow of mana and touched on the elemental air nodes, whereupon the manuscript flew to her hand. When one of Drogan's friends stepped towards them, Asil drew in the elemental power of air to her bosom and stepped forward. The she extended her hand and a gush of air knocked Drogan's accomplice off his feet. She surprised even herself with the power of the assault; she only meant to push him back slightly. Her mastery of the elements was formidable, but she did not realize that she had drawn that much power into the blow.

Drogan quickly extended each hand to shoulder height, far apart from center, and drew his hands to his own heart. Sparks crackled from his fingers the closer his hands drew together the bigger the sparks became. At last they exploded into an arc of lightning from index finger to index finger. Then, in a rush, quicker than most could comprehend, he stepped forward and extended his hands, releasing the deadly pent up energy towards Asil. The air blazed with the smell of burned ozone. Asil, manuscript in hand and recovering from the strain of summoning the wind, was oblivious to her impending doom. Before it could reach Asil, the bolt of energy exploded in a bluish flash of light taking the shape of little bunnies that ran off in every direction. A crack of thunder followed. Only then did Asil fully comprehend that a bolt of lightning had been racing towards her.

"I'm sorry," mocked Jarik with a crooked smile, "did I disrupt your spell?" Drogan, not amused in the least, began another spell.

"Children," said the Headmaster seeming to appear out of thin air, "please take your seats, you are just in time." Even though they were closer to twenty in age, the headmaster referred to all his students as his children. Either he had not noticed the brief exchange of magic or he chose to ignore it. Asil always wondered which it was.

"It will be okay," Kindle whispered, although no one was close enough to hear. Kindle stared at Drogan with eyes of hate. He had never done anything to warrant such attention from either the graduate students or from anyone else. Kindle wasn't the only one Drogan picked on, but he was the one he picked on the most. A voice in his head kept telling him that everything would be okay, but it never was.

"I don't want to miss any of the presentations and Hellion promised his would be something to remember. I promised him I would not be late." Asil took Kindle under her arm as she passed and hurried with Jarik to take a seat.

The presentation room was staged in the round. Built by the founding wizards long ago, the ancient amphitheatre was a central performance space surrounded by ascending seating, and was commonly used for lectures or presentations. A large platform of alabaster served as the stage, surrounded by marble quarter circle benches that were separated by ascending stairs. Four tunnels leading to secure rooms used to hold bigger or more dangerous objects broke up the first few rows at the cardinal points.

Asil, with the worry of being late fresh in her mind, apologized to a figure in black she had bumped into. She had not seen him until she was upon him, nearly knocking them both down the steep stairs. She found a seat for herself and Jarik, then politely asked those in the row to slide down to make additional room for Kindle, who sat down quietly trying to arrange his manuscript in the proper order. Asil tried in vain to groom his ragged hair with his fingers but it was hopeless.

Hellion had just taken the stage moments ago and was finishing his opening remarks.

"...had fallen into the wrong hands could prove deadly. For now though, allow me to start with the presentation of this artifact of legend."

From one of the tunnels two golems appeared bearing the front poles of a palanquin with two more golems bringing up the rear. A small rack designed to hold a single weapon was centered on the palanquin. They set the rack gently in the center of the platform, each taking great pains to avoid actually touching the rack, let alone the object it held. The golems then moved to defensive positions a few feet away from the Palanquin.

The rack held a single weapon, a large double bladed battleaxe. It was bound on either end of the shaft with metal clamps and the blade was secured with magical wires. The weapon, shaft to blade, was taller than most men; a testament to the size and strength of its previous wielder. The blade was inscribed with runes, but it did not appear magical. The runes did not glow or radiate and if the weapon had not been locked in the deepest division of the restricted section, one would think the blade to be a joke; something a black smith might make for a gag gift or ornamentation on a building rather than a weapon of magical might with a practical purpose.

"Stop that," Asil gritted her teeth as she yelled back to Drogan. He was having more fun with Kindle causing his manuscript to float piece by piece in the air. A hard eye from a nearby instructor caused Drogan to cease, for the moment.

Kindle didn't seem to notice, even as the manuscript fell to the ground or at the faintly glowing blue bunny at his feat. He eyes were locked on to the ordinary blade.

"Everything will be alright. Suffer no guilt..."
"What's that you said?"

~*~

Tsavik, uncontested ruler of the Kāori nation, materialized at the Northern Elemental node. There were six major elemental nodes of power; the northern and southern axis nodes, and four equatorial nodes equidistance from each other.

Missing Pieces: Bringer of Bedlam

The ground rumbled beneath his feet. It was not the first time this day. The world was wrought with disasters as if it were pulling itself apart.

Tsavin had also been to the other nodes this day. The Western node, closest to the Kāori Homeland, should have been bathed in darkness. Yet for three days the sun had not set behind the blanket of thundering clouds. The Eastern node, closest to the Nazari Ziggurat, should have had the sun beating down on him when he arrived, but it had remained shrouded in darkness for three days. Each of the other equatorial nodes, equal distant from each other, were located in what was becoming the Shadow Region, the area where the dark and the light settled upon the world.

It was not a natural phenomenon. Tsavin knew that magic of some sort was at play. Strange weather patterns plagued the world. Typhoons had been raging across the coast lines for the last three days. Volcanoes spewed the bowels of the earth into the air. No region had escaped as the ground constantly quaked. Either Gaia, the spirit of the world, was undoing itself to wipe out the mistakes of its inhabitants, or she was resetting the playing field. Neither answer made Tsavin happy.

Tsavin, never a man of many words, addressed the gathered *slaves* quickly and with little fan fair. He called them slaves, but his race viewed these beings that they had created as their children. Children were family. Family were equals. However, Tsavin had never thought of any other as an equal. Neither Tsavik, his twin brother, nor even Yyamin. That is where the brothers differed; they were polar opposites in every way.

"Something has happened," he began and even though he stated the obvious, they listened anxiously to his every word.

"We need to connect to the elemental nodes of power. All of them. I fear before the end of this day we will have a need to tap into the ley lines too." Again, the irony of there not being a day or night was not lost on him.

He issued instructions to the *slaves* to tap into the power of the elemental nodes on his command. The raw power could both aid and harm him. Elemental energy was a chaotic brew best left alone. It could be manipulated fairly easily on a small scale. The elementalists of the world could call on its power regularly with little harm. They didn't directly tap into the primal energy of the world, but rather manipulated existing elements. However, there existed some advanced elementalists who had mastered the art of bending the elements to their will and could tap into the raw mana of the world.

Tapping into the raw energy often proved fatal.

~*~

Kindle thought he heard something humming in the distance.

He tried to keep his attention on the matter at hand. Hellion had been droning on for over an hour about the various wars through history past. In some cases he was defending the artifact as being the cause of the war and in other examples he was debunking its involvement all together.

Cause? How could an object of forged metal *cause* a war? Certainly objects of wealth had been at the heart of a few wars, but that was because possession on either side prompted such conflicts. Hellion didn't imply that though. He actually was claiming that the axe itself created the chaos of the conflict. That it was in someway sentient.

Kindle watched absentmindedly as the presentation continued. The normal procedure for a thesis was to allow the presenter to finish completely and address concerns afterward. So it was unusual to say the least, when one of the instructors interrupted the presentation to call Hellion to account on one point. The rare occurrence of such an interruption could be counted on one hand throughout Kindle's years at the academy. So it was stranger still when another asked a question to confirm a date.

Kindle all but ignored the presentation as he focused on something distant. His thoughts turned in his head as he began to think about Asil. From year one Asil had watched out for him. She was one of the few to do so. He thought of Asil as more than a friend. She had grown into a very fine woman. Her raven hair hung to just below her supple breasts. He could hardly *not* notice them, she filled out nicely last year. It wasn't something he actively tracked, the growth of a woman's breasts. But one day she was his knight in shining armor coming to his rescue from bullies and the like. The next day she had definitely into a woman.

In the distance he could hear the soft breeze as it blew across the leaves, hear her laughter as she playfully ran down a beach. The crash of the waves, the rustle of the leaves and the cries of the pelicans shared the distance. He listened closely to sounds of the pelicans, tried to hone in on the noise. If he concentrated enough he thought he could hear the sounds of men arguing or conversing. He was vaguely aware that more and more people were beginning to interrupt the presentation.

Then an image of Asil came back to him. He forgot about everything else; almost everything else. Every once and a while he would think of Drogan. He pictured his hands on Asil. Drogan would look at him, stare into his eyes, as he pawed her. She seemed to like it. Somehow he bullied Kindle even in his dreams.

Am I dreaming? He thought. *I can't be dreaming, Hellion is still speaking. Why is everyone up in arms? Everyone is interrupting him.*

Asil returned to his thoughts. She was staring at him. Not at Drogan.

Drogan, always Drogan.

What he did to deserve this man's attention he did not know. Drogan appeared next to Asil again. She turned her attention to him. Why was Dragon always in his thoughts? Someone should give him a taste of his own medicine.

Drogan should be the brunt of others jokes. He should be pushed in the pond or thrown down the stairs with magic. He should be brought to justice. The righteous should judge him. Someone should punch him or hurt him.

Someone should kill him.

Kill him, he thought, *no, he didn't deserve to die. Not for some peer pranks.*

Asil returned to his thoughts.

Missing Pieces: Bringer of Bedlam

~*~

The Ziggurat of the Nazari stood far beyond time remembered, towering in the Ulterra Mountains. The high elevation coupled with the Tetons of jagged teeth ringing a lush plain of thick fertile land made it an ideal location for defense and agriculture. The Nazari wanted for nothing, but sought domination of all the lands regardless.

Protected from invasion by their natural defenses and strengthened from intrusion via the Æther realm by strong control of the magical flux, the Nazari Ziggurat stood as a testament to their dominance. With slaves of every race drugged into compliance, the Nazari nation was nearly invulnerable and growing like a virus. It was little wonder that the Nazari were near immortals.

Now machines of war and scraps of metal from objects of artifice littered the battlefield. The broken bodies of Nazari and Kāori beset the landscape offering blood instead of water for the coming harvest. Beasts of unusual size in both of spirit and nature, provided by Gaia, lay dead or dying. They had turned the once lush landscape to a field of blood, a graveyard. The once mighty defenses of the Nazari had been shattered, its gates breached and its empire felled.

Tsavin, the Carrion Inquisitionor, the Grand Imperial Legate and the Supreme Commander of the Kāori materialized at the doors of the Ziggurat. Yyamin, with her captured Nazari in tow, and the Home Guard soon materialized behind him. He peered up at the night time sky as it had been since his lord's fall. It was not natural and he made a mental note of it. He did not wait for the others and, confident of his purpose and talent, walked boldly into the Ziggurat between the two diorite stele that built the fundamental principles of the Nazari.

Yyamin followed him but paused a moment at the two diorite stele and translated again the preface of the Nazari code. *Nazari and Kāori called by name me, Kalą' Ðruñe, the exalted prince, who feared no immortal, to bring about the rule of righteousness in the land.* Yyamin reflected on these words. What the Kāori interpreted from these sacred words caused them to set upon the races of the world an equality of sorts, instructing them; mentoring and nurturing them. The Nazari used it as a justification for slavery and servitude, a birth right. They enslaved every race, but held the humans as the most favored and cherished them with brutality.

Yyamin wept.

Runes of every imaginable and deadly nature that once protected the Ziggurat from intruders were now disarmed or destroyed. Glowing balls of greenish light floated at Tsavin's mental command and duplicated when enough light could not be shed to cover an entire area. Tsavin paused at the altar in the main temple and rested his hand on the cold hard surface. It was stained with the blood of countless sacrifices, but that did not bother him. It was the unseen that caught his attention. He made another mental note and frowned at the unexpected results.

He needed no guide to the body of Tsavik the fallen. Even in death he could follow the Æthereal trail of his former lord's body to its final resting state, a curse of his profession. No, he didn't need a guide to find the body. Even in his brother's death, but Tsavik was not yet dead and yet, not alive.

He followed the Æthereal trail deep into the bowels of the ancient Ziggurat. Past the murder chambers and torture cells, down deep under the cavity where the sacrificed bodies fell and gathered from the temple's altar above and past the compartments where the Nazari stored their own claim on the stores of mana. The stored mana was now depleted in defense of the homeland. The Ziggurat descended deep into the mountain past elemental node of power and an unusually strong crossing of ley lines and Tsavin followed the trail to its end in the darkest deepest pit of nothingness, the bowels of the mountain fortress. There, in a cavernous room inscribed with runes and glyphs of ancient magics barely remembered by either race, he found the fallen body of Tsavik next to a large onyx monolith of curious size and strength.

"You are too late," came a deep, gravelly voice from nowhere and everywhere; or perhaps in the confines of his keen mind. The chamber echoed and the thick unrestrained strands of magic and elemental powers mixed as runes and glyphs glowed, throbbing with power too intense to be contained. An occasional flare connected one rune with another as an arc of power exploded and then dissipated, only to build again.

He said nothing as he entered the room and approached the body, keeping a mindful eye on the onyx monolith and deflecting arcs of stray energy with shields of Æther and light. Tsavin paused to assess the body of his fallen twin, his broken remains twisted in impossible angles with a wisp of smoke infused with mana draining from his corpse to float through the air and into the onyx. Tsavik's armor was cracked, useless and his once mighty blade at his side was now an ordinary piece of lifeless metal.

As Yyamin and the Home Guard approached, his deadly gaze turned towards the onyx monolith. It towered over him, its inky blackness seemed to absorb light even as the illuminated fluxes of power infused it with raw mana.

"My lord," said the meek voice of the captive Nazari, "what have you done?" Tsavin turned towards the man, a weak pathetic waste of a Nazari, and saw the object look of fear mixed with revulsion. Ðruñe screamed an unbearable wail of pain and anguish that sent chills down Tsavin's neck as the Nazari's eyes rolled back into his head. His life force began to extinguish as trailers of mist crept through the air from his body to the onyx monolith.

Tsavin, a master of life and death, cupped the Nazari by the throat and raised him from the ground with a powerful arm. With an ancient tongue and mastery of forces beyond comprehension he severed the connection to the death drain, and with the snap of his fingers the Nazari's eyes opened in renewed terror. Tsavin stared deeply into Ðruñe's eyes, his look of menace made it clear that he wanted answers. There was no need to ask the question and the answer came when the Nazari shifted his sight to the inky black monolith.

CRACK!

In the distance the whole of the mountain shook as a large stalactite broke free from the unseen ceiling. It split in two as it crashed into the monolith, leaving it unharmed. Tsavin pulled his hands together and the earth followed, making a protective dome to shelter the body of his fallen leader and those Kāori close enough to be in harms way. He waited for the danger to pass. With a sharp stubborn foot to the earth the shield split in two sending the remains of the stalactite in every direction. A deep gravely dooming laughter filled the cavernous room and reverberated in the hearts of all within.

Tsavin, with the Nazari still in arm, turned his attention to the monolith. He drew on the powers of the combined Kāori nation, the elemental powers of the slaves and the fluxes of mana gleamed from the nearly dead. Linked for this final confrontation the Supreme Commander should have been more than a match for the final assault on the Ziggurat. Plans seldom went as planned and once he tapped the powers of the pooled nation he could see what had gone horribly wrong. There, hidden in the deep recesses of the monolith where no mundane magic could find him, stood the leader of the Nazari. He knew what was happening, but he asked the question anyway.

"What is he doing?"

"H-he," said the Nazari through gritted teeth and a compressed windpipe, "is-drawing all power to-himself. H-h-he," the Nazari was beating at Tsavin's mighty fist trying in vain to loosen the death grip. Tsavin released his grip slightly to speed along the conversation.

Gasp.

"He has the s-sum whole of the power from the Nazari nation," he paused to take in a deep breath, "not for a day or for limited connectivity as you do when you link the Kāori, but the renewable power of all the Nazari.

A long gasp.

"T-They have sacrificed their souls to feed his ambitions. N-now he is drawing the power from all other sources. The elemental nodes, the ley lines, the ancient runes and glyphs then the world itself are being drawn upon. N-Notice that time has ceased? The sun no longer moves in the sky. A cataclysm of epic proportions is in the making and none can stop it. Mountains are rising from the earth, craters have sucked in the land, half the world will be bathed in eternal light, the other half impenetrable darkness. But long before the light side boils the oceans and the dark side freezes itself in an icy tomb, the world will be no more. He is to become a god of nothingness, as nothing will remain once he has finished.

A long gasp.

"Your Supreme Commander is even being drawn upon. He is trapped in a state between life and death, being drawn into the monolith-h.

Gasp.

"Once it is complete, the whole of the Kāori nation will be drawn to him through your connected magical bond.

Gasp.

"Once that happens, the resulting decay of magic will escalate expo-expo--.

Gasp.

"Exponentially,

Gasp.
"In a downward spiral,
Gasp.
"Resulting in the destruction,
Gasp.
"Of the world.
Gasp.
"And bey-." His final words never reached Tsavin's ears as he crushed the remaining life out of the Nazari and discarded the body without a further care.

Tsavin closed his eyes and saw through the eyes of all those attached to the link. The dog of a Nazari was correct. The world was tidally locked. One side of the world had been bathed in light for the whole of the last few days. The days he had been unconscious in his cramped cell. The other half was bathed in eternal dark leaving a swath of land between the two trapped in eternal twilight. The rest was all true, the world was pulling itself apart and in spite of his vast, nearly limitless power, there was nothing he could do about it. Tsavin, connected to the entire Kāori nation and slave races through a bond of magic, scoured the minds of each and again collectively as a whole for a solution.

None was forthcoming.

The mist and mana from Tsavik's body had nearly finished transferring to the monolith and this link he could not end. Powerful magic beyond his comprehension prohibited him from even slowing the effect. He did manage to get close to Tsavik's body though. Close enough to see the gleaming blade of high polish. Close enough to read the ancient inscription on the bloody axe.

~*~

"How can you know these words?" said an instructor on the first row of benches. It was an academic question, not a challenge. Hellion had been going on for nearly an hour detailing the known and speculated history of this object of fascination. The source of the ancient writings on the blade had always been a mystery and his proclamation of discovery had instantly sparked deep academic interest.

"I found an ancient text which predates the last war thousands of years ago of a boy who wielded this blade in battle. The barbarian king Brodock. While the language predates even this writing, his advisors often heard him whisper these words before battle."

"Surely this is not your only proof. Many scholars have researched this subject, and the runes, and found nothing to collaborate this story."

"It is true that it is conjecture. Heresy of those who loved the king and sought to make a name for him for all time. However," he said as a book flew through the air to his hand, and without looking caught the book and relied relying on magic to turn it to the correct page, "in the writings of the sage Fallin, dated only two hundred years ago, he records a merchant spoke these vary words before the merchant brandished an axe of unusual size and slew his family." He waved his hand for the coming questions, the book he was reading floated on the air to the instructor and everyone gathered in close to read it for themselves, as if the words would change if they read them with their own eyes. Another book flew from the table and opened in his hand.

Distracted by the ruffling of her papers Jarik glanced at Asil as she struggled to get comfortable on the stone seats. As she finally settled down he caught the title of her thesis.

"You're not really doing your thesis on the paternity of the decade are you?" queried Jarik in a whisper as he caught the heading on her thesis papers, "I thought I talked you out of that and you instead opted for the conversation of mana into matter?"

"Shh," she said when those nearby shot the two of them a dirty eye, "you are not the boss of me. Besides, no child has been born in a decade. It is a subject of great interest and growing into an epidemic pandemic." She was right, no births had occurred for over a decade, but that was not to say that there were no pregnancies. Women indeed were pregnant but stayed in that state, always on the cusp of labor, but unable to bear the child. She huffed and turned away from him absentmindedly placing her hands over her belly.

"You didn't," he said with all seriousness as he grabbed her hand. She pulled away from him.

"I don't expect you to understand."

"Understand?" he sputtered and then adjusted his tone so only she could hear, "Understand? I understand all too well. Those women have been pregnant for years, some in unimaginable pain and suffering, some have even died. How could you?" She turned to him with tears in her eyes. Asil had asked for him to provide his seed in a daring experiment to father a child and get a first hand perspective of the problem at hand. He had agreed, but before the act had been done, he backed out. There was a secret he kept. A secret he could not reveal to her. He could only walk away. He never thought she would go through with the act with another.

"It is my life, my body," she said as she ignored the angry looks of those few people not grossly engaged on what was unfolding below, "and you cannot tell me what to do with my body. These women have been unable to bear there children for years and no one has had any passable theory as to why. I think I do but I can't unless I understand the problem from within."

"I have heard this argument before. How coul-"

"I will never turn my back on those in need, never!" she turned her head fuming trying to hide her tears. She tried to wipe them away with the side of her index finger, her well groomed nails preventing her from using the tip of her finger without poking herself in the eye. He reached out to comfort her and thought better of it and hung his head to let her collect her thoughts. Hellion's presentation again caught his attention.

"The blade was lost to history until forty seven years ago when an expedition to the Shifting Sands came across a village of native sand riders. The village took in the expedition with open arms but a rival band of marauders disagreed with outsiders seeking refuge in their sacred lands. The following day the village was razed to the ground. We refer to this as the massacre of the Mogauna. But in this text there was one survivor from the expedition who managed to escape."

"That is not true, all died that day," came another voice higher up.

"Yes, that is historical fact, what proof do you have?"

Hellion unfolded a piece of parchment in the book with reverent hands and held it aloft for all to see.

"Forty six years ago a leader of men came out of nowhere brandishing an axe, this axe," he said as he pointed to the weapon still on the rack, "and led an army across the vast plains, slaughtering men, women and children. He left chaos in his wake and devastation second only to Kazzikdoom the Eternal. None could stop his assembled forces, not even us mages, until he died a mysterious death by an unknown illness. His name as you as know was Brogan, the Bringer of Bedlam. It is my contention that the blade found Brogan Ballin to be a worthy wielder. Here, on this manifest, are the names of those who left for the expedition forty seven years ago. Here, second to last is the name of Brogan Ballin, the lone survivor of the expedition and scrawled on the bottom of this parchment are the very words translated from this blade. "

Shouts and yells erupted from the assembled. Cries of "foul" and "blasphemy" echoed in the great hall as every assembled mage tried to state their arguments all at once. Some even came on the stage to better see the manifest and state their arguments up close and personal.

Drogan took advantage of the chaos to ignite young Kindle's papers. Asil, forgetting the tears streaming down her face, rushed up the stairs to confront him while Jarik patted the flames into submission. Kindle however either didn't notice or didn't care. He rose, oblivious to the chaos around him. He didn't notice the instructor that bumped into him or those who stood in his way. He made his way at a slow, measured pace to the stage, ignored by the people around him. Drogan, tired of the false accusations, shoved Asil down the stairs and was preparing to unleash magic on her when Jarik joined her, confronting him physically. She was with child now and Jarik was instinctively more protective of her. Asil, spun around by the shove, looked up to see the chaos erupting throughout the hall. She scanned the hall for Kindle, but he was no longer on the bench where she had left him at. She turned her sights to the stage and saw Kindle standing in front of the rack that secured the famed blade. The golems hadn't taken notice of him even though they gently ushered away others who got too close to the blade. *How odd.*

The plain looking blade caught her eye; it was nothing special to look upon. The craftsmanship was superb, only in that it had stood up to the rigors of time. Perhaps if it was polished she thought, but forty six years in the restricted section of the Wizards Keep did not improve its appearance. Marks from opposing weapons and notches where it's former wielders tried to chew off more than it could were prevalent. Asil saw Kindle raise his hand. He was speaking to himself as he reached for the handle.

"No!" she screamed, but it fell on deaf ears. Asil didn't know what would happen if kindle touched the ancient blade, but instinctively she knew it couldn't be good. She knew it was a source of great controversy to even allow Hellion to do his final thesis on the blade. The history of the carnage this weapon had brought to the world was no great secret. The mere mention of the blade caused grown men to weep. Throughout time remembered some of the greatest massacres where tied to this blade and she knew the Headmaster had initially denied Hellion's request. Hellion had presented a compelling argument in his appeal and had reluctantly been given permission so long as none touched the blade.

Kindle reached for the handle.

"Suffer no guilt," he whispered, but none could hear him through the explosion of arguments throughout the hall.

He touched the handle.

~*~

Tsavin hefted the blade in one hand. In the hands of a Kāori, it could be wielded easily with one hand. Those of the *slave races* would require two, if they could wield it at all. Instantly he felt the connection to its creator, the Supreme Commander of the Kāori, his flesh and blood, his brother. The blade he had crafted to aid in the defeat of the Nazari flowed with elemental power, but more so he could feel the flux of power flow through his many meridian pathways and there critical focal points.

The pathways of the positive and negative energy, carry on the vital communications between the various parts of the body. In the gifted, touching the meridian lines and opening them to the external power sources such as the Æthereal, elemental or Ley Lines, resulted in random and usually unexpected consequence. The blade, forged of iron from the earth, acted as a conductor, making these connections less random and more predictable.

"You are too late little Kāori," doomed the voice, "this world is dead, and you shall die too!"

Tsavin held the gleaming blade in both hands, the runes glowing brightly, a strong red. He tapped into his heart meridian, the one that represented compassion and therefore governed his emotions and spirit. It also aided in blood circulation and total body via the brain and all six senses. It also functions as the mechanism for adapting external stimulation to be used internally by the body.

Tsavin then used his connection to his heart meridian to tap into the raw power of the planet via the elemental nodes, then the ley lines and lastly the Æthereal. Tapping the emotion meridian this way would normally cause Tsavin unbearable pain and suffering. It should have instantly created a connection between him and the slave races, flooding him with their emotions.

Tsavin, devoid of empathy, was not affected. With no emotion to attach to, the pure chaos of millions instead flooded into the axe instead. Yyamin could only watch as the hopes and dreams of not only the fate of the Nazari nation but also the fate of the world rested in the hands of a man without conscious.

He then tapped into the bond with the Kāori nation, asking them for their sacrifice, the only way. For any other person, being connected to the heart and the emotion meridian through so many with the resulting flood of emotions would instantly have killed them.

"No," he said to Yyamin as she too was about to sacrifice her life to the cause, "you must not join with us. The Slave Races will need a mentor to guide them and teach them." He hand touched her belly, though she could not sense it, he could detect the life within.

"Goodbye my wife, report our cause and teach them well." Yyamin shed a single tear that seemed to burn her cheek as it slowly rolled down her face. She had never felt this alone, her bond from her people severed, she felt naked, exposed, and vulnerable.

With the Nazari all but defeated, the Kāori's time on this world was also at an end. Their sacrifice would usher in a new age for the slave races. Not one Kāori said no and as each Kāori in turn freely offered their soul and thus their mana, Tsavin grew in power, the red runes on the blade pulsed with unbridled energy.

"What are you doing little Kāori," boomed the voice, "stop that, you cannot defeat me."

"Suffer no guilt," he said. The axe had been created to be wielded with a righteous hand; an even hand; the hand of justice. To do so without cause would instantly tap into the wielder's heart meridian and the resulting inundation of emotion would lay upon the wielder such overwhelming guilt that they would usually end up taking their own life to avoid the agony. This was a defense built into the blade so it could not be abused.

The creator never thought one devoid of emotion would every wield it, thus bypassing the defenses.

As the influx of power coursed through his body, shards of light erupted from his eyes and shot through the mountain into the sky. He tapped into the ley lines and elemental nodes and stabilized the dying planet. Earthquakes and volcanic eruptions ceased, the tsunamis of the oceans calmed and typhoons and tornados died. He influenced the tide to stabilize the decaying orbits of the moons. He could do nothing for the rotation of the world, not if he was to finish the task at hand. The world would be trapped half in light and half in dark with parts trapped in a perpetual state of twilight.

A red flare of light spilt the sky, then split again and again and reached to every living being on the world. In an instant Tasvin educated his primordial children, the true embodiment of the ÆVARICE, how to maintain the world. He gifted the air elementals with the knowledge to force the winds of the upper stratosphere to bring heat from the light side to the dark side of the world. He instructed the fire elementals how to control the volcanic forces on the light side and lessen the intense heat that would surely come. With the water elementals he trained them how to use the moons to draw light, if only in a limited manner, by reflecting the sun off of the moons to the dark side. He taught the earth elementals how to move the earth in the Shadow Region, spinning part of the continent to mimic the effects of the rising and setting sun.

Now he had a direct connection to all life. Then he turned his teachings towards the *slave races*. His gift of prophecy reached each of them. He infused them with the ability of the gift, of mana and magic. He told them it would begin dormant and through discovery they would become masters of the magic, but only once they understood the mantle of power and the responsibilities that came with it, so they would not become corrupt like the Nazari. Finally he left them with hope in the form of prophecy. Events that would unfold or could potentially unfold. The greatest of these was a Prophecy of One. A prophecy which indicated that one, born of many, would change the face of the world and restore it to its former glory.

"No, what are you doing? Stop it!"

Tsavin, the red glow radiating from his body, turned his attention to the inky black onyx monolith. He couldn't sever the link of the Nazari leader, but he could divert it. He looked down at the gleaming silver blade and the inscription blazing with power unimaginable.

"Suffer no guilt he who wields this blade with righteousness hands," he screamed as he hefted the mighty blade with all his might. In an explosive burst of energy, he wielded the entire strength of a grateful world and every living being on the world shed a tear. Not for the guilt of the death of the Nazari, but rather for the sacrifice of the Kāori. Tsavin felt no guilt in his righteous wrath as he brought the mighty blade to bear on the inky blackness. A thunderous boom filled the cavernous room and the black onyx monolith split as the axe bit deep, cracking the blade by the handle. It was stuck fast, but it did not matter. The blade had served its purpose. Tsavin, still holding onto the shaft reached for his brother's body. He fingers mere inches from his brother's hand.

"NOOO!" Another large boom filled the room and the Nazari leader unleashed magic from within the monolith.

CRACK!

Another massive stalactite broke from the ceiling in hopes of destroying Tsavin before the connection could be made. Tsavin, connected to the blade and unable to react less the connection to the magic be lost forever, could only watch as the massive spear of earth dived for him. He reached again for his brother hoping to make the connection before he died. It was their only hope.

He was not near close enough.

A gale force of wind blasted the stalactite at the last second, causing the massive spear to shift barely enough to avoid killing Tsavin. It bit deep into the earth missing him by mere inches. Tsavin looked from the direction the wind had come. In the distance stood four elementals, one of each element, earth, water, fire and air. Towering protectively over them stood a fifth individual with four arms. Each arm resembled traits of one of the four elements. These elementals were not the raw substances of chaos, but humanoid in nature. These were his legacy to the world, descendants from the elemental chaos. They had elemental traits built into their genetic code which allowed them to manifest specific elemental powers. The *slave races* were the children of the Nazari and the Kāori, but these Æiherals were his children set upon the world to protect and serve the *slave races*.

First though, they came to the rescue of their father.

The pillar of earth groaned and shifted and began to fall toward Tsavin. One of the Ætherals, a figure of smooth features and flowing water for hair, under the direction of the four armed individual, squatted to the earth and drew upon forces unseen. As the pillar of earth began to fall she stood and raised her hands high and the ground rumbled. A pillar of water sprouted from the earth to match that of the pillar of earth and waged a war of gravity, bracing the pillar and preventing it from falling. Another Ætheral, with reddish features and flames for hair, drew in power to himself and stepped forward releasing a powerful burst of electricity which pulverized the earth pillar into dust. The earthbound of the five stepped forward, dust trailing from each foot step.

"Don't touch him," Tsavin screamed, "you cannot comprehend the consequences."

The Ætheral gently raised his hands and the earth below Tsavik's fallen body reverently raised to form an altar of earth. He pushed on forces unseen and gently moved the altar towards Tsavin.

"Guard them well my children," he said sorrowfully and he touched his brother. The red light turned white and the black wispy smoke traveling towards the monolith diverted and instead flowed into the blade.

"NOOO!" screamed the dying voice as the bodies of Tsavin and Tsavik transformed into light and mist and then were sucked into the blade. The inky black of the monolith seemed to absorb even the sound as the white light faded and the monolith exploded in a white flash of light.

The Quad 'Æst touched the primal forces of air and earth and settled the dust in the chamber. The monolith was completely destroyed, no trace of it remained. Tsavin's and Tsavik's body were gone. Tsavin's children searched for the blade.

It was no where to be found.

~*~

Kindle felt the unbridled wrath of all who wielded the blade before him, all through the blade's long and sordid history. He tried to avoid feeling the wrath of the second wielder of the blade, but to no avail. Tsavin's wrath had saved a world and if he could not wield the blade with righteous hands to match the unbridled wrath of one who sacrificed not only himself but an entire nation, there was no hope in mastering the pure chaos of the blade.

A flood of emotion filled him. Every wrong, every injustice that had been done to him screamed to be redeemed by blood. He hefted the mighty blade, his own anger surged strength into his limbs and the blade increased it exponentially. The world around him was abstract at best, his vision blind with pure primal wrath. He swung the axe when one of the mages bumped into him, not noticing him until it was too late. Instinctively he cut the mage, slicing cleanly through the man's waist. A look of horror filed the mage's eyes. Disbelief gripped him as he grabbed for his waist. It was useless; he fell dead in two clean pieces.

Revulsion filled Kindle instantly. He felt the guilt of it, the guilt of the dying, the guilt of killing; but did he really feel guilt at this man's death. No, he was like all the others. They were all alike. They must all pay.

The doors to the chamber slammed shut, a reflex of magic gone awry. Protective runes flared to life and shields sprang into existence. The mages quieted for only a moment.

"Boy," said the horrified Headmaster, "what have you done?"

A mage approached Kindle and was cut down without a thought before he could thicken the air around him to create a shield. Kindle's vision was focused on the source of his torment. Drogan looked directly into Kindle's eyes, the two making a connection each had never done before; Drogan the weak and Kindle the master. A bolt of fire arched towards Kindle but the blade, caught up in the vengeance of this moment, deflected the magical assault.

Suffer no guilt, said the blade to Kindle's mental connection, *he who wields this blade with a righteous hand.*

Kindle hefted the blade. It was not as heavy as it had been. With all his strength, he threw the blade through the air towards its target. The blade cut through two mages who happened to be in the way and severed the arm of another as it finally found its mark deep in the chest of Drogan. Drogan fell to the ground, blood foaming from his mouth, feebly clenching at his chest in wild disbelief.

Kindle screamed in unbearable pain. The deed done, he now paid the price for his vengeance. The guilt he never thought he had for the act he so desperately wanted; the unbridled chaos of millions of screaming souls calling to him from a time long forgotten.

Asil came to his side and tried to comfort him, tears streaming from her eyes. She pushed the other mages aside who tried to restrain Kindle and protectively used magic to push those back who did not heed her warning.

Instinctively someone brushed against the blade, trying to aid Drogan, and the blade formed a new bond. Fury filled him as he ripped into a nearby mage with a sickening splat. Three more were dead before this wielder died and the blade found its way to another.

Then another.

Mass chaos erupted, unbound magic flew and many mages died. When it was over, the doors lay asunder, the shields breached, the blade was gone.

Bedlam was free in the world again.

About the Author

An unfortunate birthing in Wisconsin eventually lead to a migration to Minnesota where he resides today with his loving wife and two adventurous children. He started out his writing career with Dragon Roots magazine to take the place of Dragon and Dungeon Magazine in the printed format and now hopes to fulfill a life long dream to share the written word from creative juices flowing within.

Learn more about Dragon Roots Magazine at www.dragonroots.net. Look for the first book of the *Wizards of War* series coming soon.

Hemingway's Challenge

Evil beguiles innocence.
Betrayed, monsters emerge.

Great swords!
(Aieee! Arrrgh.)
Darn archers...

-C. S. Marks

About the Story

The Unbroken Mirror is a juicy bit of Alterran back-story. In truth, it (and surrounding events) could easily have been turned into a novella or even a full-length novel. I have always been fascinated with the interplay between Shandor and Kotos (the 'Eagle and the Raven'), particularly with respect to the beguiling and subsequent fall of Kotos. When presented with the opportunity, I decided to indulge my fascination a little.

Shandor and Kotos play important roles in the *Elfhunter* trilogy, and I wanted to give new readers a taste of the Alterran world without 'spoiling' any future tales, hence the back-story. Assuming that my present readership shares my fascination with Shandor and Kotos, *The Unbroken Mirror* will also be enjoyed by those who are already familiar with Alterra.

The Unbroken Mirror
By
C. S. Marks

Dardis, son of the Fire-heart, was unlike his father in nearly every respect. He was, in fact, one of the gentlest and most beloved residents of Tal-Elathas, the City of Knowledge. This great realm, ruled by the High King Ri-Aldamar, was the foremost center of Learning and Lore that has ever graced the world of Alterra (so far as is known to western scholars).

Dardis' talents were nothing short of phenomenal, especially those dealing with the awakening of magical properties and placing them within objects. He had crafted numerous rings and amulets, blades and shields and armor. Driven by curiosity and the desire to try new things, he experimented with common items such as water-pitchers, shoes, belts, plates and cups, and even hairbrushes. It was a mirror, however, which vexed him the most.

At that time, Tal-Elathas had three of the ancient magic-users at her service. Known as Asari, they had been sent by Aontar (the Lord of Light) to educate and enlighten the people of the world. Twelve were sent in the beginning, but only seven had settled in the western lands. It was unusual for any realm to harbor more than one Asarla, but Tal-Elathas, being a center of enlightenment, was the exception. Baelta (the Bright), Kotos (the Perceptive), and Léiras (the Far-sighted) all dwelled within its walls.

It was Léiras who took the greatest interest in Dardis. He had, in fact, been instructing Dardis for millennia, as both the Asari and the Elves of Alterra are immortal. Slowly, and with great effort, Dardis' talents had been drawn out until he was the most gifted of all Elves—none like him had been seen before, and would almost certainly not be seen again.

There are several races of Elves in Alterra, but Dardis was of the Èolar—a race of warrior-scholars who are unexcelled in battle; taller and broader than their Wood-elven or Light-elven cousins. They are also the most learned, loving to discover the 'why' and 'how' of the world. This meant, at least for some, a great deal of time indoors. A day's pursuit might involve dismantling things to see how they worked,

Missing Pieces: The Unbroken Mirror

experimenting with elixirs and compounds, testing alloys in the forge, or simply reading and studying the knowledge already gained. Such habits are more alike to those of Dwarves, and would not be at all to the liking of Wood-elves, who enjoy wild places and open air. Nor would they appeal to the Light-elves who favor gardens with many fountains—even in their underground realms.

Dardis spent nearly all his time in his 'workshop' with Léiras, surrounded by failed projects, works-in-progress, and finished items that had yet to be tested. Dardis' works always had a benevolent purpose in the beginning, though they didn't always end that way. It was said that gentle Dardis never harbored a mean or destructive thought in his life, though none can ever know for certain. Even an object with a benevolent purpose may be turned to mischief in the wrong hands.

Because of the influence of Léiras, Dardis' creations were often works of art as well as magic. Yet one could tell if a ring or an amulet had been made by Dardis rather than Léiras. Dardis' work appeared simple, almost plain, until one examined it closely, whereupon it was revealed to be almost impossibly intricate. Léiras' tastes ran more to the obviously ornate. It might actually have been the influence of Dwarves, with whom Dardis was close in friendship, that most influenced the style of his work.

Dardis had been working for some time on what appeared to be an ordinary mirror with an oaken frame and a plain stand, such as would go upon a dressing-table. 'I would endow this mirror with the ability to show the truth of things reflected in it,' he said to Léiras, 'and yet it confounds me. All it seems to do is make things appear better than they are.'
'Show me,' said Léiras, who appeared as a Light-elf, slender and tall, with golden hair and disturbingly pale blue eyes.

'Look here,' said Dardis. 'See my reflected image? All my imperfections are gone... the lines, the pallor of my skin, even the discoloration on my chin from the ink-spot there...' (When he was making drawings on parchment Dardis had a habit of settling his chin in his right hand, which was always stained with ink. He was not the most fastidious of Elves.)

Léiras looked into the mirror at Dardis' reflection and drew in a short breath of surprise. 'You're right! It has erased all that is less than perfect. Do you know how many would desire such a thing?' He chuckled under his breath. 'It would confirm all their opinions of their perfect selves.'

'Our people have enough difficulty with self-infatuation,' grumbled Dardis, who almost never spoke ill of anyone or anything. In this case, though, it was undeniably true, at least for many. 'That's not why I tried to endow the mirror with insight. It is supposed to show the truth, not create false perfection.'

Missing Pieces: The Unbroken Mirror

'Have you tried looking at plain objects?' asked Léiras. 'For example, let me hold this water-goblet before it—I see there's a chip on the rim. Will the mirror show it as whole?'

'I had thought of that,' said Dardis. 'Unless things have changed, it will show the goblet exactly as it is. The mirror was not designed to have an effect on non-living things...unless, of course, they are bound by enchantments. I wanted to give this to the King so that he could tell an enemy from a friend, or whether an object sent to him was tainted by evil. All this will do is make him appear young and perfect again.'

Léiras patted his most treasured apprentice on the shoulder. 'Never mind,' he said. 'Sometimes it's best to put such frustrations aside for a time. When the inspiration strikes, you will work on it again. Now, tell me about this other great effort of yours!'

The mirror was set aside for many years. The great effort Léiras referred to was perhaps Dardis' most significant accomplishment, and the Fate of Alterra would turn according to its destiny. It was the wondrous, mystical, terrible, yet fathomless and beautiful Stone of Léir.

~*~

For every force favoring enlightenment there is a force which favors darkness. In the West of Alterra that force was embodied in the person of one Lord Wrothgar, an ancient, malevolent being who had sought to overcome the Light since the Time of Mystery. Why he was so driven no one knows. It is thought that Wrothgar was made stronger and more powerful when surrounded by ignorance, and that the Light of Knowledge would burn and blind him as surely as the light of the sun. He sought always to either slay the enlightened races or turn them to his service, plunging them into the darkness of self-absorption and complacency. He fared best with men, whose short lives often did not allow them the opportunity to be properly educated. Their fear of death could always be turned to Wrothgar's advantage.

Elves and Dwarves were more difficult—in fact, Wrothgar had never really succeeded in turning any of them. He came close with the exploitation of the previous Elven High King, Aincor Fire-heart, whose reckless nature and self-assurance allowed Wrothgar to lure him into a nearly hopeless conflict in which the forces of Light were all but vanquished. Wrothgar had been defeated and driven back by Shandor, the powerful Lord of the Asari, but the Fire-heart was slain. Since that conflict each side had rebuilt its forces, existing in a near-constant state of tension while attempting to take advantage of and overwhelm the other.

Now it was rumored that Wrothgar had decided to extend the hand of Peace to the Elves.

He was weary of war and was ready to share the dominion of Alterra with his enemies, for they did have common interests. He let it be known that his dark scholars had uncovered the answers to many great questions. All the Elves need do was ask, and the mysteries would be revealed. As a gift of faith, Wrothgar sent a manuscript which did, indeed, contain answers and lore unknown to the Elves, whereupon the Èolarin scholars pounced on it like starving cats. This was only a small taste of what awaited them, said Wrothgar's emissaries. All Wrothgar wanted was the chance to meet with the High King and make peace. Had Alterra not seen enough of war?
The High King Ri-Aldamar knew of Wrothgar's prior deceptions, and he was most difficult to convince. He sought the counsel of the most learned of scholars, of his battle-commanders Gelmyr and Magra, of his son Iolar, and of his three Asari. They sat together in the King's council-chamber for many days of deliberation. The emissaries of Wrothgar had been detained until an answer could be given them.

At first, opinions did not favor any parley with Lord Wrothgar, who had never shown any hint that he desired anything other than the extermination of all enlightened races.

'Why would we have anything to say to one who thrives on ignorance?' asked Baelta, a bright-eyed, dark haired Asarla who appeared as a youthful Èolarin Elf. 'Ignorance is the enemy of enlightenment.'

'Yet not all surrounding the Dark One is of ignorance,' said Kotos, who had been examining Wrothgar's manuscript. 'There are some very compelling answers to some difficult questions here.' Kotos was raven-haired, with skin like polished golden mahogany. He appeared as one of the most beautiful Elves ever seen. His eyes were inky-black, bottomless and fathomless. He was known as 'The Persuader', and the name was apt. To look into Kotos' eyes and listen to his voice usually meant capitulation in an argument with him. He was arguably the most perceptive, the most adept at seeing into the hearts and minds of others, and therefore the most dangerous of all creations of Aontar. He was the only being capable of prevailing in a debate with Lord Shandor, most powerful of all Asari, who was his good friend.

'How do we know that those questions were not answered by scholars taken by force and held against their will?' asked Magra, an enormous, battle-scarred Èolarin Elf with hair like weathered gold and piercing blue eyes. When Magra shifted in his seat at the table, everyone else could feel it shake.

'One cannot force discovery,' said Léiras. 'Thoughts and inspirations must come from free minds.'

'Free minds may also be evil minds,' countered Baelta. 'If these scholars labored in Wrothgar's service willingly, he must have promised them things. Some scholars will serve anyone if they are promised answers to questions that have eluded them.

Missing Pieces: The Unbroken Mirror

Perhaps Wrothgar offered them answers to great mysteries, and he ensnared them.'
'You sound like Lord Shandor,' said Kotos with a slight smile on his chiseled, handsome face. 'We debated for long hours over the price and value of obtaining knowledge. It was his opinion that some things should not be known. I believe that the more we know the better prepared we are to thwart deception and prevent evil influences from creeping in. Knowledge itself is not evil—only what is done with the knowledge can make it so.'

'So you have often stated,' said Ri-Aldamar, his keen grey eyes gleaming beneath pensive brows. 'What is your advice to me now? Would you have me meet this Lord of Evil with intent of establishing a peaceful truce between us? Do you really believe such a truce may be achieved? Our people have warred with Wrothgar and his thralls since before the recording of lore. Do you really believe the worm has turned?'

Kotos appeared lost in thought for a moment, resting his chin on a long-fingered, smooth-sculpted hand. 'No...I would not advise that as yet,' he said at last. 'Rather, allow me to go as your emissary. Let me assess the sincerity or threat of Wrothgar's intentions—he will not deceive me. I alone will take the risk. Wrothgar will not dare to harm me, not if he is serious about peace-making. If I do not return, well...you will know what decision should be made.'

He looked around the table at the many skeptical faces staring back at him. 'Am I not the most perceptive among you? Is there one better suited to the task? If so, then name him! I don't mind relinquishing the responsibility.'

'It's not that we do not recognize you as the most adept among us,' said Baelta, who loved Kotos as a brother. 'It's that we cannot imagine sending anyone alone into such a den of snakes.'

'Asari cannot be poisoned by the venom of serpents,' said Kotos. 'I will not allow Wrothgar to harm me. Again, if he attempts to harm me or takes me captive his plans will fail, for you will know they are false. If he truly wants peace I will know it, and he will not harm me. Is it not worth making sure?'

'But, why must you go alone?' asked Baelta, who was still worried for Kotos' safety. 'Why may I not go with you?'
'Because your spirit is not suited to immersion in such darkened realms,' answered Kotos. 'I have studied both the light and dark aspects of the mind and heart. I will be able to function there—you might not, and you would then distract me. I cannot risk the success of my quest out of worry for your well-being.'

Ri-Aldamar sighed. Kotos' words always made sense. 'If you go, you must take my armor,' he said. 'Dardis made it for me; no blade can pierce it. I must insist on that, at least.'

Kotos bowed his head in gratitude. 'I am humbled. I will gladly do as you ask. Just make certain you have additional armor.' He looked up at R-Aldamar with a prideful gleam in his eye. 'In the unlikely event that I should fail.'

~*~

Unlike the other Asari, who were reluctant to leave their protected realms, Kotos had always been a free spirit, moving wherever he would. While he made his home in Tal-Elathas, he was taken to leaving it, sometimes for years at a time, traveling the lands of Alterra disguised as a common vagabond. He was very useful in informing the King of the goings-on in faraway lands, especially with respect to the many tribes and settlements of men. Their petty squabbles did not often concern the Elves, but it was good to know of them. Kotos attempted to bring peace among them, a thing he was very good at, for he looked into their hearts and knew how to persuade them. He was known to some as 'Peacemaker', to others as 'Persuader'. He was both loved and feared by the majority of men.

On one such extended foray, Kotos sat alone by his small fire in the midnight blackness of a pine forest, recalling his last debate with Lord Shandor. Watching the two of them was riveting, especially when they wrestled with each other—Shandor's cold ivory and silver striving against Koto's warm, golden form and raven hair. Listening to their debate revealed that their differences were not merely physical. Shandor was always chilly, always logical, as though every point he made was inarguable. Kotos was hot-blooded, passionate, and very persuasive, appealing as much to the heart as to the mind.

In this last debate, Shandor had stated (with great finality) that Evil could always be recognized by the pure of heart, that it was unnecessary to explore it or understand it in order to battle against it. Kotos had disagreed. 'Evil is often hidden, and it deceives the unwary. To know one's enemy is to defeat him. How can you advocate otherwise?'

'Because the power of evil lies, to some extent, in familiarity with it. To truly know and understand its nature, one would have to descend into the depths,' said Shandor. 'One cannot come to know such things and remain unaltered by them. There are stains which do not wash off.'

'Just because one knows much of pigs does not make one a pig,' said Kotos with a smile.

'But does the average swineherd's knowledge of pigs imply real understanding of them?' countered Shandor. 'To truly understand pigs, one must become as a pig. You said you wanted to truly understand the nature of evil, but that would be most difficult for a principled person to accomplish. You would need to descend into evil yourself, and I fear you will not emerge untouched. I really wish you would turn from this obsession.'

'I would prevail,' said Kotos. 'And I still do not believe a descent into evil is necessary.'

Shandor thought for a moment. 'When you try to sway the opinion of someone in a debate, how do you do that?'

Kotos did not hesitate. 'I simply look into his mind and heart, put myself in his place, and imagine the most favorable course. Then I know how to persuade him.'

'Exactly. You put yourself in his place. You think with his mind, and feel with his heart. You have accomplished much good with this ability. But if you challenge Lord Wrothgar with the intention of actually understanding him, and try even to imagine the evil in his heart, you will be changed. Please, my friend, do not take such a foolish chance. Evil has a way of working itself into the most stalwart of souls.'

'And how would you know?' muttered Kotos under his breath. 'You've never had an evil thought in your life.'

Shandor had long since left Tal-elathas, moving southward to found his own haven. It was known as Monadh-talam, meaning 'Mountain-home', and it was quickly becoming a major center of enlightenment in its own right. Shandor was, of course, entitled to rule his own realm, but it was regrettable that he could not remain in Tal-Elathas. After Shandor had gone, Kotos had only the memory of his wise words.

For every ray of light, there is a shadow. For every happy thought, a cry of grief; a death for every birth; a friend for every foe—such is the balance of the universe. Kotos was proud, and he was powerful. He had ever used his power in the service of the Light. Now he desperately wanted to explore the realms of Darkness, to learn what he had not yet learned. The evil thoughts of men had both disgusted and tantalized him, and he would not stop now until his thirst for knowledge was satisfied. It did not matter how compelling Shandor's arguments had been, for Kotos could no longer hear them.

~*~

Dardis moved his clever, gifted hands over the surface of the crystal one last time that day, drawing and shaping the energies within it. Almost finished now, he thought, his eyes bright with the fever of accomplishment. The Stone had confounded him—in fact, this was his third attempt, as he had shattered the first two in frustration—but at last his efforts had been rewarded. This was not an easy thing.

He had banned everyone, even Léiras, from his workshop (which he referred to as his 'chamber of inspiration') for many months now. At first he did not want anyone to witness his failure, for Dardis was an Elf, and all Elves suffer from the common affliction of pride. More recently it was because the effort and concentration required was so intense that he could not afford any distraction.

The crystal was large, and at first it seemed regular in shape. But when one examined it closely, the apparent symmetry proved to be an illusion. No two faces were exactly alike, either on the surface or within. Gazing into the depths was mesmerizing, as the light caught an infinite number of planes and polygons. Only one would yield the answer to the viewer's need.

Dardis finally decided to show the Stone to Léiras. It was not yet perfect, but it was close enough to share with the Master. Perhaps Léiras could aid in finishing it.

'At last, you come forth from your refuge!' said Léiras, who had honestly been worried for Dardis and was exceptionally glad to see him. 'Have you finished what you began?'

'Come inside and you shall see for yourself,' said Dardis, his eyes shining in his pale face. He extended a beckoning arm to his teacher, and Léiras swept into the chamber in a flurry of green silken robes. Dardis approached an object on a pedestal, removed the dark cloth which covered it, and stepped back, allowing his Master to approach it. 'Behold,' he said with a weary smile. 'Behold the Stone of Léir!' Then, in a shy voice, 'I named it after you.'

'What is the purpose?' whispered Léiras, his pale hair and eyes glowing in the reflected light of the Stone. He was utterly captivated by the beauty of the shifting planes of light and shadow, the colors and shapes and faint sounds playing in the depths. 'What...who...whose reflection do I see?' He placed his trembling hands on the crystal, drawing close enough that the tip of his nose nearly brushed against it. His gaze was locked upon one of the silvery planes within.

After a moment he drew back again, a tear spilling from his right eye to touch the corner of his gentle smile. 'I saw a vision of a long lost friend,' he said. 'He was taken from me before I had the chance even to bid farewell...and he is now in Elysia, where I dare not go.' A brief melancholy washed over him, but then he smiled.

Dardis cast his eyes downward. 'What...what did you see? Please tell me,' he whispered.

'I saw my friend as I remembered him during the best time we shared together,' said Léiras. 'It was as if I was there with him—I could feel the grass, and smell the rain, and taste the ale...' His voice faded with the memory. Then he smiled at Dardis again. 'What is the purpose of this wonderful object?'

'I...I thought that it would aid in healing the terrible emptiness of souls torn by grief,' said Dardis. 'If they could re-live their happy memories, perhaps the pain would lessen. They could carry those happy memories nearer the forefront of their thoughts, and they could re-visit the Stone when their pain returned and they needed comforting.' He looked up at his friend and teacher. 'It is imperfect,' he said. 'The Stone does not always show what I would ask of it, and is sometimes unpredictable. I thought perhaps you might help me perfect it.'

'There is too much of your spiritual energy bound here, and it challenges the very nature of time and memory,' said Léiras. 'I dare not interfere. Besides, O First Apprentice, this work has surpassed anything I have yet produced. I stand in awe of my student. You quest always for the perfect thing, yet sometimes the value of a thing lies, in part, in its imperfections. This thing you have made is a wonder—do not discount it. It is my opinion that you should declare it finished, for if you try to force perfection you might just destroy the delicate energies within. Now I believe we should share a good meal—there is news which you have not heard.'

Dardis covered the wondrous crystal with the cloth, dimming its light, before following Léiras to his own chambers for food, drink, and conversation. As he passed by his dressing-table, he glanced at his reflection in the mirror. It showed a perfect image--glowing, healthy, rested, and energetic. Dardis scowled at his perfect reflection, knowing that in reality he looked pale, weary, and drained. Well, the Stone might have been imperfect, but it was certainly better than his frustrating, flattering mirror.

~*~

Kotos' descent into madness began on one dark winter's night as he sat alone and disheartened in a small cave in the Northern Mountains. An early blizzard had forced him into this refuge with no food and enough fuel for only a small fire. Though Kotos did not require food, drink, or even warmth, they did add to his general feeling of comfort and well-being. He had learned to appreciate the taste of a good meal, and he was always more contented sitting before a well-stoked fire, especially at night.

Kotos had always loved fire. He loved the beauty of the glowing coals, and the dance of the flames leaping into the night. He loved the way the wood gave up its spirit in one final brilliance of light and warmth—a display that could so quickly turn destructive under the wrong circumstances. He loved to just look into the deep gold and crimson depths of the flames to see what he could see.

On this night, a strange vision came to him in the fire. At first the flames were small, in keeping with the lack of timber, but as he looked into them they began to grow such that he could not look away. A figure appeared within them then—a figure of flames—and it began to speak, though the words were unheard.

(Lord Kotos the Persuader! At last I have found thee.)

Kotos answered with words unspoken: (Who calls to me from the flames? How is it that you know my name?)

(The name of one so powerful is known to all. Long have I sought thee, and thy desire to know Me has called Me here now. Is it not thy wish to learn the answers to all mysteries?)

(No one can know all answers. I ask again...who calls?)

(I am known by many names, but they are unimportant. I am one who can answer thy curiosities as to the nature of Evil. Was it not thy desire to learn?)

Kotos was fearful, but he would not show it. He guessed the identity of his unbidden visitor: Lord of Darkness and of Wrath, the Necromancer, whom the ancients named Wrothgar.
The Lord of Darkness tempted him from the flames. How had Wrothgar known of his desires?

(I see that thou art unafraid,) said Wrothgar. (Come then, and receive the gift of knowledge and understanding. It was always My intention to grant that gift, and with no harm unto thyself.)

(I only want to understand evil so that I may defeat it,) Kotos replied. (You may wish to reconsider your generous offer, for I will use it against you. We are enemies—I am a being of Light!)

(After I reveal the answers, I promise not to hold thee against thy will. But I must warn thee—the power of Darkness is strong, and may cause thee to re-think thy purpose. It is the ultimate power, as one so perceptive will no doubt realize. I will not hinder thee in any way.)

As Kotos 'listened' to the words of the Necromancer, he knew that he was being beguiled. Still, his pride, together with an all-consuming desire to learn and understand, would not allow him to refuse. He had longed for this opportunity, but had not known how to achieve it. Now he was being invited by the Dark Power itself! Wrothgar seemed to sense his willingness, and the flames reached out toward their intended victim like grasping golden hands, engulfing Kotos before he could hesitate, wrenching his soul from its housing. The flames bore him into the depths of Wrothgar's stronghold as his patient, lifeless body sat in the darkened cave with the stone at its back and the wild wind screaming outside.

Missing Pieces: The Unbroken Mirror

~*~

At first, Kotos did not realize that his spirit had left its body. He floated aimlessly in a chamber of dark, polished stone. In the center of the floor was a perfectly circular fire-pit with a very healthy blaze leaping forth from it, yet Kotos felt no warmth. The fire was silent and carried no scent. He looked at his own reflection in the polished, black surface of the walls, his ebon hair floating in a non-existent breeze, his 'body' adrift as though at the mercy of deep ocean waters.

A voice seemed to emanate from the fire-pit, but now the words were in the familiar, common dialect of men known as Aridani. Wrothgar wanted to lull Kotos rather than impress him.

(Welcome, Kotos the Mighty! It shall be my honor to instruct you.) From the flames there came a figure shrouded in grey. It appeared to be an old man with bright eyes peering from a wrinkled, intelligent face. It raised a gnarled right hand, palm downward, and Kotos gently settled to the floor of the chamber, standing tall upon his own feet. The old man bowed, nearly losing his balance.

(Welcome, Kotos, Asarla of Tal-Elathas. You are the most courageous of all—no other has ever dared come here to the Seat of Power. Good is easy to know, for everyone desires it and it is a simple thing. Evil, on the other hand, is far more complicated. Many are taken into its influence, but few truly understand it. That's why they are ensnared—because they don't understand. Are you ready to understand?)

Kotos' senses were phenomenally acute, as with all the Asari, yet he heard no sound—the voice was still unspoken. He reached out to steady the old man, but was denied. (It is best if you do not touch me without leave,) said the figure. It smiled, but the eyes grew cold and flinty.

(What are you called?) asked Kotos, surprised to find that, as with the old man, he made no sound.

(That is unimportant,) said the figure. (We haven't much time. Are you ready to receive your lessons? If your heart wavers, the Master can always send you back. I will not blame you—no one has ever chosen to walk this path before.)

Kotos smiled to himself. He liked being first in accomplishment. (Lead on,) he said. (I am ready and my heart will not waver.)

(We shall see,) said the old man with a sly smile. (Now you may take the sleeve of my robe.)

When Kotos' hand grasped the plain, grey fabric, a flash of light and noise startled him into yet another reality. He was shown violence, pettiness, envy, indifference, self-indulgence, and other evils too numerous to mention. They were heaped upon his spirit in wave after sickening wave. He was made privy to the dark thoughts of those closest to him—even Shandor's soul was not unstained. He felt guilty, as though he had been caught spying on a friend. Gossip, Malice, Deceit, it was all there. Brothers murdering brothers, wars fought over nothing but petty jealousies, noble souls sacrificed for the gain of the few—bodies piled up on massive funeral pyres. The killing of innocents—babes born to the wrong parents or at the wrong time—the horror of pestilence and the terrible crimes which surrounded it—the screams of the scapegoats as they were burned alive...

Kotos was overwhelmed, and he began to weep.

(For whom do you weep?) asked the old man.

(For the innocents...for the victims of violence,) said Kotos. (I did not know how many...there are so many!)

(Of course there are!) said the old man. (And do you know why? Because they are weak. They allowed themselves to be victims. There is no good done in this world that will not be turned to evil, my idealistic friend! They are not worthy of your tears. Stupidity, carelessness, delusion, vanity, selfishness—these are woven through the fabric of all men, and even Elves! You fight a hopeless battle.)

(No...not hopeless,) Kotos gasped. (Many of my efforts have averted war! I have done much of good in the world.)

(I think not,) said the old man. (I'm afraid I must now reveal your delusion...for your own sake.)

Kotos was shown a familiar scene—two warring tribes of men. He had come among them and persuaded them to make peace. Now they lived together and had not warred since. (What you do not realize,) said the old man, (is why!)

He allowed Kotos to see all that had happened after he had gone. The agents of one tribe had conspired with ambitious underlings from the other. They had murdered the clan rulers as they slept, and had formed a terrible alliance. They had not come to war with one another again, but their combined forces were now dominating and subjugating all other tribes of men in the region. There was more violence and suffering now than ever before. Kotos was horrified.

(See what your 'good works' have done?) said the old man. (It isn't your fault. All men sway easily to the side of Darkness, and they care not for the good of others. Do you see how weak--how pathetic--your precious enlightenment is? Even scholars kill each other over petty discoveries, Persuader!)

Missing Pieces: The Unbroken Mirror

(But there are those who love, and who sacrifice for love,) said Kotos. (There are beings of Light who strive to keep the Darkness from their souls.)
(And they fail!) said the old man. (Your 'Beings of Light' are just as vulnerable to jealousy, to desire, and to absurd, foolish vanity as anyone else!)

(Show me,) said Kotos.

(I will,) said the old man, (and then we shall see what you're made of. Prepare yourself!)

Kotos endured the most terrible moments of his life. He was thrown from one body to another, so that he was actually present during debaucheries, perversions, and atrocities of the worst kind. He heard millions of voices speaking the unspeakable—millions of minds thinking the unthinkable. Those voices and minds were not only of men. Elves, Dwarves--even his brother and sister Asari—were heard among the rabble. He was no mere observer—not this time. He felt the pain and triumph and ecstasy of Evil, and it overwhelmed him at last. Kotos, who had always believed in the purity of his own race, was disheartened. He sank into the depths, allowing shock and disappointment to engulf him. If even Lord Shandor harbored evil inclinations, how could the Light ever prevail?

The old man's voice drew him forth at last. (I regret having to show you some of those things,) he said. (You did not realize the darkness that lives within your own heart and the hearts of your brothers. No one can evade it—not for long. You are unmanned, adrift, and you know not where to turn. Your faith has been placed within the wrong camp, my lord. If you will but embrace the Darkness, your talents will be used to the full! The Light has always beguiled you with false promises. We promise power beyond your wildest imaginings—power and pleasure. Our promises are always kept.)

Kotos lifted a pale, tear-streaked face to the starlit sky which now appeared above him. The old man reached up with both arms. (See the vastness of heaven? The Lights are bright only because of the Darkness surrounding them. This shall be your dominion, if you agree. You shall turn the hearts of men to the service of Wrothgar, and He will reward you beyond your most fertile imaginings!)

Kotos felt then a sense of wonderful complacency. He was surrounded with sights and smells and sounds which tantalized and aroused him...and he felt sensations he had never allowed himself to feel before. Weary of fighting, he gave himself over to the physical pleasures known only to those who never question their own decency. When he finally emerged from this indulgence, the old man seemed pleased. (It is high time you were shown the folly of inhibitions,) he said. (Restraint is for lesser beings...not for you! Do you not feel most wonderful at this moment? Are you not satisfied?)

(I...do feel wonderful,) Kotos said in a languid voice, (but there is more to be experienced...things I have not yet tried. I am not yet satisfied.)

(Of course you're not,) said the old man. (But you will be. Abandon conscience! It is a set of shackles on your free will. Choose Darkness, and never deny yourself again. Remember—the world is full of those worthy only of your scorn. They can be made to serve you. It has grieved Lord Wrothgar to see your talents wasted on them, and your accomplishments, though they are many, have been brief. If all have turned to darkness in the end, what is the point of resisting?)

Kotos now stood in silent contemplation, considering all that he had seen and heard. (No one orders Lord Kotos the Persuader—not even his own conscience,) he said, (but I will not be a slave to my own pleasures. It will take a more compelling argument to convince me. I am strong—and I can still turn from evil.)

(There is one voice you have not yet heard,) said the old man.

(One more voice will not make any difference,) said Kotos, drawing himself up.
(Well then, let us listen together,) said the old man.

The voice Kotos had not heard was his own. Now he heard it...he relived every unworthy thought, every word spoken in envy, every petty, mean inclination he had ever had. This was perhaps the most difficult test of all—he had thought himself above such things. Yet as he heard them, he knew that they were true. (Do you now see?) said the old man gently. (Evil is already a part of you. It has worked its wiles even on the loftiest of souls—there is no refuge from it.)
Kotos' face was flushed with self-loathing. The old man's voice soothed him...lulled him. (Give up your shame, Kotos. It wounds you and gives you nothing but pain. You will never be free—none of you will ever be free—until you understand that. Come into the arms of Darkness, and be free! Sit at Wrothgar's right hand, and free them all!)

(Wrothgar's minions are not free...they are slaves to his will,) said Kotos.

The old man looked around furtively as though he did not wish to be overheard. He was about to reveal a great secret. (Think on this, then. As your power grows, you might even be able to defeat Lord Wrothgar one day. If that should come to pass, you would wield more power than any single being has ever known. You could order the universe to your liking then...and perhaps the Light and the Dark could exist together. You could banish the evil from the hearts of those you love. But you must first overcome Wrothgar, and to do that you must serve Him. If you return to your former life, nothing will change. All will remain as it was revealed to you. If you would change it, swear fealty to Wrothgar and aid Him for the time being. When your power grows, overthrow Him and take your place at the center of the

Missing Pieces: The Unbroken Mirror

Universe—the Master of Darkness AND of Light. You will answer to no one but yourself. It is your destiny, though Wrothgar does not realize it.) The old man looked around again. (His pride won't allow it, you see.)

(And you would aid me?) said Kotos, who had never imagined the old man would betray Lord Wrothgar.

(When the time is right, I will,) said the old man. (Think of the power and the freedom! You need never be ashamed again—need never deny yourself the answer to any question. Lord Wrothgar promised to reveal the answer to all mysteries, and as long as He believes you are at His service, that promise will be kept. You will know more than anyone has even known. Are you now ready to swear fealty to Him and fulfill your destiny?)

The old man reached out a hand, conjuring an image of a perfect sphere. The Lights of the Universe were captured inside it. Kotos looked around at the total, featureless blackness which now engulfed him. (Look at the Lights. Are they not beautiful?) said the old man. (They will move at your direction...when you are ready. Do you want this pretty thing for your own?) He held the sphere as though offering it to Kotos, who reached for it with a trembling hand. His pride allowed him to believe that he could still prevail.

He was drawn into the vastness of a thousand worlds, each one with a million souls like tiny points of light. The enormity of it overwhelmed his spirit—all these souls speaking with different voices—some pained, some even loving, but all tainted by Darkness. All touched by Evil. He reeled back, dropping the sphere and grasping his beautiful, anguished head in both hands. It was too much. Too much! The blackness folded around him, and he knew nothing more for awhile.

When Kotos awoke, his first thought was of being cold. His fire had gone out. His head and body ached. How long had he been sitting here? He was once again in the cave in the Northern Mountains, and the storm still raged outside, but it had lost some of its bite and would soon move on to the east.

He peered into the pre-dawn darkness, wondering if he had imagined the encounter with the old man. Then, as he looked on in wonder, a dark shape appeared amidst the swirling snowflakes. It grew until it stood as a black portal before him.

(Are you now ready for your next lesson?)

Kotos was, in many ways, like a very bright and unsophisticated child. This time he did not hesitate, stepping through the portal into the blackness—into a life without shame, a life without guillt, a life without consequences. He was ready to learn whatever the old man had to teach him—to gain the answers to whatever questions Lord Wrothgar would reveal. The old man and Lord Wrothgar were one and the same person, and Kotos would soon realize that, but it would not matter. The corruption of his spirit was already beyond redeeming.

~*~

In the end, Kotos had left Ri-Aldamar's armor behind. The touch of items made by the hand of Dardis had started to pain him, for their benevolent energies were counter to his own. He made his way to the encampment of Wrothgar's army, knowing that a far greater force remained hidden to all but the most perceptive scouts. None of those scouts would be returning to Tal-Elathas.

He was admitted at once, guided into the presence of Wrothgar. As always, the Necromancer spoke to Kotos from the midst of fire. Though he could assume a physical form, it drained his energies, and so he would not do so without need.

(What news dost thou bring?)

'The King is still wary, I fear. He has sent me as emissary to see if it is advisable to talk of Peace. What shall I tell him?'

(Tell him that My offer is genuine. Tell him that My forces are few, and scattered. Tell him that I apologize for the death of his scouts, but My underlings did not understand that they should not be harmed. Tell him that My delegates will meet with him tomorrow—when the sun is high. Thy loyalties are clear in this matter, are they not?)

'Of course,' said Kotos. 'Why would you believe otherwise?'
(I am pleased with thee, My servant. Soon Tal-Elathas will be thine to rule. The weak will be driven back, and the strong rewarded. While the foolish talk of peace, my legions will prepare to attack as the sun sets on the second day. Go now, and work thy charms of beguiling.)

Kotos bowed, backing away from the flames. He had learned to not ever turn his back to Lord Wrothgar. As he left the encampment, he witnessed what was left of the unfortunate scouts being torn limb from limb, but he felt neither guilt nor empathy, as he was no longer capable of either.

Missing Pieces: The Unbroken Mirror

~*~

Kotos delivered his message to Ri-Aldamar, urging him to open his gates to Wrothgar's emissaries. 'You will be the King who brings peace to Alterra at last!' he said, his enthusiasm and affection for Ri-Aldamar obvious. 'I must admit, my visit was better than I expected. Being in the presence of the Necromancer was somewhat unsettling and, needless to say, you must not drop your guard until we know for certain that all is we would have it. I would place a heavy guard over Wrothgar's minions while they are here.'

'Hmmmm...' said Ri-Aldamar. 'Yes, that goes without saying. I must admit that I had not expected such a positive reaction from you, Kotos. You are usually more wary than this.'

'I am excited at the prospect of peace, my lord, nothing more,' said Kotos. 'Perhaps I am relieved that I walked alone into that place and emerged unscathed. I cannot say it was a pleasurable experience, but Wrothgar really is on his best behavior at the moment. If things were otherwise, I would have known.'

'Yes, so it would seem,' said the King. 'And you would surely have detected any deception. I must be left alone to deliberate, my friend. I will give my answer at dawn—plenty of time to inform our would-be negotiators. Thank you for taking this risk upon yourself.'

'I live to serve you, my lord,' said Kotos, bowing low. 'Please summon me if you wish further assistance.' So saying, he left the King's chamber knowing Ri-Aldamar was not yet convinced.

A few hours later, he ran into Baelta, who knew immediately that his friend Kotos was troubled. 'You are not yourself this evening. I am not surprised, after the ordeal you endured today. How may I help you?'

Kotos sighed. 'I regret that, despite my reporting to the contrary, Ri-Aldamar still fears opening up the realm to talk of peace,' he said. 'How will we ever achieve any accord if we cannot trust? We condemn Wrothgar for his past war-mongering, but even when he comes to us asking for consideration, we do not allow him to even make his case? I had thought myself persuasive, but it seems I have not been able to convince the King. I will never forgive myself if we miss the chance for peace because my argument was weak. It might be a thousand years before Wrothgar approaches us with such an offer again.' He looked up at Baelta, and saw what he knew he would see. The bright, happy face of his 'brother' was full of genuine concern. Baelta was so easily deceived...especially by a friend.

'Perhaps I might talk to the King and lend my voice to yours,' he said.

Kotos appeared ready to weep tears of gratitude. 'If you would only do that, it might make the difference!'

'Then I shall do so, in fact, I'll go at once,' he said. 'Now, don't worry. I'll help you convince him.' Baelta smiled with his familiar optimism. 'I'll come back and tell you what the King decides.'

After Baelta had gone, Kotos closed his eyes and relaxed. All would be well now—the King trusted Baelta. Everyone trusted Baelta.

~*~

The emissaries of the Necromancer, seven learned men who had once enjoyed great reputations as scholars, were admitted at noon of the following day. They were accompanied by guardians, of course—a company of fierce Olcas commanded by men—and they appeared uneasy as they were shown to the chamber where the negotiations would take place. The Elves surrounded them all as soon as the Gates closed behind them, and they were in no mood for nonsense, armored and helmeted and bristling with weapons. The Olcas were suitably uncomfortable, even though it was winter and the sunlight was pale and weak.

'An interesting reception for a peace delegation,' hissed one of the dark emissaries.

'You will forgive us if we do not yet trust you,' growled Magra, who had been given the task of conducting them. 'Even if peace is achieved, it will be an uneasy truce for quite some time, I expect.'

'I see you bear many scars of battle. They almost justify your lack of manners,' replied the emissary. Magra said nothing more.

The delegation and their guardians were offered food and drink, whereupon the discussions could begin. Only the delegates were allowed to attend. There were seven from each side. In addition to Wrothgar's seven scholars there was Ri-Aldamar, who presided over the proceedings; his son Iomar; Baelta, Kotos, and Léiras; Magra, and Gelmyr. The Olcan guards and their Elven counterparts were forced to wait outside, where they eyed one another with loathing.

Negotiating with an enemy, especially when both parties believe they have suffered the greater offense, is wearisome in the extreme. Very little was accomplished in that first awkward session, and the 'guests' were soon shown to their quarters for the night.

The following day proved little better, though the delegates had gotten beyond mutual accusations, at least for the time being. Supper had been brought in for

Missing Pieces: The Unbroken Mirror

everyone as the afternoon waned and evening drew nigh, whereupon Kotos rose and stretched. 'I must go out and take the air,' he said. 'I am not hungry for supper, so I might not return until later. I bow to you all in respect.' He turned and made his departure, for he had several important tasks before him.

First he went to the Chamber of Dardis, knowing that he most likely would be there. Kotos would tell Dardis that his presence had been requested in the negotiating chamber by his friend Léiras, who wanted his opinion on an important matter. Once Dardis had gone, Kotos would steal the Stone of Léir for his Master, who coveted it. Then he would make his way outside the realm by secret paths, allowing the servants of Wrothgar to enter. They would slay the Gate-keepers, opening the realm to the Dark Army. Kotos would be long gone by then, and no one would know of his duplicity. They would probably assume he had simply been misled, as had they all.

Dardis knew of no reason why he should not allow Kotos to enter, and he received him as he would a friend. 'I regret disturbing you, but your presence is requested in the council-chambers,' said Kotos. Dardis turned even paler than usual—he did not like being thrust into important gatherings.
'Why me?' he asked.

'Léiras did not explain, he only sent me to fetch you,' said Kotos. 'I know he would appreciate it if you would attend him with all haste.' He raised an eyebrow at Dardis. The Elf was as disheveled as an Elf could ever be; his hair was untidy and his clothing was careworn and rumpled. 'Come on, now, and let's get you presentable.' He took off his own beautiful robe, offering it to Dardis. 'This will dress things up a bit,' he said. 'And comb your hair! You don't want to stand before the King so unkempt.' Dardis flushed red, and he moved to his dressing-table, scowling at his reflection again. Though he had worked on the mirror several times, he had never managed to prevent it from showing false perfection—his hair appeared perfect in the glass. He picked up a comb and worked through the tangles, noticing the reflection of Kotos, who was standing behind him.

The comb froze in his hand.

Kotos did not look like himself at all—he was a monster with leering, grinning snarl, narrow, malevolent eyes full of ill will, and a dark and unhealthy cast to his skin. This was a being filled with ugliness and malice. Dardis gasped in spite of himself, all the remaining color draining from his face.

Kotos had also been surprised at his own reflection, for he was among the vainest of creatures. But more than that, he knew he could not allow Dardis to draw another breath. His hands closed around Dardis' slender throat, throttling him easily, extinguishing the brightest Elven Light the world had ever seen. The hurt remained in Dardis' eyes even after he lay dead on the floor before his enemy, still expressing a final, shocked question: (*Why?*)

'Kotos...Why?'

This time the question was not unspoken, and it came from the mouth of Léiras, who had followed Kotos from the peace chamber. He had arrived too late to aid Dardis, and now Kotos turned to him, snarling.

'Your face...look at your face!' cried Léiras, his horror unimaginable. Kotos lifted Dardis' mirror and smashed it on the floor beside its creator. Léiras wailed, knowing then that they had all been deceived. Kotos' face had been forever changed—it was now the same horrific visage that had so terrified Dardis, gentle Dardis, who only wanted to use his gifts for the good. Kotos would never be beautiful again.

Léiras stood between Kotos and the Stone. His wailing had drawn attention—Kotos could hear footsteps hurrying toward him. He bolted from the chamber without his prize, running past those rushing to Dardis' aid. They hardly noticed him. Kotos the Persuader, the Beguiler, now forever known as the Deceiver, escaped as he had planned, opening the Gates to Wrothgar's waiting legions. The rest of this tragedy is known to every Elf, though they will not sing of it.

The Elves rushed into Dardis' chamber to find Léiras holding his beloved apprentice as one would a child, rocking him and weeping. At last he understood—the mirror had not been flawed after all. Dardis' reflection had appeared perfect because it showed him as he truly was.

Missing Pieces: The Unbroken Mirror

About the Author

C.S. Marks has often been described as a 'Renaissance Woman'. The daughter of academic parents, she holds a Ph.D. in Biology and is currently as a Full Professor of Equine Science at Saint Mary-of-the-Woods College. She is also a gifted artist, singer, songwriter, and author of the award-winning Elfhunter trilogy (Elfhunter; Fire-heart; Ravenshade). She enjoys archery, and makes hand-crafted longbows.

Horses are her passion, and she is an accomplished horsewoman, having competed in the sport of endurance racing for many years. One of only a handful of Americans to have competed the prestigious 'Tom Quilty' Australian National Championship hundred-mile ride, she has described that moment as her 'finest hour'.

Throughout the Elfhunter trilogy, the world of Alterra unfolds in classic epic style. It has been well received by readers and reviewers, winning several Reviewer's Choice awards. Available on Kindle, it consistently ranks among the top 100 sellers in Epic Fantasy. C.S. Marks is not afraid to put her own 'stamp' on the classic fantasy tropes. Her books have been described as character-driven, fast-paced, beautifully written, and appropriate for readers of all ages.

The Unbroken Mirror is taken from the pages of Alterran history, giving the reader a glimpse into a world of Elves, dwarves, mortal men, and delightfully intelligent horses. As with the Elfhunter trilogy, it blurs the line between Light and Darkness, love and obsession, free will and fate. (www.elfhunter.net)

COMING TO GENCON 2011

PRESENTS

MISSING PIECES II
Untold tales from your favorite Bards in GenCon 2011 Author's Avenue

Volume 2

Please visit
www.dragonroots.net
to learn more
about how to submit material
or pre-order your copy today.

Made in the USA
Charleston, SC
16 July 2010